ALSO BY RACHEL DEL GROSSO

Eleanor & Sam

Fine, But Not Finished

Another Kind of Green

FREE SHORT STORY OFFER

Want to see what Harriet was up to before
Harriet In Waiting?

Subscribe to my newsletter at www.racheldelgrosso.com to receive the free short story, *Before Everything Broke*. It's the perfect way to meet the women at the heart of the series—before their full stories unfold.

PRAISE FOR ELEANOR & SAM

"Rachel Del Grosso is a gifted and natural storyteller whose debut is sure to please readers who enjoy layered novels about writing and women's relationships."

CAMILLE PAGÁN, BESTSELLING AUTHOR OF *GOOD FOR YOU*.

"I absolutely flew through this book. Compulsively readable and wholly satisfying, *Eleanor & Sam* is a love letter to authors, to books, to the creative process, to friendship—especially the unique, often tricky, bond that forms between artists. I loved every minute of it."

SUZY KRAUSE, BESTSELLING AUTHOR OF *SORRY I MISSED YOU* AND *I THINK WE'VE BEEN HERE BEFORE*

"A powerful story of two women and the choices they make that affect their lives forever. Two very different women bond over their love of story and how difficult it can be for women to find their way as writers in a world that still doesn't make it easy for creatives. A riveting page-turner you don't want to miss!"

JANUARY BAIN, AUTHOR OF THE *ANNA HALE P.I.* SERIES

PRAISE FOR FINE, BUT NOT FINISHED

"[A] Realistic and emotional story of midlife and a marriage in crisis."

KATRUN, *AMAZON REVIEWER*

"An absolute gem…raw, witty, and deeply relatable. Del Grosso has a rare gift for creating perfectly imperfect characters, and Hazel's journey of unraveling and self-reinvention captured my heart from page one."

JEN B., *AMAZON REVIEWER*

PRAISE FOR ANOTHER KIND OF GREEN

"A heartfelt, beautifully written exploration of marriage, friendship, and self-discovery."

JEN B., *AMAZON REVIEWER*

Harriet in Waiting

Harriet in Waiting

LOST AND FOUND
Book One

RACHEL DEL GROSSO

Harriet In Waiting
Paperback Edition

Love N. Books Press
An Imprint of Wolfpack Publishing
1707 E. Diana Street
Tampa, FL 33610

www.lovenbookspress.com

Edited by My Brother's Editor

Paperback ISBN 979-8-89567-689-9
Ebook ISBN 979-8-89567-688-2

To Jordan, for all her help...even though she will claim only 4.6 percent of the credit

Harriet in Waiting

PROLOGUE

The frame hit the tile with a sharp, splintering crack. Glass scattered across the kitchen floor, tiny sparks catching in the overhead light.

Harriet kneeled, her bare knees against the cold porcelain, reaching for the shards. A sliver bit her thumb, and she pressed it to her lips, tasting the sting of metal.

She stared at the fractured photograph: Alex's half-smile, the twins mid-laugh, her own eyes shining with a happiness that no longer felt like hers.

The edges cut into her palm as she gripped the frame too tightly.

Something was breaking, she knew. Maybe it already had.

PART ONE
HARRIET

1

BEFORE

Every morning upon waking, Harriet Langley's first thought was how much she loved the silence. No snoring, no blaring alarm, no whispered "Did you hear that?" when the only things to hear were the neighbor's sprinklers and the cicadas humming in the thick, late-August heat. The king-sized bed was hers, all hers, and she sprawled across it dramatically, limbs akimbo, like a starfish. Through her slightly ajar window came the faint smell of salt from the ocean.

Her second thought was about her schedule. Namely, what she'd do with her glorious, child-free day. The house was already spotless—naturally. She had the kind of clean house people in Instagram ads claimed was impossible with children. Counters gleamed, throw pillows were artfully fluffed, and not a single sock was draped over a banister.

She padded into the kitchen—half naked, of course, because why not?—slippers shushing against the tile, and admired her perfectly organized fridge. Rows of neatly labeled containers greeted her, the culmination of last night's highly unnecessary but deeply satisfying meal prep for one. Who needed anyone else when you had kale chips alphabetized by flavor?

Her phone buzzed, the moment of peace shattered. She glanced at the screen, groaning when the caller ID read Grayson, her son.

"It's nine a.m.," she said by way of greeting. "Aren't you supposed to be unconscious until noon?"

"It's an emergency. Dad's fridge is empty. There's a jar of mustard, three olives, and oat milk. Oat milk, Mom. He's trying to kill us."

Harriet pinched the bridge of her nose. "I sent groceries on Thursday. What happened to them?"

It had been a lapse in judgment, the groceries. She wouldn't make the same mistake again. There were so many habits needing to be broken.

"I don't know. Maybe he ate them?"

"Oh, right. Your father, renowned for his ability to eat his body weight in frozen waffles and chicken nuggets."

Grayson sighed dramatically. "Can you just—"

"Call him and yell at him?" she cut in. "No. I'm no longer in the business of managing his life. Good luck with your olives."

Grayson groaned. "You're impossible."

"And yet, you called me."

Before Grayson could launch into more complaints, her daughter Olivia's voice cut in on the line. "Mom, hi! Quick question—hypothetically, what happens if someone accidentally explodes a blueberry smoothie in a blender?"

Harriet took a deep breath and stared at her immaculate kitchen. "Hypothetically," she said, "*someone* should clean it up immediately before it dries and turns into cement."

"Okay, but what if it's already dried...hypothetically?"

"Then ask your father, the adult in charge this weekend."

There was a pause. Then Olivia asked in a small voice, "Would you maybe come ov—"

"No," Harriet said firmly. "Enjoy your oat milk. Love you, goodbye!"

She hung up, pleased with her resolve.

Harriet stared at her phone for a long moment, debating whether she should call Alex to check. Not to fix it—*definitely not*—but to ensure the twins wouldn't end up living on condiments for the rest of the weekend. Then she shook her head, steeling herself. Alex could figure it out. For once, she wouldn't be the one to swoop in and fix everything.

She poured her coffee into her favorite mug, the one that said, "This is why we can't have nice things," then wandered through the pristine house. Sunlight bounced off the perfectly arranged gallery wall she'd curated after Alex left. Still, the space felt airless, as if his presence lingered in the corners.

She turned toward the master closet. Enough avoiding it.

The double doors opened on rows of color-coded hangers and perfectly folded sweaters, yet the air still smelled faintly of Alex's cologne. Once crammed with his loud ties and ill-fitting polos, it now felt like a mausoleum.

Harriet pulled clothes from the shelves, stacking them with mechanical precision. Each hanger scraped the rod like a reprimand. The guest room closet was smaller, a downgrade she accepted without hesitation. A pink silk blouse from date nights. Black heels that once made her feel invincible. A blue sweater Alex had chosen. Her chest tightened. Pieces of a life she no longer wanted to inhabit.

She shoved the last hanger aside and shut the door harder than she meant to. "It's a start," she said to the empty room.

Her phone buzzed again. This time, it was a text from Olivia.

Olivia: Grayson says he'll eat the olives for $20. Should I let him?

Harriet grinned.

Harriet: Make it $50. He's going to need therapy after.

She rolled her eyes and tossed the phone aside. They were fine. Better than fine, probably. Teenagers bounced between drama and laughter like it was a sport.

She pushed the final stack of clothes into the cramped guest closet. The master bedroom stood hollow behind her, heavy with silence she'd once craved and now found unbearable.

"What the hell do I do now?" she asked the empty room. The silence, as always, had no answers.

There had never been a question of keeping the house. The twins needed stability, and Alex hadn't fought her—maybe because he knew he'd forfeited the right. He'd taken the couch, the coffee machine only he could work, even the wedding-gift Vitamix, declaring he was "getting into smoothies," as if that explained anything. She'd never felt much of an attachment to any of these items, so what did it matter if he wanted to take them to decorate his sad little rental house five blocks away?

Harriet bought a bright-blue knockoff blender out of spite, its gritty margaritas a small act of rebellion. Redecorating was supposed to be a fresh start—her couch, her walls, her choices. But the shine wore thin, and friends Carrie and Laura had tried (and failed) to hide their winces at the bare rooms.

Redecorating felt like a fresh start anyway. Now she could buy the couch she'd wanted in the first place! Use the kitchen counters for more than making coffee! Now she could park her SUV in the middle of the garage! Now she could replace the hideous vertical blinds Alex had put in without consulting her! God, she hated those things.

But by the time Alex moved out and she could assess the gap between what she owed versus what was needed, the shine had already begun to wear off. And then her friends, Carrie and Laura, had come over for wine and charcuterie, and their expressions, which they had tried hard to control, had confirmed everything Harriet had worried to be true.

She'd kept the good car, at least. The shiny, electric thing had been, like so many things, Alex's idea. He hadn't fought her on it, but she hadn't given him much of a chance to.

Harriet hadn't needed time to think it through. Leaving him had been an easy decision. She had been unhappy but in love until the moment she found out about the affair.

The breaking of plates had come later, after dinner, while Alex buzzed around her, hysterical, as though he hadn't been the one to blow up their entire life. That Alex appeared unable to keep it together was what eventually led Harriet to throw a dinner plate at his feet. The sound it made as it hit the floor was so satisfying, she did it again and again.

Eventually, Alex had done what he should have in the beginning and left her the hell alone.

The closet now conquered, it was time to subdue the week ahead with meal plans and a fresh grocery list.

Sundays were for planning. No exceptions. The dining table was strewn with the tools of her ritual: her leather-bound planner, a stack of printed meal ideas, and her laptop open to a spreadsheet with tabs like "Easy Dinners," "Low-Carb Lunches," and "Things Olivia Will Actually Eat." Harriet chewed the cap of her pen as she cross-referenced recipes, jotting down ingredients in neat columns on her grocery list.

Once the week's meals were mapped out, Harriet pulled the first basket of laundry from the dryer and began folding with mechanical precision. Whites, darks, towels, and delicates—each one had its place. She didn't believe in the chaos of communal baskets. If she could control *this,* at least, then she could control something.

Her phone buzzed with a text.

Olivia: Can we get donuts after school tomorrow? Please?

Harriet smirked. *Donuts.* She added "low-sugar snacks" to her grocery list before typing back.

Harriet: We'll see.

Olivia's response came immediately.

Olivia: That means no.

Harriet: No, it means we'll see.

The day wound down with the hum of the washing machine and the satisfaction of a neatly stacked pile of folded laundry. The house was quiet again, her life folded and stacked into something almost manageable.

It wouldn't last, of course. It never did.

2

Harriet's Monday morning began not with silence but with the unmistakable roar of a leaf blower outside her window. It had to be Greta's house. She was the only neighbor stubborn enough to cling to real grass in a sea of drought-tolerant landscaping. Harriet squinted at the clock and groaned. If she were a braver woman—or at least a more aggressive one—she might have marched over there at some point in the last decade and mentioned how Greta's landscapers were single-handedly ruining her Monday mornings, but the woman was a fifty-something widow, and Harriet wasn't quite ready to be the villain in her story.

Harriet dragged herself out of bed and into the shower, which lasted approximately eight minutes. After which, she dried and styled her hair, dressed, and ate breakfast: a sensible bowl of oatmeal topped with fruit. She loathed oatmeal, but that never stopped her from eating it most mornings ever since she'd read that doing so could prolong her life. This had been neither confirmed nor denied since, but she was nothing if not a creature of habit.

After breakfast, Harriet eyed the empty coffeemaker on the counter. Normally, she'd brew a quick, no-fuss cup at home—cheap and practical. But today, a flicker of rebellion sparked in her chest. She would stop for a coffee on the way to the office and buy something sweet and expensive as a treat, even though these were the kind of indulgences she was supposed to be limiting now that she was on her own.

Or was she now deserving of these kinds of indulgences *because* she was on her own?

A little while later, she slid into her car and headed down the familiar La Jolla streets. Cliffs glowed in the distance, the ocean flashing silver between gaps in the houses, and traffic was the usual mix of polished Teslas and beat-up hatchbacks dusted with beach sand.

She pulled into the drive-thru and ordered a caramel latte with extra caramel drizzle. The sweetness hit her tongue like a revelation, and for once, she didn't feel guilty about indulging in something simply because it made her happy.

Caught at a red light known to last a solid five minutes, Harriet pulled out her phone and tapped to open Instagram. She knew she shouldn't, that whatever she saw would leave her feeling suddenly less than. But she couldn't help herself. She scrolled past photos of families on vacation, advertisements for curling irons and turmeric face pads, past a tutorial for styling the perfect messy bun, and an ad for a viral color-changing foundation. She stopped when she spotted a familiar face.

Upon closer inspection, it was two familiar faces, Carrie and Laura, to be specific—and she always preferred to be. They were angled toward each other, coffees in hand and big smiles on their faces. Harriet recognized the coffee shop.

There had been a time they wouldn't have dreamed of going to Rosemere's Café without her, but clearly things had changed. Not *things.* Her. Or rather, her marital status. She'd always thought that if she were to lose her friends one day, it would be because she was finally too particular for them, not because she was no longer Alex Young's wife.

Harriet stared at the photo, her thumb hovering over the screen as if double-tapping it for a like would brand her with some mark of pathetic approval. She could almost hear their laughter, the way Carrie's cackle always startled strangers while Laura's quiet snort made everyone crack up even harder.

Her throat tightened as she skimmed the caption. *Catch-ups over cortados! <3 Nothing better than time with my bestie. #friendshipgoals*

Harriet locked her phone with a sharp jab of her thumb and tossed it onto the passenger seat like she'd been burned.

Hadn't she?

Harriet hadn't noticed the light had turned green. The car behind her honked, a sharp, impatient sound jolting her out of her spiral. Harriet had always thought of La Jolla as a bit of a sleepy town...but the driver behind her was wide awake.

She accelerated down the familiar route to work, the quiet hum of the air conditioning failing to fill the silence in her mind. The thought of texting Carrie or Laura flitted in and out, like a fly she couldn't swat away. She could send something breezy, like, "Looks fun—next time invite me!" or "Missing you guys!" But the idea made her stomach twist. What if they didn't respond? Or worse, what if they did, with some halfhearted "Of course! Let's plan something soon!" that never materialized?

The last time she'd seen them was months ago at a dinner party hosted by one of Alex's colleagues. He'd begged her to go with him even though they had already separated. Something about needing to appear solid and settled in front of his boss. The only reason she'd agreed to go was because she hadn't seen Laura and Carrie in months.

An hour into the night, it was clear that, though they tried to hide it, they knew about the separation. They'd smiled too much, their voices too bright. Harriet had left early, claiming exhaustion, and hadn't heard from them since.

Pulling into the parking lot at work, she sat for a moment. The office building loomed ahead, sterile and uninviting. For a brief second, she considered calling in sick. But she couldn't, not today. A meeting with a senior manager meant putting on her game face, even if inside, she felt like a loose wire sparking out of control.

Her phone buzzed, and for a fleeting moment, her heart lifted. Maybe it was Carrie or Laura reaching out. But no, it was an automated text about a sale at her favorite department store.

Wanting to prolong her last minutes of silence, she flipped down her visor and studied herself in the small mirror. Her deep brown curls were behaving themselves for once, falling in soft, defined spirals framing her round face. She smoothed a stray strand behind her ear, noticing a faint streak of silver peeking through at her temple. Harriet's light-brown eyes, though tired, held a spark of warmth and curiosity, the kind that made people instinctively feel at ease around her, which was funny considering she often felt the opposite. She was too sensitive to people's energies—reading too much into every sigh, every raised eyebrow—and most left her feeling anxious, like she was perpetually trying to balance on shifting sand. It was exhausting, but she hadn't yet figured out how to turn off this part of herself.

Harriet adjusted her shirt, tugging it down over her

midsection with a resigned sigh, the fabric snug against her soft frame. Being forty felt like stepping onto a whole new terrain—familiar in some ways but with odd, unexpected twists. On one hand, it was liberating. For the first time, Harriet felt a confidence she hadn't known in her twenties or thirties. She no longer had the constant urge to impress anyone. She'd outgrown the fear of what others thought of her clothes, her hair, and even—to an extent—her decisions.

But then there were the realities that came with aging. Suddenly, she could walk into a room and be the oldest person there. She was no longer the one effortlessly in tune with trends or the music playing in the background. It was strange to be the age her own mother had once been—grown-up, responsible, *officially* an adult in the eyes of anyone younger. And even though her body was familiar, it came with some new quirks that kept her on her toes. She could feel aches in places she didn't even know had muscles, and suddenly had to factor in things like calcium, fiber, and back support.

More than anything, forty was a paradox. She felt wiser and more secure with herself, but the world had new ways of reminding her that she was no longer in her twenties. It was its own odd blend of freeing, humbling, and, in its way, hilariously enlightening.

With a deep breath, Harriet grabbed her bag, smoothed down her skirt, and got out of the car. Time to focus on work, where everything was neat, organized, and relatively free of feelings.

Harriet pushed open the office door, the familiar scent of stale coffee and printer ink greeting her as she stepped inside.

Working in HR was the perfect fit. It was all about control—an area where she thrived. Policies to enforce, complaints to mediate, candidates to size up in interviews—it was like her own little arena where she could keep everything in order. She had her moments of power, too, like brandishing the company handbook in a meeting, her version of a scepter. It was as close to ruling a kingdom as she was likely to get.

Of course, there was the downside: far more "smiling at strangers" than she would prefer.

Harriet plastered on her professional grin as she passed the break room, but her step faltered when she spotted Clare leaning against the counter, stirring sugar into her mug. Clare—the only person in this office with whom maintaining a friendship with didn't feel like work.

"Harriet," Clare greeted warmly, lifting her mug in salute. "Good morning! Fancy coffee today? Look at you living dangerously."

Harriet smirked, holding up her caramel latte like a trophy. "One small act of rebellion at a time."

Clare chuckled, stepping closer. "You know, I'm proud of you. You've been through so much lately." Her head bounced this way and that, making sure no one else was around. "It can't be easy figuring out who you are without Alex in the picture."

"Olivia says I need to reclaim my identity."

"Smart girl."

Harriet's grin faded into something softer, more self-aware. "Of course, reclaiming my identity sounds noble until I remember I don't even know where I left it. Possibly somewhere between the kids' carpool schedule and picking up Alex's dry cleaning."

Clare laughed gently. "One latte at a time," she said.

"I hope so."

Clare studied her for a moment, then shrugged, as if

letting go of something. "Maybe you don't need to put it all back together the same way. Maybe you can build something new instead."

"Great. I'll add 'rebuild my entire life' to my to-do list right next to 'find the missing sock from the laundry' and 'figure out how to properly apply eyeliner.'"

3

Work was work, which is to say that Harriet generally experienced few to no problems during her work hours. She began her day by reviewing new applications and scheduling interviews for some new positions. After a lunch of chicken salad eaten at her desk, which she'd prepared in bulk the day before, she worked on onboarding session notes and then had her meeting with the Senior HR Manager. By the time the meeting was over, she had only an hour to respond to a few employee questions about benefits enrollment before five p.m. rolled around.

The second she was back in her car, however, Harriet felt her anxiety creeping in. The kids would be home from Alex's by now, and the thought of walking into a shifting emotional minefield made her chest tighten. Teenagers were unpredictable at the best of times, but fifteen-year-old twins? It was like trying to juggle two live grenades without knowing which one might go off first.

There was also the fear she might run into Alex dropping them off. She'd somehow managed for four months now, to never cross his path. It wasn't about missing him. It was the humiliation and anger that she couldn't escape. It was like an invisible weight clinging to her every step. The thought of facing him made her skin crawl. She didn't want to know if he was doing better, thriving even, while she was here, trying to hold it all together.

She couldn't shake the feeling that one of the kids—likely Olivia, the more perceptive of the two—might say something, casually mention something about Alex upon her return, and it would break the dam she'd built around her heart. What if they told her he was happy? What if they'd seen him with someone else, someone new?

She didn't want to know. She couldn't.

Harriet squeezed the steering wheel tighter as she turned onto the familiar road to the house. She had to keep her guard up. She couldn't let anything slip, couldn't let the kids see how much this was still eating her up. They needed her strong. They needed her to be steady.

Her house—she'd found it easy to drop the *our*—sat along a quiet, winding street in a La Jolla enclave of sun-washed stucco homes with terracotta roofs and carefully manicured bougainvillea climbing every wall. She'd once scoffed at the curated charm of it all, but had softened over time. Once the kids were old enough to run off on their own, they'd started meeting friends at the neighborhood park or heading down the bluff to the beach to poke around tide pools, and Harriet had quickly come to see the steep property taxes and HOA dues as a fair trade. Her neighbors were nice enough and tended to mind their own business most of the time, save for Greta next door, which was great once Alex moved out. She wouldn't have been able to bear all their questions and concerned expressions.

Not when she got enough from her friends and family members.

Not when she wanted to tell them all, "No, no, it's a good thing. Believe me."

Harriet had come into contact with other separated people, the kind who *were* deserving of a concerned expression or words of condolence. But she was not one of them. She refused to be one of them. Yes, she had been married, but now she was not. She didn't need to spend months with a therapist breaking down what had happened. What had happened was that Alex had gone and done something Harriet could never forgive him for.

He'd moved out two days later.

By the time she retrieved the mail and pulled into the driveway, Harriet had already mentally cataloged what needed to be done: check homework, cook dinner, remind Grayson not to leave his cleats in the hallway lest she trip over them again, and talk to Olivia about her sudden obsession with wearing oversized hoodies to school every day, despite the heat.

As she stepped through the door, Olivia was sprawled on the couch, earbuds in, scrolling through her phone with the kind of scowl that made Harriet's stomach sink.

"Hey, Liv," she said cautiously, setting her bag and the mail on the counter. "Everything okay?"

Olivia didn't look up. "Fine."

Harriet perched on the armrest of the couch, trying to read her daughter's expression. "You sure? You look like something's bothering you."

Olivia huffed and yanked out her earbuds. "It's just... forget it."

"Come on, you can tell me. Whatever it is, it can't be that bad. I mean, we all have rough days."

Olivia's head snapped up, her face darkening. "You don't get it, Mom! You *never* get it!"

Harriet blinked. "I only meant—"

"Whatever," Olivia snapped, shoving her phone into her hoodie pocket and stomping toward the stairs. "You'll never understand."

"You haven't even told me what it is!" Harriet called after her, a note of desperation creeping into her voice. "At least give me a chance!"

Olivia stopped halfway up the stairs and turned, her face a mix of anger and disbelief. "Why? So you can tell me I'm overreacting again? Forget it, Mom!"

The words hit Harriet squarely in the chest, and she could only watch as Olivia stormed up the remaining steps, her door slamming moments later. Harriet stood there, a familiar ache settling in her chest, the kind that came from trying so hard and still getting it wrong.

She let out a slow breath. *Mother of the Year, right here. Someone get me a trophy.*

From upstairs, Grayson's voice rang out, breaking the silence. "Mom! What's for dinner?"

Harriet sighed, shoulders sagging, and shuffled toward the kitchen. "I guess we're all having feelings today," she muttered, pulling open the fridge.

Over dinner, Harriet tried her best to hold a normal conversation with her children. Once she convinced—read: threatened—them to put their phones away, it was only marginally easier to keep their attention. Grayson was shoveling his second helping of miso salmon into his mouth, while Olivia ate her chicken nuggets dipped in honey as slowly as she had as a five-year-old. Her bad mood from earlier appeared to have passed.

"Slow down, Gray. No one's going to take your dinner away from you." She studied her son, shocked to find he looked as though he had grown during his weekend at his dad's. Was it possible he had?

She looked at Olivia. Same curly hair, though hers was lighter and much longer, same light-brown eyes she shared with her brother. Both their kids had Alex's nose and the same catlike eye shape, but the similarities to their father seemed to end there.

"Are you trying to beef up for soccer?" she asked, even though, realistically, didn't it make more sense to be smaller and lean? Wouldn't that make him, as a right forward, faster and therefore harder to catch?

Harriet never cared much for soccer or any team sport. Tennis, however, had been her first and only love for a long time. But that was a long time ago.

Grayson went still. As soon as he shot his sister a look, she knew something was up.

"What?"

Again, Grayson looked at his sister, who shrugged.

"Just tell her."

Grayson set down his fork with a sigh. "I think I want to take a break from soccer."

Harriet forced herself to count to three before responding. "But you love soccer."

He nodded, but his heart wasn't in it. "I can love something and still need a little space."

Isn't that the truth.

"Does your dad know about this?" She knew she shouldn't care, but the instinct to run things by Alex was hard to shake. She was still subconsciously checking with him like some old habit she couldn't break, no matter how much she tried.

Grayson smirked. "Not yet. I figured I'd wait until he's in a good mood. So...like, Christmas?"

Olivia snorted.

Harriet leaned back in her chair, crossing her arms. "Great. I get to be the bad guy. Again."

"Why are you always so dramatic? It's not a big deal."

"You've been playing soccer since kindergarten. What are you going to do instead?"

Grayson shrugged. "Honestly, I'm looking forward to having more free time."

"Free time?"

"Yeah. I mean, soccer's fun and all, but it takes up a lot of time. Practice, games, all that stuff. I could use a break. You know, just *chill* for a while."

Harriet felt a rush of confusion. "So you want to quit soccer so you can, what, do nothing?"

"Not nothing. Just…less running around," he said with a casual air, as though it was the most obvious decision ever. "I could sleep in on Saturdays, maybe play some more video games, or, I don't know, relax. It's the *chill* vibe I'm after."

Olivia snorted again. It was the kind of thing she would only do in front of her family, never her friends. "Grayson's idea of 'chill' is sitting around and talking about how much he hates his homework, or whatever it is he does with his door locked all the time."

Harriet sighed. Nope, she was *not* going *there.* "You're really going to quit soccer so you can play more video games?"

"Well, it's not forever. Just a break. Like when you take a nap and then you feel rejuvenated."

Harriet fought back a smile. "I swear, you two are going to be the end of me."

Olivia brought herself to standing. She looked at her brother pointedly. "Don't mind Mom. Just because she can't function without a plan or a schedule doesn't mean the rest of us need one."

The comment would have stung Harriet if it weren't so true.

4

The kitchen was quiet, save for the hum of the refrigerator and the rhythmic clinking of Harriet's glass as she sipped her wine—Pinot Grigio, chilled to a perfect forty-five degrees. A storage bin sat open on the floor, its lid leaning against the counter. *HOLIDAY DECOR*, the bold black label read, though the contents were far from festive right now. She crouched beside it and pulled out a crumpled string of lights. The faint scent of dust and plastic wafted up as she worked to untangle the wires, their tiny bulbs catching the glow of the overhead lights. Harriet stared at them for a moment, letting the weight of the task settle over her.

It wasn't Christmas, not even close, but Harriet had seen the box in the garage and had the strange desire to poke around inside of it. She pulled out a ceramic reindeer, its antlers glued back on more times than she could count. Alex used to insist it go on the mantel, front and center. She frowned and set it down a little too hard, the sound echoing in the empty room.

What was the point of dragging all this out now? She ran her hands over a battered garland still carrying the faintest scent of evergreen. She wouldn't even host this year. No big dinner, no pretending everything was fine.

Her gaze caught on a familiar envelope tucked beneath a mess of ornaments. She pulled it out slowly, her name scrawled across the front in Alex's handwriting. It was a card. Five years old. She didn't have to open it to remember the words. *To the best wife, partner, and mom. You make this house a home.*

Her laugh was dry, almost brittle, as she set the card on the counter. "The best wife," she muttered. Funny how little that had mattered to Alex in the end.

The sharp chime of the doorbell broke the quiet, making her flinch. Harriet wiped her hands on her jeans and walked to the door, her bare feet cool against the tile.

The delivery driver gave her a polite nod and handed her a large envelope. "Sign here."

She scrawled her name quickly and took the envelope, offering a distracted "thanks" before closing the door. Back in the kitchen, she slid her finger under the flap. The glue gave way with a faint crackle, and she tugged the contents free.

Harriet unfolded the thick fold of papers, the paper cracking and popping.

Petition for Dissolution of Marriage.

Her eyes scanned the page again and again, her mind taking far too long to catch up with the words she was reading.

No, no, *no.*

This was all wrong. Harriet wasn't supposed to be the one receiving divorce papers. She was supposed to be the one sending them. She was supposed to be the one selecting what was wrong with them from a predetermined list of acceptable reasons. Grounds for divorce: incompatibility.

Alex wanted to fuck women other than his wife, but she had taken her marriage vows more seriously.

Harriet read the first lines again, willing the words to rearrange themselves. They didn't.

Heat climbed her throat. Her pulse thudded in her ears. The refrigerator hummed, maddeningly steady.

Anger surged—sudden, physical. She wanted to hurl something, to hear it break.

Her gaze landed on the family photograph propped on the counter: the four of them, frozen in a summer long past, all smiles and sunburns.

Before she could think, her hand swept it up and flung it.

The frame hit the tile with a sharp, splintering crack. Glass scattered across the kitchen floor, tiny sparks catching in the overhead light.

Harriet kneeled, her bare knees against the cold porcelain, reaching for the shards. A sliver bit her thumb, and she pressed it to her lips, tasting the sting of metal.

She stared at the fractured photograph: Alex's half-smile, the twins mid-laugh, her own eyes shining with a happiness that no longer felt like hers.

The edges cut into her palm as she gripped the frame too tightly.

And then her gaze moved to the stack of papers on the counter.

Petition for Dissolution of Marriage. Such neat, quiet words for something that roared in her ears.

She'd known her marriage was fraying, but she hadn't expected this. Not now. Not yet. Not Alex choosing the last word. Not a surprise like this.

She was the one who'd been blindsided, not him.

She was the one who'd been "no longer compatible" with a guy who apparently thought marital problems could be solved with a strategic disappearing act. She should be the one calling the shots about when enough was enough.

Harriet paced the length of the main floor, the divorce papers clutched tightly in one hand, her phone abandoned on the kitchen island. She didn't scream, throw something, or give in to the urge to post a scathing social media takedown about the sanctity of marriage and the men who ruined it. Instead, she did nothing.

Nothing except letting her brain run circles around itself, playing and replaying the same questions. When had he decided to file for divorce? And why hadn't he at least warned her?

The words felt imprinted on her mind: *Petition for Dissolution of Marriage.* The finality of it. The simplicity of it. As if their entire relationship could be distilled into a few tidy phrases, no mess, no blood.

"God," she muttered to the empty room. "How did we even get here?"

She didn't expect an answer. But the silence that followed made her shiver.

Harriet looked down at the papers again, determined to see what she'd missed the first time. There was always fine print in these things, right? Something that would explain how Alex had gone from *maybe this separation is for the best* to *let's serve my ex with divorce papers with zero warning just to see if I can kill her rather than have to deal with her for a second longer.*

Her eyes skimmed the document, scanning for a sign, a reason, something that would make this all make sense. And then she saw it.

> *The Petitioner agrees the Respondent shall have primary physical custody of the children...*

She froze.

What?

She sat there, still as a statue, her heart pounding erratically in her chest, blinking at the page, hoping it might rearrange itself into something comprehensible. This couldn't be right.

But there it was, in cold, unfeeling legalese.

The Petitioner, Alexander Young, respectfully requests that primary physical and legal custody of the minor children, Grayson Young and Olivia Young, born 04/21/2009, be awarded to the Respondent, Harriet Langley Young, with the following terms for visitation and parental responsibilities:

1 Custody Agreement:

The Petitioner agrees that the Respondent shall have primary physical custody of the children, as well as primary legal custody, granting the Respondent the authority to make decisions regarding the children's health, education, and welfare.

2 Visitation and Parenting Time:

The Petitioner requests regular parenting time consisting of visitation with the children every second weekend, beginning on Fridays at 4:00 p.m. and ending on Sundays at 6:00 p.m., or as otherwise mutually agreed upon by both parties.

3 Parental Responsibilities:

The Petitioner acknowledges that the Respondent will retain primary decision-making authority in all major matters concerning the children's upbringing, including but not limited to their schooling, medical care, extracurricular activities, and other significant aspects of their welfare. The Petitioner requests to be informed and consulted on major decisions whenever possible, but defers final decision-making authority to the Respondent.

4 Child Support and Financial Obligations:

The Petitioner agrees to fulfill financial obligations, including child support, as determined by the court in accordance with state guidelines, ensuring the children's financial needs are met.

5 Statement of Understanding:

The Petitioner acknowledges that this request reflects an effort to maintain a consistent and stable environment for the children while fostering their relationship with both parents. The Petitioner understands that the proposed visitation schedule and custodial arrangement are in the best interests of the children, providing continuity and minimizing disruptions to their daily lives.

Harriet glanced at her wineglass, wanting a large drink but worrying about the thin, fragile glass in her trembling hands. Her cheeks burned. Who the hell did Alex think he was? Slipping this in like a hotel mini-bar charge she'd blindly pay? Not a word, not a hint of warning!

This was the man who used to do midnight diaper runs like some kind of exhausted superhero. The same guy who taught their daughter to ride a bike, running alongside her so fast he ate pavement...and got up laughing. *That* guy was now trying to clock out of fatherhood? What the hell happened to him? Did he wake up one day and decide, *You know what? I think I'd rather parent part-time.*

Harriet pressed her hands to her eyes like she could reboot her brain with enough pressure, but the panic was already setting in. How was she supposed to tell the twins?

Maybe she wouldn't. Maybe Alex would explain it himself, preferably while wearing a "World's Okayest Dad" T-shirt. She snorted bitterly at the thought.

She opened her eyes and glared at the papers again. They didn't glare back, but she could practically hear their smug little legalese voices taunting her. And all she could think—loudly, clearly, and with an intensity that might have singed the edges of the pages—was *Fuck you, Alex Young.*

5

Harriet had always been fascinated with the various ways people respond to bad news. Take her coworker Clare, for example. Last year, when Clare's boyfriend of seven years broke up with her over brunch, she didn't cry, scream, or even blink. Instead, she calmly finished her eggs Benedict, wiped the corners of her mouth with surgical precision, and asked the waiter for the dessert menu. "If I'm going to be blindsided, I may as well get a crème brûlée out of it," she later told Harriet with a shrug.

Then there was Harriet's neighbor, Mrs. Patel, who fainted when she found out her son had dropped out of med school. Just collapsed right there in her driveway, grocery bags and all, the disappointment short-circuiting her entire nervous system. Harriet helped her up, of course, but couldn't stop wondering if the fainting spell had been entirely genuine, or simply a strategic performance. And Harriet's college roommate, Sophie? Sophie got mad. Not regular mad, either, but the kind of mad involving meticulous planning and borderline illegal retribution. When Sophie's boss demoted her, she responded by sneaking into the office one night and swapping out all the coffee beans with decaf. It was months before anyone figured it out. Sophie said the chaos was worth it.

It was this fascination with reactions, her own and others', that kept Harriet staring at the ceiling too many nights to recall, cataloging them like some macabre hobby.

Her own response to most anything negative was almost always the same. It started in her hands, which tingled and shook, and then spread slowly through her arms, all the way to her shoulders. Then came the steep rise in her body temperature, not unlike what she imagined she'd soon experience in menopause. It was around this time that she began to feel as though she wasn't in control of her own body. If she were stubborn and gave in to the anxiety attack, it would continue to take over, and then there was little she could do except ride the wave for the night. If, however, she willed her body to stay calm, if she was successful in convincing herself she was not, in fact, in mortal danger, her symptoms would continue for little more than fifteen minutes before subsiding.

Tonight, she stood little chance against her anxiety. And it was all Alex's fault.

Upstairs in the guest room, which she had done her best to decorate with items that brought her joy, Harriet sank onto the bare mattress. Through the cracked window came the faint whoosh of palm fronds shifting in the night breeze, and somewhere close by a neighbor's surfboard rattled against a fence, a reminder of the ocean just beyond her walls. Across the hall, her freshly laundered sheets sat forgotten in the dryer. She made no move to retrieve them. Instead, she lay motionless, staring up at the ceiling, her breath shallow and uneven.

Anxiety had always been a shadow in her life. In middle school, it showed up as endless worrying, restless fidgeting, and stomachaches, leaving her doubled over. By high school, it had evolved into constant irritability and the feeling of being crushed under the weight of it all. By the time she graduated from college, she was juggling all of these symptoms on a near-daily basis. It wasn't until years later—married, with kids—that she finally sought help.

Her mother had been no help. Whenever Harriet tried to explain how she felt—the constant knot in her stomach, the buzzing restlessness in her limbs—Susan Langley waved it off. "It's all in your head," she'd say. Harriet stopped trying to explain after a while. It wasn't worth the fight.

Susan's dismissiveness wasn't limited to Harriet's anxiety. Her mother had a way of downplaying anything not fitting her narrow view of the world. Harriet's fears were "silly." Her aspirations, unless practical, were "childish." Even her accomplishments were scrutinized for flaws rather than celebrated.

As an adult, Harriet found it particularly frustrating. The deeper she dug into her anxiety, the more she realized how much of it had been exacerbated by her mother. The tension in her own chest felt hauntingly familiar to the sharp, impatient sighs of her childhood home. The fear of being too much or not enough had been her constant companion for years, and Harriet could see now how much of it had been planted in her.

It was maddening the way someone so central to her life had been both the origin and the accelerant for so much of her pain.

Susan's weariness extended to almost everything, especially Harriet's marriage to Alex. From the beginning, her mother had been skeptical—not of Alex himself, but of the concept of marriage. "You're rushing into this," she'd said with a sharpness lingering long after the words. "You're too young to tie yourself to someone. You don't even know who you are yet."

It wasn't that her mother disliked Alex. In fact, she'd been cordial enough during the engagement, smiling at family dinners and asking polite, surface-level questions. But Harriet knew what lay beneath: her mother's unwavering belief that no man could be trusted.

Harriet hadn't changed her last name when Alex and she married, a fact he'd always hated but hadn't bothered to admit until they were already near the end. By then, it had become another item to add to the list of complaints.

Susan had been married twice, and after the second marriage ended, she made her daughter promise she'd never choose a man's name over her own. "These men take so much from us. The least we can do is keep our name," she'd said.

Alex thought this was ridiculous, which only strengthened Harriet's resolve to follow her mother's advice this one time.

Now she was glad she wouldn't have to go through the hassle of changing it back, of rebranding herself once again—first as a wife, as belonging to someone else, and now, not.

Harriet exhaled sharply, her breath stirring the stray hairs tickling her forehead. The ceiling stared back, unflinching in its indifference to her swirling thoughts.

You're okay. It's just an anxiety attack.

She repeated the mantra over and over until the trembling in her hands slowed and the prickling heat beneath her skin began to fade.

Finally, she pushed herself upright, legs unsteady but functional, and shuffled to the dryer to retrieve her linens. Her movements felt hollow and mechanical, arms and legs obeying commands her mind hadn't fully issued. By the time she made the bed, she wasn't sure if she felt better or just… numb.

How could Alex do this? How could he blindside her like this? How could he do this to his children? He could be so fucking narrow-minded and selfish sometimes.

She shook her head. No. No, she wouldn't do this. Calling

him names wasn't going to help. It wouldn't undo what had happened or make the ache in her chest any less raw.

But even as she tried to pull her thoughts back in line, they veered somewhere darker, heavier. It wasn't just Alex. It wasn't only the betrayal or the way he'd blindsided her. It was the life she was now officially losing, the ground crumbling beneath her feet. She'd built so much around him—around their marriage, their routines, and shared history. The family they'd created.

And now, it was like he'd taken a match to it all, leaving her to sift through the ashes. What was left?

She'd prepared herself for a lot of things in life—raising kids while balancing a career, existing peacefully among people who didn't share the same political beliefs, and navigating the occasional marital argument. But this? This hollow, unpredictable future? She wasn't ready. She didn't even know how to be ready.

She wasn't sure she was ready to be alone. It wasn't the solitude that scared her, not exactly. She liked her own company well enough, and she wasn't the kind of person who needed or even enjoyed being part of a crowd. But there was a difference between choosing to be alone and having it thrust upon you.

Harriet sank back onto the bed, her hands gripping her knees. Her chest tightened again, the edge of panic creeping back in. She sighed and reached for the remote. Distraction. She needed a distraction...and some peanut butter. That always helped.

She flipped through the channels aimlessly, not really paying attention to anything in particular. A sitcom laugh track grated against her nerves. A true crime show felt too bleak. And then, she stopped. On the screen was the unmistakable blue-green of a tennis court, lit brightly under stadium lights. The US Open. The camera zoomed in on Radu

Albot, sweat dripping from his brow as he steadied himself for Novak Djokovic's serve.

For a moment, she just stared, letting the familiar rhythm of the match pull her in. The sound of the ball meeting the racket, the precise movement of the players' feet, the muted hum of the crowd—it all wrapped around her like a long-forgotten comfort. It took her back to her childhood summers, sitting cross-legged on the living room floor, eyes glued to the matches. She'd idolized the players, their strength, precision, and grit.

Her own history of playing the game felt so long ago now.

Harriet relaxed further into the pillows, her focus narrowing. Djokovic's serve was relentless, and Albot scrambled to keep up, his returns sharp but a hair too slow. Harriet couldn't look away.

She didn't notice the hours slipping by.

Somewhere between the second and third sets, she realized her pulse had slowed, her breathing steady and deep. It wasn't peace exactly, but it was something close to it—a quieting of the noise in her head, a reminder of something she used to love.

6

Harriet woke the next morning, two minutes before her alarm was set to go off, to find ESPN still playing. A rerun of last night's match was on, the commentators' voices low. For ten blissful seconds, she lived in a world where she hadn't just been served divorce papers. A world that hadn't been turned upside down.

And then she blinked, and it all came flooding back.

Her chest tightened, the way it always did when she thought about anything terrible for too long, so she swung her legs out of bed and pressed her feet to the cool floor. No time to wallow. The kids needed to get to school.

She padded to the kitchen, poured herself coffee, and then went to the twins' rooms.

"Liv, time to get up," she called, knocking once before moving on to Grayson's door. "Gray, let's go. School."

Both of them groaned their discontent in unison, and Harriet almost smiled at their symmetry. It wasn't often they were so in sync.

By the time they'd eaten and shuffled out the door, backpacks slung over their shoulders, Harriet had drained her coffee. The drive to school was quiet. Olivia had her headphones in, and Grayson stared out the window with the same sullen expression he'd worn for months now.

Harriet felt their absence the moment they were gone. She couldn't help but think this was the part where other people, normal people, might call a friend. They'd vent, cry, maybe even scream. But Harriet was in short supply of friends these days, ever since she'd moved from a *we* to an *I*. She couldn't think of anyone to call—well, except for Charlie.

With a resigned sigh, she asked her fancy car to call her soon-to-be ex-sister-in-law before she could overthink it.

"Harriet?" Charlie answered after the third ring, her voice groggy.

"Sorry, did I wake you?"

"No, no, I was...what's going on?"

Harriet took a steadying breath. "Did you know?"

"Did I know what?" Charlie's voice sharpened.

"About Alex." Harriet's throat constricted around the name. "That he was going to serve me divorce papers."

There was a pause, and for a moment, Harriet thought the call had dropped.

"No. No...he didn't say a word to me."

Harriet's grip loosened, the tension in her chest ebbing slightly. "Okay. I thought maybe you...I don't know. Never mind."

"I'm so sorry, Harriet. I can't believe—"

"Please don't apologize for him. I just needed to know if you knew." She considered bringing up the custody arrangement. Alex had barely fought for the kids and relegated them to every other weekend, as if they were an inconvenience. But no. This was his mess to explain, not hers. Talking to his family wasn't her problem anymore. "I have to go," she said instead. "Work."

"Harriet..."

"We'll talk soon, okay?" She ended the call before Charlie could say anything else.

Harriet's hand rested on the steering wheel, her heart racing as her conversation with Charlie replayed in her mind. The disbelief in Charlie's voice hadn't soothed her. If anything, it only made her angrier. She'd spent the last fifteen hours trying to keep it together—for the kids, for herself—but something inside her snapped.

Alex. This was his mess. His choice. His wreckage. And he dared to hand her divorce papers?

He wasn't going to just drop this bombshell and slink away.

Before she could think better of it, Harriet unlocked her phone, found his number, and hit call. The line rang once, twice, three times before going to voicemail.

"Unbelievable," she muttered, her anger bubbling hotter. She hit redial. Again, it went to voicemail.

Her phone buzzed with a text before she could call him again.

> Alex: I think it's best if we communicate through the attorneys moving forward.

Harriet let out a laugh, sharp and humorless. Communicate through the attorneys? That's how he wanted to play this?

Her hands trembled as she hit call for the third time. This time, she didn't care when it went to voicemail.

"You're a coward, Alex," she snapped into the phone, her voice low and icy. "A cheater and a liar, too, but more than anything, a coward. You don't want to talk to me? Fine. But you're not going to run away from this. You're going to sit down with our children and tell them what you're doing... what *you* are doing to this family. And don't even think for a second you'll be doing it alone. I'll be there. Because those kids are going to need their mother when their father shatters their world." She stopped, her breath coming fast and hard. "You don't get to walk away, Alex. Not like this."

She ended the call and tossed the phone onto the passenger seat with more force than necessary. Her chest heaved, the quiet of the car pressing down on her as the weight of her words sank in. She didn't regret them. Not a single one. If Alex wanted to slink away into the shadows, that was his problem. But Harriet wasn't about to let him disappear without facing what he'd done.

Harriet didn't think much of the red two-door sedan parked across from her driveway until she pulled into the garage and, in her rearview mirror, saw Alex step out from behind the driver's seat.

He was tall and broad-shouldered, the kind of build that made him seem commanding even when he wasn't trying. His dark-blond hair, now streaked liberally with gray, was shorter than the last time she'd seen him months ago, a clean cut that somehow made him look sharper. He had those same striking blue eyes, catlike in their shape, giving him a piercing, almost unreadable expression she used to find magnetic.

If she weren't so angry, she might have been able to admit he looked good. Better than ever, actually. But she *was* angry, and so she arranged her expression into one that displayed as such as Alex maneuvered his way up the driveway toward her.

He kept his head lowered as he greeted her.

She crossed her arms, raising a brow. "Look at you, lowering your head like a badly behaved golden retriever. Only difference is, dogs usually feel guilty when they've done something wrong."

"Harriet..."

She lifted her hand to stop him from speaking. She didn't want to hear it. What she wanted to do was go inside and get through the next hour as painlessly as possible.

Alex's jaw tightened, but he said nothing. Instead, he glanced toward the house, his gaze darting back to Harriet's with an unspoken question. She didn't answer. Instead, she turned on her heel, marched up the driveway, and unlocked the front door, leaving it ajar behind her. She hadn't even closed the door to the living room when Olivia appeared from the hallway, her expression twisting in confusion.

"Dad? What are you doing here?"

Grayson came next, sliding into the room with his hands stuffed into his hoodie pockets. His eyes narrowed as he glanced at his father.

Harriet said nothing. She simply turned her gaze to Alex, arching a brow in a way that said, *Go ahead. This is your doing.*

Alex hesitated, his hand brushing through his short-cropped hair, a telltale sign of his nerves. He stepped forward and sat on the edge of the loveseat, his shoulders stiff. The twins exchanged a glance, then slowly sat across from him on the floor.

Harriet really did need to go couch shopping.

Harriet stayed in the corner near the fireplace, her arms crossed tightly over her chest. Watching Alex seated in the middle of the home they had shared for a decade made her stomach twist. She'd never thought she'd see him there again, certainly not so soon. Her eyes lingered on the way his broad shoulders curved inward slightly, how he leaned forward with his elbows on his knees as though bracing for impact. She was taken aback by how *familiar* he looked, sitting in that same spot he used to sit every evening to read or to watch TV after the kids went to bed.

But this wasn't the same.

"Dad?" Olivia prompted again, her voice uncertain.

Alex cleared his throat and glanced briefly at Harriet. She didn't move. Just stared at him, her expression sharp and unyielding. He was quiet for a moment, as though steeling himself for an uphill climb. Then, with a stiff exhale, he began, his tone measured and almost clinical. "Your mom and I…" His voice wavered for a fraction of a second before he forced it steady. "We've decided we should be apart."

Olivia frowned, leaning forward. "You're already living in separate houses."

Alex hesitated.

There was no easy way to say what had to be said. Truthfully, Harriet was glad not to have to be the one to say the word.

"We're getting a divorce."

And there it was.

It landed like a boulder in the middle of the room, the silence stretching unbearably thin.

Olivia sat back, stunned. She and Harriet had had enough discussions for her to know that there was probably no going back on her and Alex's separation, but to hear it now, coming out of her father's mouth, still had to be a bit of a shock.

It was Grayson who said, "What? Why?"

"It's complicated," Alex said tightly.

Harriet snorted and then tried to pretend like she hadn't. "You're talking to our *kids,* Alex. Not strangers at a cocktail party."

"Mom, stop." Grayson's voice was low, edged with a quiet frustration that made her wince.

Alex cleared his throat again. "I want you both to know this doesn't change how much we love you—"

"Oh, don't," Harriet interrupted, her voice trembling now, though with anger or something else, she wasn't sure. "Don't act like this is some noble, mutual decision…"

"I don't think this is the time," Alex said, his voice even but his shoulders tense.

Grayson stood abruptly. "This is stupid." His tone was clipped, his voice steady, but the redness creeping up his neck betrayed him. "You're not even saying anything real."

"Gray, it's real. This is happening," Alex said, but his son was already heading for the hallway.

Olivia sat frozen, her eyes wide and glassy, darting between her parents. "So…is that it?"

Alex leaned forward, his hands braced on his knees. "We're still your parents, Olivia. That doesn't change."

But Olivia wasn't looking at him anymore. Her gaze was locked on Harriet, waiting for confirmation…or denial.

The urge to shield her kids from this sterile, stilted conversation clawed at her. But she didn't move. She couldn't. "I think you've said enough, Alex," she finally said. "Maybe it's time to go."

Alex hesitated, his lips pressing into a thin line before he stood. For a moment, Harriet thought he might argue, but instead, he gave a slow, reluctant nod.

"I'll call you and your brother tomorrow," he said softly, his eyes lingering on Olivia.

He turned and walked out, shutting the door behind him.

In the silence following, Harriet looked at Olivia, who hadn't moved from the floor. She wanted to say something—anything—to make the hurt on her daughter's face go away, but the words refused to come.

7

The kids were quiet for days, and Harriet couldn't blame them. She remembered what it felt like to be the tender age of fifteen—the age where everything already felt impossibly big and out of your control. When she was their age, a single bad grade could ruin a week, and a fight with a friend could feel like the end of the world. Parents are getting a divorce? Tectonic.

At dinner, the usual chatter of school gossip and requests for second helpings was replaced by the dull clink of forks against plates. Olivia poked at her salad, her brows drawn tight in concentration. Grayson ate quickly and methodically, without lifting his eyes from his plate.

Harriet wanted to say something, to offer them a thread of comfort, but the words tangled up in her throat. She didn't know how to help them navigate this.

Harriet herself hadn't been much older when her parents split, and even then, it had left a mark. But she worried about Gray and Liv. She worried they'd take it personally, that they'd start to question what love or stability meant.

That night, Harriet stood in the hallway, caught between

their bedrooms, hesitating. She wanted to knock on both doors. To ask Grayson if he was okay. To sit on the floor with Olivia and talk about nothing until the nothing became something. But she didn't want to push. Didn't want to risk making it worse. Instead, she went to her own room, closed the door, and leaned against it.

The house was too quiet, the weight of all their unspoken feelings pressing against the walls. Harriet had always prided herself on being the glue for her family—the steady, dependable presence who kept everything from falling apart. But tonight, she felt like she was the one cracking.

God, she hated Alex so much right now. Him and his smug new haircut and shiny midlife crisis sports car. He was such a cliché.

Harriet slid down to sit on the floor, her back still pressed to the door. Her thoughts were a storm she couldn't quiet, circling endlessly around Alex and the kids. Her gaze bounced around the room, landing on the remote sitting atop the nightstand. She pushed herself up, grabbed it, and collapsed onto the bed. The TV blinked on, its glow the only light in the room. This time, she knew exactly what kind of distraction she was looking for.

On ESPN, the replay had Madison Keys up one set to Elize Mertens. The women moved across the court with a kind of relentless focus Harriet envied. Back and forth, back and forth, every shot deliberate, every swing purposeful. There had been a time she had been like them, moving with purpose and confidence on the court. But that was before Alex came along. Before she'd traded her racket for the kind of life she thought she was supposed to want.

Harriet let out a slow breath and tried to match the rhythm of her breathing to the steady cadence of the game. Something about the precision, the order of it, soothed her. Points were won or lost, clear as day. No gray areas, no passive-aggressive silences. Just the clean sound of a racket hitting the ball and the occasional outburst of applause.

She wondered if her life could ever feel like that again—measured and in control. For now, she let herself sink into the calm monotony of the game, letting it carry her away from the wreckage of her evening, pretending she wasn't the human equivalent of an unforced error.

She fell asleep once again to the rhythmic grunts of the players, their exertions slowly melding into something more...suggestive. By the time the ball bounced for the fifth time in her dream, Harriet was half-watching the match, half-wondering if ESPN had secretly switched to a late-night channel.

Saturday morning. Harriet had already been up for hours, the quiet house stretching around her as she worked in the kitchen. She'd made Olivia and Grayson's favorite breakfast—pancakes, bacon, and eggs—because at least *this* she could control.

The kids hadn't said much since Tuesday night, and while she'd given them space, the silence was driving her crazy. She needed to know what they were thinking and how they were feeling.

The table was set, the food waiting. Harriet stood by the counter, forcing herself to take a deep breath before they came in. Grayson shuffled in first, eyes still heavy with sleep. He slid into his chair and picked up his fork without a word. Olivia came in a moment later. She dropped into her seat with a huff, crossing her arms over her chest. She was wearing an old and faded John Mayer concert tee she'd long ago stolen from her mother.

"Good morning." Harriet tried for casual, but it came out tight.

"Yeah," Olivia muttered, barely glancing up from her phone. "Good morning."

Harriet spooned a portion of eggs onto her plate, trying to keep her hands steady. "You know, we haven't had a proper breakfast together in days. Thought it'd be nice to start the weekend right."

"Sure, Mom. Whatever."

Harriet felt the frustration rising, but she fought it down. She had to be patient.

"Gray, you need some more syrup?" She pushed the bottle closer to him without waiting for an answer. "Remember when we used to make breakfast together on Saturdays? You two were always so much help. Gray, you used to be in charge of the bacon, and Liv…well, you were always in charge of the syrup. You'd pour it all over the pancakes like you were trying to drown them or something."

Olivia snorted. "I'm pretty sure I was only doing it because you told me to."

Harriet's smile faltered. *Okay. Ouch.*

Grayson shrugged, still quiet. The silence felt like it was thickening, each second stretching longer than the last.

Olivia finally looked up from her phone, her eyes narrowing. "Are you really gonna pretend everything's fine?"

Harriet sighed. "I don't want to push you guys to talk about it if you're not ready. I'm certainly not trying to pretend everything is fine. I know it's not."

"You're the reason Dad doesn't want to live with us!" Olivia's words cut through the air, venomous and raw.

The fork Harriet was holding clattered against her plate. Her breath caught in her throat as anger, guilt, and pain rushed to the surface, but she couldn't quite find the words to fight back. Instead, she stared at her daughter.

Grayson said nothing, his eyes focused on his food like he was trying to disappear into it. The tension between them was thick, and Harriet's heart was heavy, unsure how to keep her balance in the midst of it all.

Harriet pulled in a shaky breath, fighting the urge to lash out. "That's not fair." Her voice trembled. "There's so much you don't know."

"Then tell me."

"It's not so simple, honey. It's between your father and me. I know you don't understand, but someday you will."

Harriet could see the hurt in her eyes, the layers of confusion and anger. Guilt gnawed at her.

Harriet opened her mouth to speak, but was interrupted by the shrill ring of her phone across the room. She recognized the tone. And if she didn't answer it the first time around, the caller would keep calling until she did.

Harriet answered on the fourth ring. "Good morning, Evelyn."

"Harriet, hi. Good morning."

Harriet waited for her mother-in-law to get to the point of her call. After a few beats of silence, she adjusted the phone against her ear and forced her voice to remain steady. "Is everything okay?"

There was a brief pause, the kind that hinted Evelyn was searching for the right words—or maybe just the least offensive ones. When she finally spoke, her tone was heavy with a cloying mix of concern and condescension that Harriet had come to expect.

"I heard about what happened between you and Alex…the divorce papers." Evelyn's voice was soft yet deliberate, as though Harriet might shatter if spoken to too loudly. "I wanted to…check in."

"How kind of you," Harriet said, her words measured. "We're managing as best we can."

"Oh, I'm sure you are, dear. You've always been so resilient. But, well, you know Alex. He's always carried so much on his shoulders. Work, the kids. I'm sure this decision wasn't easy for him."

Harriet's fingers tightened around the phone. Evelyn wasn't calling to offer sympathy. She was calling to rationalize, to smooth over her son's decision like it was some minor misunderstanding.

"I'm sure it wasn't."

"It's just...when I spoke to him, he said he's been unhappy for a while. And, well, these things don't happen overnight. Sometimes people grow apart, and it's nobody's fault. You understand, don't you?"

Harriet bit the inside of her cheek, keeping her tone even. "I understand that's what he told you."

Evelyn hesitated, clearly sensing the frost creeping into Harriet's voice. "Harriet, I'm not saying this is easy for anyone. But Alex is still the father of your children, and I hope...I hope we can all stay civil. For the kids."

There it was. The implicit reminder of what Harriet stood to lose if she didn't play nice: her place in the family, in the world she'd spent years building around Alex and his relatives.

Evelyn's words were a subtle weapon, wrapped in the guise of concern.

"Of course," Harriet said. "I've never been anything but civil."

Evelyn hummed, a placating sound. "Good, good. That's all I wanted to hear. You're such a good mother, Harriet."

The words should have felt like a compliment, but instead they felt like a goodbye, a way to let Harriet down easy before fully stepping away.

Harriet glanced at the clock. She couldn't endure much more of this. "Thank you for checking in, Evelyn."

Evelyn hesitated again, as though considering whether to say more. But in the end, all she said was, "Take care, dear."

"You too."

Harriet set down the phone with deliberate care. The silence of the room rushed back in.

Harriet glanced over at the kids huddled over the remnants of their breakfast, trying to decide whether she felt angry or sad or just empty. In the end, it didn't matter. Evelyn's polite deflection was another reminder she was, slowly but surely, being erased from the life she'd once thought was hers.

Harriet barely had time to catch her breath before her phone buzzed again. This time, it wasn't Evelyn's name on the screen but Charlie's. Harriet hesitated, thumb hovering over the screen.

"Charlie, hi."

"Oh my god. I'm so sorry," Charlie blurted, skipping any preamble. "I heard Evelyn call you. Please tell me she wasn't awful."

Harriet smirked despite herself. "She wasn't awful. Polished, maybe. Guilt-adjacent. Pretty on-brand for Evelyn."

Charlie groaned. "I knew it. I told her to stay out of it, but you know her. She heard part of our call the other day, and suddenly she's Dr. Phil."

Ah. That explained it. "So she was eavesdropping?"

"I was on speakerphone because I was folding laundry, and she wandered in like a Victorian governess, catching every other word and *completely* missing the point."

"It's fine, really. It's not like I didn't see it coming."

Charlie huffed. "This is why I can't stand living here anymore. Every phone call is a family conference. If I'm not careful, she'll start chiming in on my group texts. And don't get me started on Dad's nightly lectures about budgeting or Evelyn's *helpful* commentary on my love life. It's like being sixteen again but with a lot more responsibility and no curfew."

"Sounds like a dream," Harriet quipped.

"Oh, it's magical. But seriously, I'm so sorry about her. She's way better at making things weird than fixing them."

"You don't have to apologize for her, Charlie. That's not your responsibility."

"I know, but I feel bad. You've always been good to me, Harriet, and Evelyn has this way of making things harder for everyone without even trying." She let out a short, sharp exhale through her nose. "If it's any consolation, she's probably on the phone with Alex right now giving him the same lecture. She loves to play mediator, even when no one asked her to."

"Well, at least she's consistent."

"Oh, consistently maddening," Charlie said, her voice brightening a little. "But hey, here's an idea. Let me make it up to you. Dinner. Somewhere with carbs, wine, and no Evelyn. Chuck's?"

Harriet smirked. "That sounds good."

"Perfect. I'll text you the details. And don't worry, I promise not to tell Evelyn where we're going."

"Deal." Harriet laughed softly. Even in the mess of it all, Charlie's humor felt like a lifeline—small and imperfect, but enough to remind her she wasn't completely alone.

8

When Harriet left the house the following evening, the kids were both in their rooms, their faces lit up by the glow of their phones. She felt like a terrible cliché as she walked out the door, imagining a better world for her children, one where screens never existed and their imaginations soared. But such were the times.

Charlie was already seated at a small table on the patio when Harriet arrived at Chuck's. She was sipping some kind of daiquiri, and as Harriet approached, she nudged the other glass toward her sister-in-law.

Harriet drank it greedily, bolstered by the sugar and alcohol. "I needed a night out." She studied Charlie across the table, her eyes narrowing. "How do you always manage to look so put together? I essentially slapped on some mascara and called it a day. You're lucky I changed out of my pajamas."

Charlie smirked, brushing an imaginary speck off her sleeveless linen shirt. "Oh, this? Just something I grabbed from the laundry pile. I like to call it 'effortless chic.'"

Harriet snorted. "If that's your laundry pile, then mine should be condemned."

"Laundry pile or not," Charlie said, raising her glass, "we both showed up. I'll toast to that."

"To showing up," Harriet echoed, clinking her glass against Charlie's.

They sipped in silence for a moment, the faint chatter of other diners filling the space between them. Harriet opened the menu in front of her and let her gaze wander over the options.

"This is nice," she said finally. "No lists to make, no dishes to do. Just a drink and some happy hour sushi."

Charlie tilted her head. "You really don't take enough nights off."

"I don't have your kind of time." She was only half-joking.

Charlie rolled her eyes. "Oh, please. I have my hands full, too, you know. Only with things that don't nag me every five seconds."

"You mean your job at a high-end boutique where you're constantly hit on by gorgeous, rich men? Yeah, my heart bleeds for you, Charlie. How do you even get out of bed every morning?"

Charlie grinned. "It's tough, but someone's gotta do it. Besides, most of them are twice my age and just looking for someone to stroke their ego…and maybe something else."

"Poor thing. Having to fend off sugar daddies while surrounded by designer suits. Truly, the struggle is real."

"Exactly," Charlie said, "You get it."

They both laughed, the easy rhythm of their banter cutting through the weight of their respective lives.

"Speaking of the struggle, what did my mother dearest have to say for her precious golden child?"

Harriet rolled her eyes. She was going to need another drink. "Oh, you know. Poor Alex has always carried so much on his shoulders, blah, blah, blah. I'm sure this decision wasn't easy for him."

Charlie's eyes closed. "He can do no wrong in her eyes. It's pathetic."

Harriet couldn't relate. An only child, she never had to compete with anyone but herself.

"She also felt the need to remind me that sometimes people grow apart, and it's nobody's fault."

"God, she's condescending."

A waiter materialized in front of them, and Charlie was quick to order for them both. "My treat."

After the waiter had gone, Harriet swirled the last of her daiquiri. "You'd think after twenty years of marriage, Alex could've found a less clichéd way to end it. I mean, an affair? How original."

Charlie lifted her thumb to her mouth and chewed on her nail, her expression somewhere between sympathy and scrutiny. "Do you really think it's just about the affair?"

Harriet sat up straighter. "What do you mean?"

Charlie shrugged, tracing the rim of her glass with her finger. "I mean, I've always thought you've been a little fixated on Alex's screw-ups."

It struck Harriet, as it often did, how sharp Charlie could be for someone still figuring out her own life. But then there was the upward lilt at the end of her sentences, the hint of uncertainty reminding Harriet her sister-in-law was still, in so many ways, just a girl.

Charlie was still talking. "Not saying they're not valid, believe me. But you talk about him like he's the only one who messed up."

Harriet's cheeks warmed. "What are you saying?"

Charlie leaned forward. "I guess…maybe the whole 'Alex is the villain' narrative is doing you more harm than good. Maybe you're so busy being angry at Alex, you're missing a chance to figure out what *you* actually want now. You know, instead of making him the center of the story."

Sharp as a damn tack, this one.

"You deserve better than to let him live rent-free in your head."

Harriet wished their food had arrived so she'd have something to do with her hands. "Since when did you get so wise?"

Charlie smiled and leaned back in her chair. "Since I decided not to let any guy—rich, gorgeous, or otherwise—ruin my vibe."

Harriet couldn't help but laugh, a short burst that felt good but quickly gave way to thought. Charlie's words began to morph, echoing in her mind, taking on a life of their own. Had she let Alex ruin her vibe? Maybe ruin was the wrong word, but change? Absolutely.

She could still picture the younger version of herself—vibrant, full of ambition, and, yes, a little stubborn. Tennis had been her outlet, something she'd excelled at through high school and college. She loved the rhythm of the game, the adrenaline of a close match, and the camaraderie with her teammates. Back then, Saturday mornings meant hitting the courts with her friends, followed by long brunches filled with laughter and mimosas.

That all changed once Alex came along. He didn't like tennis. He found it boring, their grunts unnecessary and dramatic, and over time, her Saturdays became more like his—errands, social events he wanted to attend, or simply staying home because he preferred a quiet weekend.

Even the small things had shifted imperceptibly at first. The way she dressed, choosing clothes she knew he liked. The vacations they took were always to places he found relaxing, never the bustling cities she'd dreamed of exploring. Harriet's entire world had been sculpted, consciously or not, to fit into his.

She'd done exactly what Charlie worked so hard not to do. She'd let a man change her wholly, from the inside out.

"So what you're saying is it's time to stop playing the victim and reclaim my identity?"

Charlie's brows furrowed. "I wouldn't say it quite like that, but yes." She paused for a moment and then chuckled. "Wait… reclaim your identity? What self-help podcast are you secretly listening to? Please tell me it's something with a host named Serenity or Moonbeam."

Harriet laughed, shaking her head. "It's not from a podcast, thank you very much."

"Mm-hmm. Well, whatever works. Just don't start quoting them at dinner, or I'll have to order something stronger."

"Like I could stop you."

Later that evening, after dinner with Charlie, a spirited argument over homework with the kids, and enduring her daughter's expertly honed arsenal of scathing looks after Harriet dared to ask who Liv was constantly texting, Harriet finally sank into the loveseat with a fresh cup of coffee. The house was quiet, relatively at least, and she flicked on the TV, deciding she'd earned a break from her habit of curling up with a book.

It hadn't taken much to ditch the ritual lately. All it took was the discovery that watching tennis players grunt in HD was oddly satisfying.

Tonight, Frances Tiafoe was playing Alexei Popyrin. Popyrin she vaguely remembered, but Tiafoe? She didn't recognize the name. How many players had risen through the ranks while she'd been too busy with carpools and PTA meetings to notice?

She reached for her phone, planning to Google the American, but the doorbell interrupted her. Harriet froze for a moment, debating. She glanced at the Ring camera out of habit but didn't wait for it to load before heading to the door.

Swinging it open, she found Charlie on the front porch, illuminated by the porch light. A well-loved suitcase sat at her side and she had a backpack slung over her shoulder.

"Hey." Charlie's voice was light but her expression was uncertain. "Since we had so much fun at dinner…any chance you'd be open to a houseguest?"

9

"Aunt Charlie! You're here early!" Olivia practically skipped into the kitchen to hug her aunt, then pulled back, studying her. "Wait, did you stay here last night?"

Charlie smiled at her niece. "Hey, kiddo. Yeah, I did. I'm going to be staying here for a while."

From the other end of the kitchen, Harriet rolled her eyes. "Well, we've talked about it being an option," she clarified.

Olivia was practically salivating. "Oh my god, we're going to have so much fun!"

Of course they would. Charlie, being the ripe age of twenty-seven, meant she was more like a big sister to Olivia than an adult figure. And the simple fact that Charlie wasn't her mother meant they would surely get along like gangbusters.

"Can you take us to school then?" Grayson asked.

Charlie looked down at her clothing—a ratty white T-shirt over a pair of old gray joggers—and laughed. "If I don't have to get out of the car, you have a deal."

Olivia reached for her aunt's cup of coffee, stealing a quick sip. "Your timing sucks, though. We're at Dad's for the rest of the week."

Charlie tore her gaze away from her niece to meet Harriet's eye. It was a look that clearly said, *Oh, fuck.*

Harriet moved slowly across the kitchen and took a seat across from her kids. "Your dad didn't talk to you?"

The twins exchanged a look of confusion.

"No. What is it?" Liv asked.

Harriet glanced between Olivia and Grayson, their faces still full of youthful innocence despite the undercurrent of teenage defiance that was ever-present these days. Her heart tightened as she thought about Alex and his sudden pivot. Every second weekend? How had they gone from splitting time equally to this? The kids deserved more than halfhearted gestures.

Harriet opened her mouth to explain, then hesitated. The words stuck in her throat.

Why was this on her? Why was it her job to clean up Alex's mess, to soften his choices for their children?

Finally, Harriet sighed and leaned forward, resting her forearms on the table. "You're not going to Dad's this week."

Olivia frowned. "Why not?"

"That's something your dad will have to explain."

Grayson frowned. "He didn't say anything when we saw him last week."

"Well, he'll talk to you soon, I'm sure."

The tension in the room thickened as Olivia exchanged another glance with Grayson.

"Whatever," Olivia muttered, leaning back in her chair.

Harriet pushed herself to her feet, her mind already racing. She crossed the room, picked up her phone from the counter, and quickly typed out a text.

> Harriet: You need to tell the kids what's going on. They deserve to hear it from you, not me. I won't cover for you, and I won't let you hide behind me. Be an adult and handle it.

She stared at the message for a moment before hitting send, her thumb pressing the button with more force than necessary.

Charlie spoke up from her spot by the sink. "You okay?"

Harriet let out a sharp breath, placing the phone down with a solid *thunk*. "I will be. If your brother would stop being such a—"

"Coward?"

"It's like he thinks parenting is optional."

Harriet fought the urge to pace. The text was sent, the ball now in Alex's court.

Charlie turned, pressing her back against the sink. "So what time do you brats need to head out?"

The moment everyone left, the house sank into a blissful, almost sacred silence. Even the overpowering trace of Grayson's cologne couldn't taint the deep, calming relief of solitude. Harriet adored her family—truly, she did—but the noise and constant presence of others could be a lot. Sometimes it was too much, just the sheer weight of *people*. And with Charlie moving in, Harriet doubted peace would be a frequent visitor.

She moved to the dining table where her laptop sat waiting, surrounded by a carefully arranged chaos of notebooks and sticky notes. It was rare for her to work from home, but today she was thankful to be home and in her pajamas.

Harriet set her coffee down, opened her laptop, and stared at the glowing screen. The email notifications were already piling up, little red numbers multiplying like bacteria. Harriet adjusted the glasses she only wore in the safety of her own home—how had she let the saleswoman convince her that she would pull off oval frames?—and tucked a strand of hair behind her ear. She had a presentation due by the end of the week and a handful of tasks she was already behind on. But for now, for a moment, she let herself sit in the quiet, the ticking of the clock the only sound, and appreciate the fleeting calm before the day's demands began clawing at her.

Charlie's arrival would surely throw a wrench into her carefully constructed balance. Call it crazy, but Harriet could already feel the shift. The girl had a knack for turning the most mundane mornings into a flurry of forgotten keys, mismatched socks, and dramatic exits. It was almost endearing how Charlie could create chaos just by existing.

She took a deep breath and pulled her to-do list closer, fingers poised over the keyboard. Time to work before the noise came back.

After a lunch of reheated chicken tikka masala, Harriet washed and dried her dishes and wiped down the kitchen counters. From the corner of her eye, she noticed the discarded pile of mail she'd collected on Saturday night, and right on top, where it couldn't be missed, was a letter from her neighborhood HOA.

Harriet opened the letter, cursing under her breath.

Dear Mr. and Mrs. Young,

As part of our ongoing efforts to keep our community beautiful and welcoming, we'd like to remind all residents of our guidelines regarding trash can storage.

It has come to our attention that your trash cans were left out beyond the designated time for collection this past week. As outlined in the HOA Rules and Regulations or CC&R Section...

Harriet stopped reading. And then she promptly threw the letter and its envelope into the garbage and, just for a kick, poured the dregs of her coffee over top. Satisfied, she sat back down to work.

The doorbell rang, slicing through the quiet. Harriet sighed, already half-dreading whatever solicitor or package mix-up awaited her. Sliding her chair back, she padded to the door in her socks and swung it open, only to find Greta standing there, arms crossed over her chest, wrapped in a scarf that probably cost more than Harriet's monthly grocery bill.

"Morning," Greta said briskly. "I thought I'd warn you that your trees out front are starting to look like they belong in a jungle exhibit. The HOA's going to be breathing down your neck if you don't handle it. Trust me, I know. Those nuts like to come after me all the time."

Harriet blinked. "Good morning to you too, Greta."

"Also," Greta continued, leaning against the doorframe. "I know you recently got a notice about your garbage cans. I'd hate to see you get written up twice in one month." She paused, studying Harriet with a sharpness that made her feel both scrutinized and—oddly—looked after. "I came over to keep you out of trouble, but honestly, you look like you could use a friend. And I don't have anything better to do."

Harriet stared at her. "So you showed up to tell me my yard's a disaster and then invite yourself in?"

Greta grinned. "Pretty much."

Harriet hesitated. It was the middle of her workday. She had things to do. But then she thought of Carrie and Laura, their easy laughter over coffee—the kind of warmth she was never a part of anymore—and suddenly, letting Greta in didn't seem like the worst idea.

She stepped back. "Fine. But only because anyone my age seems to want nothing to do with me."

"Deal." Greta breezed past her into the house. "And while I'm here, you're going to tell me what happened with you and Alex. Don't think I haven't noticed he hasn't been around."

Harriet arched a brow. "Straight for the jugular, huh?"

"You've lived here what, ten years? And we haven't graduated past small talk. Maybe it's time to stop caring so much about what everyone thinks and start figuring out what you want. You know...before you turn into me."

The door clicked shut behind them, and to Harriet's surprise, a small smile tugged at her lips. Greta could be intrusive, exasperating, and nosy—but maybe, just maybe, that wasn't the worst thing at the moment.

10

The kettle let out a sharp whistle, and Harriet moved to switch it off. Mondays were bad enough without Greta commandeering her kitchen, but there she was, perched at the table with her tea and her ever-present opinions. Harriet almost wished she hadn't let her through the front door.

Greta stirred her tea with a clink of the spoon against porcelain. "You going to stand there all day, or are you going to top me off?"

"I should get back to work," Harriet replied, pouring herself a cup. She hesitated a moment, then joined her at the table. She didn't need the older woman looking at her like she'd committed some kind of social crime.

"Your spreadsheet can wait. Tea first. Sanity later."

Harriet took a small sip, wincing at the bitterness she never quite got used to. Why anyone would drink tea when coffee existed was news to her. "Not sure this is doing much for my sanity."

"It's not supposed to taste good. It's supposed to slow you down."

Harriet gave a faint smile but didn't reply.

"How are things?" Greta raised an eyebrow. "And don't say fine. You say you're fine every time I see you. You'd think with Alex gone, you'd have a little more to say for yourself."

Harriet stirred her tea to buy herself a moment. "What's there to say? He's gone, I'm busy, and parenting teenagers sucks."

Greta studied her. "You don't miss him, do you?"

Harriet shook her head quickly. "No. Not at all."

"Good. Because that man never looked happy. Spent the last few years walking around this place like he was allergic to being home. If you ask me, you're better off."

Harriet blinked, the words landing heavier than she expected. *Allergic to being home?* That wasn't the way she'd ever thought of Alex—even in the ugliest moments.

"I—" Her mouth stayed open, soundless. The right response had been vacuumed out of the room. Surprise flickered into something closer to hurt, though she couldn't quite name why.

Greta practically leaped on her. "I see you. You've been holding this family together for years, and for what? You need to let go of this need to do everything."

"I'm not holding on to anything," Harriet snapped. "I'm trying to keep things stable...for the kids, for me."

Greta tilted her head. "Are you keeping things stable, or are you avoiding change? What's your plan? Spend the next ten years being miserable?"

Before Harriet could answer, the front door opened and Charlie breezed in. Her entrance was as effortless as always, her cheap flip-flops clicking against the tile floor. She tossed her bag onto the counter, looking fresh despite the summer heat.

"Hey, who's this?" Charlie said brightly, making a beeline

for the fridge. She grabbed a bottle of water and leaned against the counter, giving them both a curious look.

"Charlie, this is my neighbor, Greta. Greta, this is my sister-in-law, Charlie."

Greta's eyes traveled the length of Charlie, taking in her perfect beach wave hair and crop top right down to the silver toe ring on her right foot. "Your parents named you Charlie?"

Charlie barked out a laugh.

"Obviously not. Could you imagine Evelyn Young naming her daughter after a man? Not even if hell froze over." She turned to Greta. "I'm Charlotte, but prefer Charlie." She sipped from her bottle, her eyes on Harriet. "What's going on? You look tense."

"Nothing's going on," Harriet said a little too quickly.

"Your sister-in-law is still in denial."

Charlie said, "Ah. You're talking about my brother, then."

Harriet glared at Greta. "She doesn't need to know every detail of my life."

"You can talk about it, you know. It's not like I'm going to defend him."

"I'm not having this discussion," Harriet said, though her tone lacked conviction.

Greta studied Charlie thoughtfully. "What do you think? Is Harriet making the most of her new freedom?"

Charlie considered this, twisting the cap off her water bottle. "Probably not. But I can't blame her. Alex didn't exactly leave her in a good place."

"He didn't leave me," Harriet muttered, more to herself than to them.

Greta barreled on. "My guess is she's too busy cleaning up his mess that she's forgotten she doesn't have to. It's time to do something for herself."

"Like what?" Harriet knew she shouldn't have asked, but she couldn't help herself.

"Start small," Greta said. "Stop trying to do everything for everyone. And before you ask how I know that's what you're doing, let me remind you, I'm a mother too. Let the kids handle more of their stuff. And for God's sake, do something that makes you happy."

"She's not wrong," Charlie added.

Harriet stared at them, torn between irritation and the uncomfortable sense they might be right. She looked down at her tea, swirling the liquid absently. Then she walked straight over to the sink and dumped the vile liquid down the drain. She turned back to the women with a smile. "There. That made me *very* happy."

She walked back to the table and slid into her chair, smiling faintly. Greta raised an eyebrow, while Charlie let out a low whistle.

"Well, it's a start," Greta said.

"Small victories."

Charlie leaned forward, her chin resting in her palm. "So… what's next on the list of life transformations? Maybe you're finally open to the idea of having fun now?"

"Fun?" Harriet shot her a look. "What exactly do you mean?"

"You know," Charlie said, grinning. "Not working yourself to death, not micromanaging everything, maybe even—brace yourself—socializing."

Harriet groaned and leaned back in her chair. "I'm not a hermit. I talk to people all the time."

"Work doesn't count," Charlie said. Her expression turned serious. "Liv told me your friends are ignoring you."

Greta's smirk disappeared. "Let me guess…they're busy, right? Lives to live, schedules to keep?"

Harriet shrugged. "People move on. It's not personal."

"Not personal?" Charlie gave her a sharp look. "I get

people grow apart, but if they were real friends, they wouldn't have left you high and dry when things got hard."

Unsurprisingly, Greta agreed with her. "Are you even trying to connect with anyone?"

Harriet's cheeks flushed. "I don't have time to—"

"You have time," Charlie interrupted. "You just don't want to risk it. But you can't complain about being lonely if you don't put yourself out there."

Harriet blinked. "I don't recall saying I was lonely."

"It's written all over your face, Harriet," Greta said, not unkindly. "You're in a house full of people, and I'd bet my left kidney you've never felt more alone. I've been there. And you know what helped?"

Harriet glanced at her neighbor warily. "What?"

"Deciding to stop giving a damn what anyone else thinks and do what I needed to feel human again. It starts with one step—one. Talk to someone new. Say yes to an invite. Or hell, make the invite yourself."

Harriet looked between Greta and Charlie. "I don't even know where to start."

"You just start," Greta said.

Charlie raised her mug in a mock toast. "And remember, if it makes you happy, it's probably the right thing."

Harriet leveled a finger at her sister-in-law. "Oh no. Absolutely not. You do not get to hit me with some Pinterest wisdom and get away unscathed. You owe me some information if you want to stay here."

Charlie blinked innocently. "What do you mean?"

Harriet gave her a look, the kind that said *I was born at night, but not last night.* "Come on. Welcoming you into my house without at least one round of aggressive questioning as to why you are here is literally against my entire brand."

Greta snorted. "Yeah, no kidding. I'm honestly shocked you don't have a guest questionnaire by the door. 'State your business, list three references, and for the love of God, don't touch the thermostat.'"

Charlie joined Greta in a bout of laughter.

Harriet crossed her arms. "Ha. Ha. You're both *hilarious.* Remind me to laugh when I'm kicking you both out onto the street. I'll even provide snacks for the journey. Maybe a little sign that says *Will mock for shelter.*"

11

Despite her initial reservations, Harriet grew accustomed to having a new person living in the house more quickly than anticipated. Once she got over the shock of seeing Charlie's navel most days—seriously, how many crop tops could one person own?—her sister-in-law actually turned out to be a fairly helpful house guest. She cleaned up after herself, took over the carpool most mornings, and even helped with homework.

As directionless as Evelyn liked to assert she was, Charlie was surprisingly equipped at teaching algebra in a way that didn't have the twins pulling out their hair. They actually sat at the kitchen table for longer than twenty minutes when their aunt was teaching them. Another item to add to Harriet's list of parental failures—right up there with believing she could bond with them by saying "slay" unironically.

And if Charlie wasn't ready to spill whatever had sent her fleeing here in the first place, Harriet would try to respect her wishes. Even if it *did* go against every fiber of her being.

Even after Charlie teamed up with Greta to shame her for her antisocial, controlling ways, Harriet was still glad not to be alone with the kids. Having Charlie around offered a strange sense of relief, like a human shield in a Nerf war she hadn't realized she was losing.

Ever since Alex finally revealed to them his sudden change of heart regarding parenting, the twins had taken the words moody and distant to heart. Olivia seemed to spend all her time in her room, blasting melancholic pop playlists Harriet didn't recognize. When she *was* around, she remained glued to her phone, hiding her screen any time Harriet came remotely close to her. It was a real test of Harriet's patience.

Gray was sulking around the house more than ever. It didn't quite seem like the *chill vibe* he'd been aiming for, but who was Harriet to judge?

Dinner had become an exercise in endurance, with Harriet picking at her food while the kids communicated in glances and subtle shrugs, excluding her entirely.

Charlie, however, appeared unfazed. "At least they're not throwing things," she had said that morning, perched on the kitchen counter and sipping coffee like she already belonged there.

Harriet wanted to laugh at the absurdity of it. How Charlie, the *second* most chaotic influence in her life, was suddenly playing the role of the calm in her storm. But she couldn't muster the energy.

Instead, she sighed and leaned against the counter. "I have no idea what I'm supposed to be doing. It's like…like Alex dropped a bomb and left me to clean up the fallout."

Charlie set her mug down and regarded Harriet with a rare seriousness. "Granted, my big brother is not making the best choices lately, but…maybe stop trying to clean up after him?"

Harriet blinked. "Um, *hello*. You know I can't help it." Telling Harriet to stop running around after everyone was like telling the sun not to shine.

"You're trying to fix everyone's feelings. But what if they don't need fixing? I mean, it's only been a week. What if they just need you to sit in the rubble with them for a bit?"

It was such a Charlie thing to say. So nonchalant, yet uncomfortably on point.

Harriet looked at her coffee, her reflection distorted on the surface. "I don't know how to," she finally admitted.

"Well," Charlie said with a shrug. "Lucky for you, I have nothing better to do. Consider me your designated rubble-sitter." Then she flashed a grin so mischievous, so thoroughly *Charlie,* Harriet couldn't help but let out a dry chuckle.

After a few beats had passed, Harriet looked at Charlie over the lip of her mug. "Is that what you and your mom are doing? Sitting in the rubble?"

Charlie scrunched up her nose. "We were talking about your rubble."

"And now we're talking about yours."

Charlie gave Harriet a mock glare. "Okay, therapist. Didn't know this came with a side of hypocrisy."

"Oh, please. I'm not qualified to be anyone's therapist. My only credentials are a bachelor's degree and the fact that I once cried so hard in a Target that a stranger hugged me."

Charlie laughed, a sharp burst of sound. "How tragic."

"Tragic is my brand. And speaking of, can we circle back to your rubble? Or are you just here to laugh at my pain?"

Charlie straightened, brushing imaginary dust off her sweater. "I prefer to call it *deflecting with style.* But fine, since you insist...yes, my mom and I are *technically* sitting in our own rubble. Except I bet she's telling anyone who will listen she's 'giving me space.' I'm surprised she managed to stop texting me twenty times a day to ask if I've eaten."

Harriet raised a brow. "Have you?"

"Mostly chips. But the gourmet kind. You know, the ones with words like 'kettle' and 'artisanal' on the bag."

"Oh, well, in that case, you're thriving."

"You should try it. Buy something tasty, ignore your feelings for a bit, and call it progress."

Harriet shook her head, unable to stop a reluctant smile from creeping across her face. "This is why you're single, you know."

"Please. I'm single because the world isn't ready for this level of greatness. And also because I keep ghosting people."

Harriet snorted. Maybe Charlie was right. Maybe fixing everything wasn't the point. Maybe surviving the rubble was enough.

She worried over this as she sat at her desk in her square, 267 square foot office later that day. A stack of performance reviews sat in front of her, ready to be inputted into the system.

Records management was the least sexy part of her job, so she usually left it for Tuesday mornings—not Monday, the most vile day of the week, or Fridays, when she couldn't wait to get through work and spend two glorious days in her little home bubble. Tuesdays were easier to manage, easier to get through, easier to stomach.

Harriet stared at the spreadsheet on her monitor. The reviews were all neatly listed in the system, each tied to a color-coded cell indicating its status. Reviewing these files should have been a simple, straightforward task, precisely the kind of orderliness Harriet usually appreciated. But today, the words on the screen blurred into an indistinct mess.

She blinked hard and straightened in her chair, resolving to focus. One by one, she typed her notes, carefully weighing her feedback on each employee. No shortcuts, no skimming over details. It wasn't just about diligence. Harriet found a certain satisfaction in knowing she'd accounted for everything.

She had finished reviewing the third record when an email

notification popped up in the corner of her screen. The subject line: "Urgent Request: Benefit Dispute."

Harriet sighed and clicked the email open. One of the junior employees had filed a complaint about her health benefits, claiming discrepancies in her deductions. This was technically payroll's responsibility, but Harriet knew how these things went. If she didn't step in to smooth it over, it could snowball into a bigger issue.

Harriet's fingers hovered over the keyboard. She typed a short response asking Candace to stop by her office, and within minutes, there was a knock at the door.

"Hi, Harriet." Candace's voice was tentative as she stepped into the office. Her blonde hair was slightly frazzled, and her blouse had a small coffee stain near the hem. "Thanks for seeing me so quickly."

"Of course." Harriet gestured to the chair across from her desk. "Let's go over this together."

Candace launched into an explanation about the deductions, and Harriet nodded along, her mind already mapping out the next steps: check the payroll system, compare it to Candace's records, follow up with finance if needed.

Halfway through the conversation, Candace paused, fidgeting with her hands. "I hope I'm not bothering you. I know you must be swamped."

"It's no bother. These things are important."

Candace looked relieved, but as Harriet continued to reassure her, a small voice in the back of her mind whispered, *Why am I the one handling this?* She had a team for a reason, but she'd always been bad at delegating. What if they missed something? What if the issue escalated? It was easier, safer, to do it herself.

When Candace left the office, her concerns mostly resolved, Harriet leaned back in her chair and exhaled deeply.

Later that evening, Harriet returned home to the smell of Charlie's experimental cooking—a combination of garlic, something burned, and possibly...peanut butter?

"Dinner smells oddly good."

"Relax, it's pasta," Charlie called from the kitchen. "I'm trying a new sauce recipe. If it's bad, we can order pizza."

Charlie was twirling a wooden spoon in a pan. She looked up and grinned. "Long day?"

Harriet only sighed and glanced at the TV in the corner, which was muted but displaying highlights from the weekend's US Open finals. Jannik Sinner had beaten out Taylor Fritz for the trophy in a crowd, including Taylor Swift and Matthew McConaughey. Harriet had watched every minute from bed.

"You still into that?" Charlie asked, nodding toward the screen. "You used to play, right?"

Harriet's mind slipped back to her junior year of college, playing Long Beach State. Her opponent, Vanessa, had been quick, relentless, and impossible to wear down. Harriet remembered the second set vividly, tied at 4-4, 30-30. She'd taken a deep breath, tossed the ball high, and slammed her serve down the T. Vanessa returned it, but Harriet had already moved, driving the ball sharply to her opponent's weak backhand. The point had been hers, a brief thrill of triumph electrifying her as the crowd cheered. She'd lost the match in the third set, but that rally, her calculated risk, had stuck with her. She'd felt bold, capable.

Harriet blinked back to the present. "I forgot I'd even told you."

A thoughtful look crossed Charlie's face. "You ever think about picking it up again?"

"I don't know. I haven't played in years. I probably

wouldn't even know where to start. My racket is ancient and my knees aren't what they used to be."

"Oh, please. You're acting like you're eighty. You can still move, can't you?"

"Barely," Harriet quipped, but a flicker of nostalgia crept into her voice. She remembered the rush of a perfectly timed serve, the satisfying thwack of the ball hitting the strings.

Charlie grabbed her phone and started typing. "There's a sporting goods store nearby. We'll get you a new racket, some gear, maybe even those cute little wristbands—"

"Whoa, whoa, whoa. Who said anything about buying new gear?"

Charlie raised an eyebrow. "You did. In your heart. I can tell."

Harriet rolled her eyes but couldn't suppress a small smile. Maybe revisiting tennis wasn't such a terrible idea. But the thought of stepping back onto the court, rusty and out of practice, filled her with hesitation.

Charlie turned back to the stove. "Remember what Greta said last week. It might be nice to do something for yourself for a change. And who knows, you might even have fun."

Harriet didn't respond immediately, but as she sat down to dinner, the idea lingered. Maybe it was time to reclaim a piece of her old life, even if it was only for an hour on the weekends.

12

Harriet hadn't set foot on a tennis court in over seventeen years. She ran a hand across the smooth handle of the racket, feeling an odd mix of nostalgia and nerves.

In high school and college, she'd been good. More than good, actually. Tennis had been a part of her identity, if not nearly all of it, a thrill in the rush of serves and rallies. But then came Alex, with his easy charm and endless opinions, the kind that started off sounding like lighthearted banter until they didn't. She stopped playing one week, then two, and before long her racket sat untouched, gathering dust. Even watching the tournaments lost its appeal, Alex's commentary turning her excitement into a slow, reluctant retreat.

But now, standing on the court, she felt something click back into place. The faint squeak of sneakers on the court floors, the muffled thud of rackets hitting balls…it was like coming home after a long, confusing trip. She could play whenever she wanted to! Maybe even buy a new racket! And a new outfit to make her at least look the part!

Harriet scanned the courts, her gaze sweeping across the

faces of various men and women, until she spotted a lone player. She had the sense she'd seen him before, but it was unlikely.

He was impossibly tall with dark hair and eyes so light they were almost clear, and he was dressed as she'd expected: athletic shorts and a matching sweat-wicking T-shirt. His shoes looked new.

As she took him in—his flawless footwork, the way he anticipated the ball's bounce—she couldn't help but wonder what he'd make of her. Would he assume she was a tennis mom, tracking her kids' drills and making polite small talk?

She imagined the conversation, his polite but disinterested questions about her children, her awkwardly explaining how the twins weren't into tennis at all. She was afraid he might mistake her for one of *those* wives. That he might think she was only here to fill up the hours between hair and nail appointments.

It couldn't be further from the truth. She hated sitting in a chair for hours to have her hair colored, and she had never been one to paint her nails.

He tossed the ball into the air again, his wrist flicking at the perfect angle, and she found herself smirking. She got the impression that he was the kind of guy who had a ritual for everything—every serve, every grip, every glance at his watch. Would he make his smoothies with precision too? Track his steps obsessively? He didn't know her from any of the other players, but she felt like he would find a way to analyze her all the same.

He practiced his serve with calm, mesmerizing precision. He didn't need a team or a partner—just him and the ball and the confident ease in his movements. It was the kind of confidence she associated with someone who never had to wonder if they'd made the right choices or replay conversations long after they'd happened.

In short, the opposite of herself.

She could almost feel the energy coming off him as he moved. And it wasn't the usual dad-at-the-club energy, where they lunged around the court half-heartedly to justify their beer afterward. Each swing of the racket was controlled and powerful. Harriet was impressed. If she wasn't careful, he'd see her looking and mistake it for...she didn't know what. Some kind of interest that wasn't exactly why she was here.

But still, it was hard to look away. He didn't just play tennis. He commanded the court.

Finally, Harriet took a deep breath and stepped forward, squaring her shoulders, feeling, at last, ready to start swinging.

He turned and looked right at her. "Harriet Langley?"

Here, now, she was granted a full, unobstructed look at him. He had a rare, natural look about him, the kind that made her wonder how many hours he'd spent in the sun without ever worrying about wrinkles. It struck her how attractive he was.

No, attractive didn't cover it. He was *beautiful.*

But then, as quickly as she had the thought, she tossed it aside. She reached for his hand, surprised by its chill, despite the heat.

"I'm Liam. It's nice to meet you. Are you ready to show me what you've got?"

Harriet knew with certainty that she'd follow this man anywhere. To the ends of the earth, off a cliff, even. All the way to Ireland, which she was certain he was from. Right into his bed...

She set down her water bottle and adjusted her sunglasses, still feeling oddly self-conscious. She hadn't been around someone quite like him since...ever, really. Tall and athletic wasn't her type, or maybe it had never been in her orbit. But here he was, unmistakably impressive and irritatingly nonchalant about it.

Liam tossed a tennis ball lightly between his hands as he studied her. Harriet squirmed under his gaze, feeling like a kid in gym class all over again. She adjusted her visor, then tugged at her skirt, wondering if it had always been this short or if the past seventeen years had made her more modest. If she'd known what Liam looked like, she might have sprung for some new clothes after all, something designed in this decade.

"All right, Harriet. We'll start simple. No need to be nervous."

"I'm not nervous," she lied, gripping the racket like it might fly away otherwise. "Just…a little out of practice."

"Out of practice is fine," he said, his voice lilting in a way that made her stomach flip. His accent—it *was* Irish, she was sure now—wrapped around his words like a cozy sweater. "We're not aiming for Wimbledon today. Let's see what you've got."

He stepped back, standing behind the service line. "We'll start with a few volleys. No pressure to get it perfect, this is just to get a feel for where you're at."

He bounced the ball once, then sent it her way with an easy swing. She managed to hit it back—barely. The ball wobbled over the net before plopping unceremoniously onto his side of the court.

"Not bad," he said, his voice kind but neutral, the kind of tone a teacher used with a struggling student. "Your follow-through's a bit stiff. Try loosening your grip and letting your arm swing naturally."

Harriet nodded, adjusting her grip.

He sent another ball her way, and this time she managed a cleaner return. Not perfect, but it felt less awkward.

"Much better. Let's do a few more."

They volleyed back and forth for a while, Liam keeping his movements slow and deliberate.

Harriet found a rhythm, though her body protested every swing. By the tenth or eleventh exchange, her arms were already aching.

"How long has it been since you last played?"

"Oh, seventeen years," Harriet said, her voice tight as she caught her breath.

Liam chuckled, the sound low and easy. "Well, you're doing better than most after so long. Let's try a serve next."

Her confidence wavered at the word serve, but Liam was already demonstrating, his movements slow and exaggerated to show her the proper technique. When it was her turn, she sent the ball flying straight into the net. Twice.

"Not to worry. We'll work on it. Baby steps."

Harriet felt both reassured and mildly insulted. Baby steps. The phrase made her think of toddler playdates and spilled juice boxes, not the sleek, coordinated swing she'd hoped to emulate.

But when Liam smiled at her, she found herself forgiving the comment.

"Besides," he added, tossing the ball back to her. "You've got plenty of potential. I can tell."

His words were simple, but they landed with surprising weight.

Harriet squared her shoulders, determined to prove him right—or at least not make a total fool of herself. She tightened her grip on the racket, the awkward weight of it making her palms sweat.

"Relax your grip." Liam's smile made her stomach do a small, traitorous somersault. "You'll wear yourself out before you've even hit the ball."

She adjusted her hold, feeling his eyes on her as she tried to mimic the stance he'd demonstrated minutes ago. It didn't help that his effortless ease on the court only amplified her nerves.

When she finally looked at him, his smile widened, full of irritating charm, like he hadn't a clue what failure—or divorce—felt like.

I hate your smile, she thought, *mostly because I like it too much.*

He tossed her a ball, the bright yellow blur spinning through the air. Harriet swung too early, sending it ricocheting into the net. She retrieved the ball, feeling the burn in her legs from bending over. Tennis, it was now clear, was less forgiving than it had been at twenty-three.

"Ready?"

She nodded, though she wasn't, and this time, when she swung, the ball soared over the net. A hollow *ping* echoed in the quiet of the court. Harriet's heart leaped.

"Perfect form. See? You've got this."

It wasn't much—just words, a smile—but something flickered inside her. A faint, unfamiliar excitement. She wasn't sure if it was the sport or the coach, but for the first time in a long while, she felt seen. Not as Alex's ex-wife or Olivia and Grayson's mom. Just Harriet.

The sun bore down as they continued, and Harriet grew more comfortable, even laughing when she missed an easy shot. "You're not going easy on me, are you?" she teased, adjusting her visor.

"I wouldn't dare."

His grin was disarming. Harriet hated it again. And liked it even more.

By the end of the session, she was drenched in sweat, muscles aching. She reached for her water bottle, glancing at

Liam as he gathered up the balls with effortless efficiency. She wasn't sure how she would ever tear her eyes away from him.

As she left the court that day, her step felt a little lighter, like the start of something she couldn't quite name.

13

Harriet's tennis skills improved quickly. Not quickly enough to go pro or even make her way into the tennis club's doubles tournament, but quickly enough that Liam started complimenting her forehand instead of wincing at it.

Unfortunately, Harriet's real workout wasn't mastering her backhand. It was keeping her eyes off Liam's tan, muscular arms, and the way his shirt clung to his chest like it had a crush on him. How nice it was to be able to look at another man. And not feel guilty about it.

"Nice form," Liam said, tossing her another ball.

Harriet wasn't sure if he meant her swing or her sudden habit of zoning out whenever he bent to pick up a stray ball. She blamed her impending divorce. That was the real issue here, wasn't it? She was *rusty*. Certainly not *thirsty*.

"Thanks." She steadied her grip on the racket. She was definitely not picturing him shirtless, sweaty, and holding a towel. "I've been practicing."

She hadn't.

"Let's try volleys."

Harriet tried to keep her focus on the fuzzy yellow ball he'd tossed her way, but then he smiled—a devastating, movie-star smile—and all her focus evaporated like mist off the sunbaked cliffs of La Jolla.

She whiffed the ball entirely.

"You okay?"

"Oh, fine. Totally fine." Her voice was an octave too high. "Just distracted by…um…" She looked around, searching for an excuse. "Cloud formations."

There wasn't a single cloud in the sky.

Liam gave her a patient grin.

Harriet adjusted her grip again and told herself to *focus*. She was here to learn tennis, not to star in her own personal rom-com.

Well, not yet, anyway.

By the time Harriet got home, her post-tennis glow had been replaced by the simmering frustration of walking into what could only be described as *chaos meets college dorm chic*.

The culprit was obvious—Charlie.

The living room, which Harriet had left pristine, now looked like the set of a reality show where contestants competed to create the most creative mess. A half-assembled IKEA chair sat in the middle of the room, flanked by an open toolbox and what looked suspiciously like a half-empty bag of peanut M&M's spilled across her cream-colored rug. A stack of clothing teetered precariously on the back of her new couch, and the coffee table was buried under magazines and nail polish bottles.

"Charlie! Why does this room look like a thrift store exploded?"

From somewhere in the kitchen, Charlie's voice rang out cheerily. "I'm reorganizing! It's part of my process!"

"Your *process* is giving me a nervous breakdown." She stepped over a pile of mismatched shoes to rescue a framed family photo dangerously close to toppling off the edge of a shelf.

Harriet poked her head into Grayson's room first, where music blared loud enough to shake the walls. He was lying on his bed, headphones on despite the full-volume speakers, staring at the ceiling like he was trying to merge with it.

"Gray," she called. He didn't hear her…or pretended not to. She tapped the doorframe until he pulled off one earphone.

"Yeah?" he asked, not looking at her.

Harriet hesitated. What she wanted to say was *Are you okay? Do you want to talk about your dad?* But the way Grayson's face set in a stony, unreadable expression told her the answer was still *no*.

"Can you turn it down a little?"

He reached for his phone to adjust the volume.

Harriet closed the door, her heart heavier than before. She longed for the days when the kids spent all their time outside in the fresh air, or followed her around like she was the most interesting person in the world. Now, they were only interested in her when they wanted something.

Olivia's room was next, but the door was shut tight. Harriet could hear the faint hum of some YouTube video playing. She didn't bother knocking; Olivia would tell her she was fine. They both would.

But Harriet knew better. She was desperate to tell them about her own experience with her parents' divorce, but Charlie's words echoed in her head. *What if they just need you to sit in the rubble with them a bit?*

Back in the living room, Charlie had emerged, holding a

bowl of almonds. "You look tense," she said, plopping onto the couch.

"That's because my house is a war zone." Harriet sat down and grabbed a handful of nuts.

"Eh, it's temporary chaos. You need a little clutter in your life. Loosen up!"

Harriet gave her a look, but it was hard to stay mad at Charlie for long, even if her idea of *loosening up* involved Harriet's meticulously organized life being turned into a Jackson Pollock painting of stuff.

Still, as she glanced at the stairwell, Harriet couldn't help but feel the real mess wasn't in the living room. It was in the silence between her and her children, the words they weren't saying, the pain they weren't sharing. And as much as Harriet wanted to fix it, she knew Charlie was right.

She'd have to wait for them to come to her. All she could do was let them know she was here, should they want to talk.

Charlie's nose turned up. "From the smell of you, I'd say you got one hell of a workout this morning."

Harriet tossed another almond into her mouth. "First off, rude. Second, it turns out taking seventeen years off means you're a bit rusty."

"Sounds about right."

"It's a bit intimidating, actually. I was a completely different person the last time I played. Not to mention I had a lot more stamina." She shrugged. "At least the trainer is hot."

"Details, please," Charlie said through a mouthful of nuts.

Harriet tucked her left leg under her bum and angled her body toward her sister-in-law. "Tall, muscular, dark hair with impossibly light eyes, and an Irish accent that makes you want to confess your sins even though you're not Catholic."

Charlie's eyes widened. "I'm coming to watch next time. To support you."

"Uh-uh. I've got dibs."

"No fair."

"Seems perfectly fair to me."

"How old is he?"

Harriet made a face. "That's the only hitch. I'm pretty sure he's closer to your age than mine."

"Okay, I like that for you. It would be a good change of pace from my brother."

Harriet grabbed another handful of almonds and then pushed away the bowl. "You can't be serious. He's nice to look at, which makes our lessons more fun. I'm not looking to hook up with the guy."

Charlie slapped Harriet's thigh. "And why the hell not?"

Harriet stood and went into the kitchen to wash her hands. "I could give you about a hundred reasons, but all you need to know is it's not happening."

"You really are no fun."

"So I've been told," Harriet said. "Now clean up this mess before I change my mind about letting you stay here."

Later that evening, Harriet sat on the living room floor, her back against the couch, watching the soft glow of the TV flicker across the room. Grayson was sprawled across the carpet, long legs stretched out, absently scrolling on his phone, while Olivia perched on the arm of the couch, earbuds dangling from her neck. A bowl of popcorn sat untouched on the coffee table between them, its buttery scent hanging in the air.

"I told Coach I'm quitting soccer," Grayson said suddenly.

Harriet raised an eyebrow but kept her tone breezy. "Oh? Big decision. Are you planning to retire completely, or holding out for a better contract?" She plunged her hand into the bowl of popcorn.

Grayson smirked but didn't look up. "Retire completely."

"Interesting. Any plans for post-soccer life? Maybe pickleball? Crochet?"

He stretched, setting his phone aside. "I told you already. I want more free time. Soccer's not fun anymore."

She hesitated, unsure if she should push or let it go. Was this truly about wanting a break from soccer, or something else entirely? The divorce, maybe, or the way their dad only showed up every other weekend now? She decided to test the waters.

"Not fun? This is the sport where you get to kick things and not get grounded for it." She brushed a stray kernel off the couch. Alex always hated when they ate on the couch.

Another thing she didn't have to worry about anymore.

"Did something happen? Or do you feel done with it?"

Grayson sighed the kind of sigh only a teenager could muster, implying his mother was both clueless and ancient.

"Maybe you're burned out. Or maybe something happened? Fight with a teammate?"

"He just wants more time to spend with Mea—"

"*Stop!*" Grayson bolted upright, his face flaming. "You're literally the worst."

Olivia stuck her tongue out at her brother.

"You're one to talk! I bet Mom doesn't know about—"

"*Stop!*" Olivia shrieked.

Harriet's gaze widened with interest, her mind teeming with questions she didn't dare voice, knowing they'd scatter like startled birds. She needed to be calm. Cool.

She tilted her head, her smirk mischievous enough to make Grayson squirm. "You know, there's a fine line between 'hanging out' and 'dating.' Usually, it's when one of you starts picking up the other's favorite snacks without being asked. Has it come to that yet?"

Grayson's ears turned red. "We're not *dating*, okay?"

Harriet hid her grin. "Sure, sure. Just let me know when I need to start stockpiling sour gummy worms for someone else."

"You're so weird," Grayson muttered, but his lips twitched as he picked up his phone again.

"I try my best." Harriet leaned back, relieved by the flicker of a smile. "So no crochet then? Too bad. I hear it's all the rage."

"I just don't want to play anymore, okay?"

"Fair enough," Harriet said softly. "I get it. Sometimes it's better to spend your time on things you actually enjoy."

Olivia looked up from her phone. "Dad's gonna freak."

Grayson huffed a laugh. "Yeah, well, maybe if he cared more than every other Saturday, I'd care about his opinion."

Harriet's heart clenched, but she kept her voice calm. "I know it's hard, Gray. For all of us. But it's okay to feel how you feel. You don't have to explain it to anyone if you don't want to."

"Thanks," he said so softly she almost didn't hear it.

It wasn't much, but it felt like something. A tiny crack in the wall he'd been building for the past two weeks.

Harriet didn't push any further, content to let the moment settle.

She barely had time to enjoy the moment of connection before Charlie strolled into the room, barefoot and wearing a hoodie two sizes too big. It was still August. How she wasn't melting under all that fabric was one of life's unanswerable questions. At least they were granted a respite from having to stare at her midriff for a day.

Charlie paused in the doorway and took in the scene—the dim lighting, the half-eaten bowl of nuts, and Grayson sprawled out on the carpet.

"Movie night?"

"Maybe," Harriet said, her voice measured. "We were deciding what to watch."

"Cool, cool," Charlie said, flopping onto the arm of the couch. Then she turned to Harriet. "But, uh, I wasn't talking to you."

Harriet blinked. "Excuse me?"

Charlie gestured vaguely at her. "It's Saturday night, and you're sitting here like a hermit. You're still remotely young, H. You should go out, not spend the night third-wheeling your kids."

"I'm not third-wheeling!"

Charlie stood up, pointing toward the stairs with exaggerated authority. "Go. Get dressed. Call one of your friends, hit a bar, something. You'll thank me later."

"Charlie—"

"Nope, no excuses. You're going. It's sad at this point. I refuse to let you wallow."

Harriet groaned but allowed herself to be nudged toward the stairs. "You're being ridiculous. I'm not going to—"

"Go! We'll handle the movie. You go handle being an adult with a social life."

Olivia snorted from the floor. "Bold of you to assume she has one."

"Olivia Marie Young, you take that back, or I *will* start asking a lot more questions about your love life."

Once upstairs, Harriet lingered in her room, staring at her phone on the nightstand. Call one of her friends. Sure, it sounded great, except for the glaring fact that she didn't have anyone to call. Not anymore. Her married friends had distanced themselves like she was contagious, and the one adult she could count on was already downstairs pushing her out of the metaphorical nest.

She sat on the edge of her bed, running a hand through her

hair. The truth was heavier than she cared to admit. She didn't only lack plans for the night, she lacked people, period.

Harriet flopped back onto the bed with a heavy sigh. She'd wait a few minutes to make it look like she tried to rally her friends, then go back downstairs and reclaim her spot on the couch.

Charlie could lecture her all she wanted, at least there'd be popcorn.

14

Harriet felt a flicker of her old self as she volleyed the ball over the net, her forehand crisp, her footwork nimble. The morning sun cast long shadows on the tennis court, and for the first time in weeks, she felt light. Not weighed down by her usual worries.

She had won the last two games, which might explain the extra spring in her step. The gorgeous weather didn't hurt, either.

Her opponent Diane met her at the net. "That's more like it. You're on fire today."

Harriet laughed, toweling off her face. "Maybe I'm finally shaking off the cobwebs." She could see Liam from the corner of her eye and hoped he had been watching.

When she returned home, Olivia was sulking on the couch, scrolling through her phone.

She barely glanced up when Harriet walked in, her tone acidic as she said, "Nice of you to come back. Guess you don't care that Gray's been whining about Dad all morning."

Harriet sighed. "Good morning to you too, Olivia."

"Whatever," Olivia muttered, storming off to her room.

Lately, she'd been lucky to spend five minutes in the same room with her kids, including dinner.

Harriet dropped her tennis bag by the door, the earlier calm replaced with the dull throb of familiar frustration.

The day only spiraled further.

Grayson, who had been quiet over a late breakfast, broke down during dinner, yelling about how his father didn't care about them and that Alex had promised to take him to the movies the night before but canceled at the last minute.

Olivia's eyes narrowed into slits as she added her own bitter commentary, blaming Harriet for "not doing anything about it."

Harriet had tried to keep her voice steady, but Charlie could see the strain when she arrived home later that evening. Harriet was still dressed in her tennis outfit—a new one she bought shortly after her first lesson with Liam—a half-empty glass of wine perched on the counter. She looked like she wanted to disappear into the background.

"I'm fine," Harriet said before Charlie could ask. "It's been a long day. The kids...It's not their fault. They're hurting."

Charlie raised an eyebrow. "They're hurting, sure. But so are you, and you can't pour from an empty cup."

"I know." Harriet shook her head, her voice unsteady. "I hate how I can't fix it for them. Or even for myself."

The truth was, she hadn't been dwelling much on Alex as her ex-husband lately. It was the other Alex—the one who was supposed to be their father—she couldn't stop thinking about, and the ways he kept letting them all down.

"You need a break," Charlie said firmly, "A real one. Not just a morning at tennis or an hour to yourself. Get away for the weekend."

"A weekend? I can't—"

"Yes, you can. You don't have to go far. Even just a hotel

downtown or somewhere nearby. Recharge a little, Harriet. You'll come back better for it."

Harriet paused, thinking. "The only weekend I could possibly make work is next weekend, but I have the kids. The last thing I want to do is ask Alex to switch—"

"I'll watch the kids."

Harriet hesitated, clearly toying with the idea. "I don't know. It feels selfish."

"It's not selfish to take care of yourself. It's smart. Look, worst case? You get a couple of nights of peace. Best case? You come back ready to deal with snobby teenagers and baby daddy drama."

Harriet laughed, though it sounded a little fragile.

Still, Charlie could see the idea taking root.

"Maybe you're right," Harriet said finally.

"I'm definitely right." Charlie grinned. "And I know the perfect place. I'll send you the details."

"Don't worry about it. I'll figure out something."

Charlie stepped forward, reached for Harriet's wine, and tipped the last of the liquid into her mouth. She set it down with a bemused smile. "Uh-uh, you're going to overthink it and end up canceling at the last minute. Like I said, I know where you should go. Leave it to me. You just need to show up at the address I send you at the time I tell you to."

Harriet looked at Charlie through her lashes. "Why am I suddenly scared?"

Charlie smirked. "It's hard letting go, isn't it?"

In the end, Harriet had decided to do something unusual and took a half-day at work so she could get on the road sooner. Charlie had told her nothing other than to take the CA-52 E to I-15 N and text when she reached Temecula, which she did like a good little girl vying for an A+ grade—even if not knowing where she was going was making her left eye twitch.

Charlie: Sent a location.

Charlie: Text me again when you're there.

The address ended up being a fast-food restaurant. Harriet went through the drive-thru and ordered a vanilla milkshake. She texted Charlie and waited for a response.

Charlie: Don't forget to watch your car charge. Can't have you running out of juice.

Harriet smiled to herself, grateful to have let go and let Charlie plan this weekend for her. It was tough not knowing where she was headed, but even she could acknowledge it was all part of the thrill.

Twenty minutes later, Harriet's phone chimed again.

Charlie: Continue on I-15 N and let me know before you hit Menifee.

Harriet: How on earth do you have time for this? Don't you work?

She meant it as a joke, but really…how *was* Charlie pulling this off?

Charlie: Don't you worry your little face off about that, H. I've literally wanted to do something like this for you for. Ever.

Harriet started up the car with a bemused smile and scrolled through the SiriusXM stations, looking for something to listen to, stopping when she heard Christina Aguilera singing about what makes her stronger and work a little bit harder. She tried not to think about where Charlie was sending her, mostly because that's what Charlie would want her to do.

When she'd agreed to let Charlie plan her weekend, Harriet had envisioned something simple—two nights at a nice enough hotel in Laguna Beach, a massage, and a steady stream of room service. Relaxation on a platter.

When she finally saw the sign for Menifee, Harriet instructed her fancy car to text Charlie and tell her so. A moment later, the car read her incoming text.

Charlie: 25210 Fern Road.

Idyllwild? It was certainly further than she'd expected to be driving, but she had to hand it to Charlie...it was different, all right. And Harriet fully planned to make the most of it.

As soon as she pulled up to The Pinewood Hotel, something in Harriet's shoulders softened. Maybe it was the way the cabins were tucked gently into the trees, the dark wood blending into the tall pines like they'd always belonged there. The whole place felt quiet, not only in sound but in spirit, like it understood how tired she was. Bright flowers peeked out from beneath the trees, little pops of color that made her smile without meaning to. Paths wound through the property like they were inviting her to explore, but gently, without any urgency.

There was a shared courtyard with a long wooden table, the kind you'd imagine gathering around with strangers who become friends by the end of the night. Comfortable chairs circled fire pits that promised warm conversations under chilly mountain stars. She could already picture herself there, mug in hand, wrapped in a blanket, not saying much—just being.

Out back, the pool shimmered, heated and serene, while a small sauna and cold plunge waited nearby, like secret rituals tucked into the trees. A mural—soft, sweeping, full of movement—drew her eye and made the whole spa area feel a little more magical.

The whole place felt like it had been built by someone who understood solitude and connection in equal measure. It wasn't showy. It was sweet, thoughtful, and deeply kind, like it was made for people who needed a break but didn't know how to ask for one.

Harriet tried to push aside the worry of what this weekend was costing. That was a discussion for future Harriet and Charlie.

She checked in and handed over her credit card for incidentals…and then was promptly informed her room wasn't quite ready.

Harriet glanced at her watch. "What time is check-in?"

"Three p.m. But I must apologize, we had some issues with the previous couple occupying the space. I've gone ahead and discounted your stay to make up for the inconvenience." The woman's response was practiced but sincere, and Harriet found herself assuring the woman there was no issue.

"We can hold on to your belongings if you'd like to explore the city? Your room should be ready in an hour or so. I can give you a ring when it's ready if you'd like?"

"Sounds great." She tucked her wallet back into her purse and met the clerk's eye. "Any coffee shops around here that might still be open?"

As it turned out, there were a few. Harriet chose one at random and headed toward it.

In the car, a text came through from Charlie.

Charlie: Welcome to Idyllwild, H. I went ahead and took care of booking a couple of things for you while you're there. Tomorrow morning, you have something I know you'll love: a facial and body treatment at a nearby spa. I've also secured you a reservation at a great restaurant in town. Stay tuned for Sunday's events. For now, relax and enjoy. Everything's set up, so no excuses!

Harriet felt her stomach flutter. *This is good for you,* she thought. *You need this.*

Harriet: You're the best. Thank you.

She was in a different state, after all. She could be whoever she wanted to be.

Maybe, for once, she wasn't the woman who constantly second-guessed herself, who planned every moment down to the smallest detail, who made endless lists just to feel like she had some control. Maybe in Idyllwild, she was someone who *liked* having things planned for her. Someone who didn't agonize over decisions and didn't feel the need to research every possible option before committing.

Maybe she was someone who could strike up a conversation with a stranger in the hotel lounge without overanalyzing every word as soon as it left her mouth. Maybe she was even the kind of person who *enjoyed* small talk, who could swap travel stories with fellow guests over breakfast, laughing easily without mentally rehearsing her responses in advance.

She liked the idea more than she expected.

With one last glance at her phone, she tucked it away in her bag. Maybe this weekend wasn't only about relaxation—it was about trying on a new version of herself, even if only for a few days. And who knew? Maybe she'd like this version enough to bring a little bit of her back home.

At the Café Aroma, Harriet indulged in a latte and a chocolate croissant. She tried to ignore the blissful conversations of those around her, but it was difficult.

For the first time since the separation, Harriet felt truly lonely. Not just the kind of loneliness that came from sleeping in an empty bed or having no one to share a funny text with. This was deeper, heavier, a gnawing ache that whispered she was unmoored and drifting.

She leaned forward, resting her elbows on the table, and let the feeling wash over her. Maybe this was part of the process, letting the sadness in instead of pushing it away.

Or maybe this was her life now.

As she bit into the croissant, a cascade of crumbs rained down her shirt. Harriet brushed at the crumbs, only succeeding in smearing chocolate onto her sleeve.

She glanced up and froze. A man at the next table was watching her with a bemused expression, his coffee cup paused halfway to his lips.

His kind of handsome didn't quite fit in nature-soaked Idyllwild. His dark-blond hair was neatly trimmed, his jawline sharp enough to cut glass, and his tailored button-down looked wildly out of place in a town where hiking boots were practically the uniform.

"You're really committing to that croissant, huh?" His voice was warm with amusement.

Harriet felt a flush creep up her neck. "I like to leave a trail. You know, in case I get lost."

The man chuckled, setting his coffee down. "Good strategy. But if you need a map, I think they sell them next door."

"Noted."

His grin widened, and Harriet felt an unexpected flutter in her chest. She wasn't sure if it was his smile or the fact that someone was looking at her like she was more than a frazzled mom or a woman trying to piece her life back together.

"I'm Nate, by the way," he said, holding out his left hand. She clocked the shiny gold ring on his finger immediately, her stomach sinking a little. Of course he was married. Men who looked like him weren't wandering around single. Somewhere, there was probably a picture-perfect wife waiting, maybe even kids.

Harriet forced a polite smile as she shook his hand. "Harriet," she said, trying to ignore the flicker of disappointment she had no right to feel. It wasn't like she'd been hoping for anything. She hadn't even noticed him until twenty seconds ago, and she was *definitely* not the kind of woman who went around daydreaming about strangers at cafés.

Still, it stung a little. Not because she wanted him—but because he represented something she no longer had and wasn't sure she'd ever find again.

But then, as she leaned back in her chair and watched him return to his coffee, she felt a spark of defiance rise up. Why did she care? It wasn't like she was on some magical vacation rom-com trajectory where the handsome stranger sweeps her off her feet. Her life wasn't a movie, and the truth was, even if he were single, it wouldn't change anything. She wasn't looking to get involved with anyone yet.

Harriet picked up the last piece of her croissant, popped it into her mouth, and brushed her hands clean of crumbs. "Well," she said, mostly to herself, "guess I'll leave the romance tropes to someone else."

Nate glanced up from his coffee. "Did you say something?"

She shook her head, smiling faintly. "Nothing important. Have a good day."

As she stood and walked out of the café, the crisp air filling her lungs, she felt oddly lighter.

The old Harriet—the one who tied her worth to other

people's attention—might have let his gold ring ruin her day. But the new Harriet? She wasn't going to waste her time worrying about someone else's husband. She had more important things to figure out.

Like what on earth Charlie had planned for her next forty-eight hours.

15

Harriet's cabin was its own little sanctuary, complete with wood-beamed ceilings, big windows letting in light and pine scent, and an old fireplace waiting to be curled up beside.

The moment she entered the space, a sense of peace washed over her. She could already feel the weight of the world lifting as she stood there, her breath deepening as the peace of the tranquil retreat settled over her. It was clear this would be the perfect place to unwind and reconnect with herself.

Of course, she'd probably spend too much time over-thinking the quiet, wondering if it was too quiet. Or, worse, if she was somehow doing relaxation wrong. She couldn't even remember the last time she'd let herself *be,* without the constant hum of to-do lists.

Still, for now, the peaceful surroundings were a welcome distraction from her usual chaotic inner monologue.

Because she couldn't help it, she took a few moments to empty her suitcase and strategically position her various moisturizers and lotions around the bathroom sink—in order of use, of course. On the bed, where she removed the provided pillows and set down her own, she promptly fell asleep.

Later, as the evening light softened into a warm amber glow, Harriet pulled out her phone and ordered dinner from DoorDash. After her meal, she lingered with a cup of herbal tea, cradling it in both hands as if it might make her feel better about having willingly chosen tea over coffee. Was this what relaxation did to a person? Stripped them of their caffeine dependency and left them sipping chamomile like someone who had their life together?

Eventually, exhaustion from the long day of travel set in, and she changed into her softest pajamas before slipping into bed. The mattress was like a cloud, the sheets crisp and cool against her skin.

For once, Harriet didn't scroll through her phone or make a mental list of things to worry about. Instead, she let herself drift off, the peaceful stillness lulling her into the best sleep she'd had in ages.

Harriet woke to the golden morning light filtering through the curtains. For a moment, she simply lay there, cocooned in warmth, letting her body wake up at its own pace. It wasn't until her stomach grumbled that she finally pulled herself out of bed and into the bathroom, splashing cool water on her face before getting dressed.

> Charlie: You have a massage booked at the Grand Idyllwild Lodge at eleven. Grab some breakfast there first. Don't be late.

Breakfast was delicious and exactly what Harriet needed. As she sipped her coffee, she felt something unexpected—a sense of contentment.

As much as it pained her to admit it, Charlie had been right. This was exactly what Harriet needed. She needed to clear her head, to silence the noise that had become her constant companion.

She needed to have someone massage her body from top to bottom and leave her mind silent.

In the waiting room, Harriet tried to fire off a quick check-in text to the twins, but the message refused to send. Frowning, she waved her phone around in a desperate attempt to find a single bar of service. Nothing.

"Of course," she muttered. It figured that in this supposed oasis of relaxation, she was completely cut off from civilization. She'd try again after her massage.

Reluctantly, she pocketed her phone and stepped up to the counter where an impossibly tiny woman stood, dwarfed by the counter she stood behind. Her impossibly serene voice greeted Harriet. Moments later, a woman who introduced herself as Sonya appeared, all business.

"You're here for the deep tissue massage?"

Harriet hesitated for a second. "I think so?"

Deep tissue sounded effective. Luxurious, even.

Sonya gave a curt nod and gestured for Harriet to follow her into a dimly lit treatment room. Harriet dutifully lay face down on the table, resting her head in the cradle as she took a deep breath. This was going to be great. Relaxing. Healing.

Then Sonya's hands landed on her back.

Harriet barely had time to register the pressure before Sonya *dug in.* It was like the woman had spent years honing her craft in an underground fight club. Her thumbs found knots Harriet didn't even know existed, and she attacked them like a woman avenging a personal vendetta.

Harriet's breath hitched. Her fingers clenched into the sheets. *This is fine,* she told herself. *This is probably normal.* After all, wasn't deep tissue supposed to be intense? That was the point, right? Then Sonya found a particularly stubborn knot in Harriet's shoulder and went after it with the determination of someone trying to break a rock with their bare hands. A muffled *oof* escaped Harriet before she could stop it.

"Very tight here," Sonya noted.

Harriet could only grunt in response. Tears prickled in the corners of her eyes, but she bit her tongue. What was she supposed to say? *Please stop trying to rearrange my skeletal structure?* That felt rude.

By the time Sonya moved to her lower back, Harriet had fully transcended into another plane of existence, one balancing precariously between pain and the distant hope that maybe this was, in some twisted way, good for her. She tried to focus on the calming spa music playing in the background, but all she could think about was that she might never be able to lift her arms again.

Finally, after what felt like a lifetime, but was only forty minutes, Sonya stepped back. "All done."

Harriet slowly pushed herself up, wincing as her muscles protested. She felt like she'd been hit by a bus. Or maybe several buses.

Sonya smiled. "Drink lots of water. You may feel a little sore later."

Harriet nodded weakly. *A little sore?* She was fairly certain she had bruises forming as they spoke. But instead of saying anything, she forced a smile, thanked Sonya, and hobbled out of the room, vowing to never let politeness put her in physical danger again.

The moment she reached the lounge, she fished out her phone. Still no service. Fantastic. If she was going to suffer, the least she could do was make sure her children weren't also in crisis.

With a sigh, she grabbed a glass of cucumber water and headed for the changing room. Once dressed, she made her way back to her room, all the while thinking about how excited she was to pick up her copy of *The Paris Apartment* she'd brought along with her.

She read until it was time to head to the restaurant for dinner and then tucked it into her purse to take along with her.

The drive wasn't long, and soon Harriet found herself pulling into the restaurant's parking lot, clutching her book like a security blanket. Charlie had made the reservation, so she hadn't thought to check what kind of place it was. The moment she stepped inside, she realized her mistake.

The restaurant was striking—soft golden lighting, greenery draping from the ceiling, minimalist wood tables set with delicate ceramic plates. But it smelled…earthy. Too earthy. A waiter glided up to her, all serene smiles and linen-clad elegance, leading her to a small table by the window.

She opened the menu and immediately regretted it. *Fermented walnut pâté. Spirulina foam. Jackfruit carpaccio.* She flipped the page, hoping for something normal, but it was more of the same—ingredients she didn't recognize and descriptions that sounded like science experiments.

She swallowed hard. Maybe she could order a drink and pick at something small.

A waiter appeared. "Would you like to start with our kombucha flight?"

She forced a smile. "Just water, thanks."

When her entrée arrived—something involving dehydrated mushrooms and a "creamy" sauce that was very much *not* cream, she tried a bite and immediately regretted it. It tasted like a forest floor.

Harriet set her fork down, stomach tightening. Between this and the deep tissue massage, it was beginning to feel as though the trip was falling apart.

She stared at her barely touched plate, then down at her book. Maybe she should have ordered DoorDash again.

When Harriet woke the next morning, the soft glow of yesterday's relaxation had dimmed, replaced by the more familiar buzz of anxiety. She grabbed her phone and scrolled through the itinerary Charlie had texted her sometime in the night. How was it that Charlie's messages could get through, but she was still unable to send anything?

Charlie: 9 a.m.: Guided hike.

Harriet groaned aloud. Of all the things Charlie could have booked—a yoga class, another spa treatment, even pottery painting—this was what she'd chosen?

Her first instinct was to roll over and ignore the text. Maybe she could pretend she'd never seen it. She didn't even have the right clothes for hiking anyway. Charlie wasn't here to argue with her or give her one of her "this is good for you" pep talks. She didn't *have* to go. The thought of scrambling up steep trails with a group of strangers felt less like an adventure and more like a punishment.

Harriet sighed and flopped onto her back, staring at the ceiling. She didn't *want* to go on the hike, but skipping it outright felt like admitting defeat. Besides, the fresh air and movement would be good for her.

With a resigned groan, she swung her legs over the side of the bed and stood. She didn't have hiking clothes, so leggings and sneakers would have to do. Tugging on a T-shirt, she made her way downstairs to the front desk.

"Excuse me," she said to the receptionist, a woman with a sleek ponytail and an ever-present aura of calm. "Do you know where the guided hike meets?"

The receptionist gave her an apologetic smile. "Oh, actually, that's been postponed due to the weather."

Harriet frowned. "Weather?"

The woman gestured toward the wide front windows. Harriet turned. Sure enough, the sky, which had been bright and clear yesterday, was now a thick, unbroken stretch of gray. Heavy clouds loomed over the horizon, dark and swollen with impending rain.

"Oh," Harriet said, struggling to summon anything resembling disappointment. "Well. That's a shame."

The receptionist nodded sympathetically. "You can check back later to see if it's rescheduled, but it looks like it'll be raining most of the day."

Harriet thanked her and made her way back to her cabin, feeling almost *relieved*. She kicked off her sneakers, climbed back into bed, and reached for her book. The room was blissfully quiet, save for the faint rustling of pages as she settled in.

Eventually, Harriet had to tear herself away from her book to pack her things. She zipped up her suitcase, glancing around the room to make sure she hadn't left anything behind.

Before getting on the road, she decided to stop at the coffee shop she'd gone to when she first arrived. That latte had been one of the best parts of her trip, and she figured she at least deserved one more for the road.

The café was as cozy as she remembered—warm wood tones, the scent of espresso and cinnamon in the air. She stepped into line and ordered her drink, answering the barista's question about what she was doing with her night—

"Headed back home to La Jolla," she'd said—then stood off to the side, waiting.

"How'd you like Idyllwild?"

She turned. A man stood beside her, smiling. Tall, dark-haired, a little scruffy in an intentional way. There was an easy charm about him, the kind that set off alarm bells in her head.

"Yeah," she said, keeping her response short.

"Shame. If I'd met you earlier, I would've offered to show you around."

She gave a polite smile, then glanced down. A gold band, unmistakable, on his left hand.

"You're married," she said flatly.

He followed her gaze, then looked back up with a casual shrug. "I am, but it doesn't mean I can't have a nice conversation with a beautiful woman I meet at a coffee shop."

She thought, *Alex*.

Something in her snapped. There was simply no other way to put it.

"Oh, give me a break. A *nice conversation*? That's where it starts, right? Do you *men* ever get tired? Is it *so* hard to love the person you vowed to love? Or is the thrill of being a sleazy, cheating pig just too good to resist?"

The man's smile faltered. "Whoa—"

"No, *you* don't 'whoa' me," she cut in. "You should be ashamed of yourself. You have someone waiting at home, trusting you, and you're here, throwing out lines at strangers like it's nothing. Do you even *like* your wife? Or is she some obligation you keep around while you chase whatever looks good that day?"

The man took a small step back. And then another. The confidence had drained from his face, replaced with something between shock and mild fear.

Harriet's name was called. She spun on her heel, grabbed

her latte, and bolted out the door, heat creeping up her neck as the realization hit.

She'd unloaded *all* her baggage on some random guy in a coffee shop.

She practically threw herself into her car, heart still hammering. Hands shaking slightly, she pressed play on a familiar playlist—soft, comforting music she always put on when she needed to reset.

But it didn't work. The whole drive back home, the embarrassment sat in her stomach like a rock.

Maybe I've finally lost it.

16

Harriet pushed open the front door, the familiar creak echoing through the house. The air inside was blissfully cool, laced with the rich, savory scent of something bubbling on the stove.

"Finally!" Charlie's voice rang out from the kitchen. "I was starting to think you'd ditched us for good."

Harriet dropped her suitcase with a dramatic thud and kicked the door shut. "Believe me, I considered it. But I figured I'd better return and reclaim the chaos."

"Smart move." Charlie leaned around the corner, wielding a wooden spoon like a scepter. "I'm making dinner. And before you ask, no, not a single vegetable was harmed in the making of this meal."

Harriet followed the sound of clattering pans, already feeling some of the Idyllwild stress start to dissolve. Home might be a circus, but at least it was her circus.

"Where are the twins?"

"In their rooms, pretending to do homework. Liv let me help with her science work for about five minutes before she realized I was making it worse."

Harriet sighed. She wanted nothing more than to walk into Grayson's room and squeeze him like she used to when he was little, back when he actually needed her. And Olivia—she missed when her daughter would greet her with a high-pitched "Mommy!" instead of a suspicious, "What do you want?"

Ah, nostalgia.

"They're fine, you know," Charlie said, reading her face like a cheap novel. "We had a good weekend."

Harriet huffed. "How do you always do that?"

"Do what?"

"Know what I'm thinking before I even think it?"

Charlie grinned. "I'm gifted like that. You better watch yourself, or I'll start charging you for my services."

"Don't threaten me with a good time," Harriet muttered. She collapsed onto a barstool.

Charlie gave her a once-over. "You don't look all that relaxed for someone who just spent a weekend away."

Harriet groaned. "Oh, I was relaxed. Incredibly relaxed. Nothing says relaxation like sitting alone in a hotel room, reading *The Paris Apartment* while listening to the soothing sounds of rain pelting the window."

Charlie frowned. "What happened to the hike?"

Harriet sat up, giving her a pointed look. "Oh, you mean the scenic, soul-cleansing hike? Yeah, that got canceled. Because apparently, hiking in a torrential downpour is frowned upon."

Charlie winced. "Yikes."

"Yeah. So instead of becoming one with nature, I became one with my bed and read three hundred pages of my book, which I'm not complaining about. It's been ages since I last read a book so quickly."

Charlie raised an eyebrow. "And was that…relaxing?"

Harriet shrugged. "I mean, it was a break from the norm, right? And no one tried to talk to me, which was nice."

Charlie smothered a laugh. "What about the dinner reservation I made for you?"

Harriet shuddered. "Charlie, I bit into something I swear was rebranded mulch. I don't know what it was, but I will never emotionally recover."

Charlie burst out laughing. "It was vegan! I thought you'd be adventurous."

"I was. And I regret it deeply."

Charlie wiped a tear from her eye. "At least the spa visit was good. Right?"

Harriet stretched her neck, wincing. "You ever been physically assaulted by someone with a wellness certification? Well, I have. I think she relocated my spine."

Charlie gasped, delighted. "So what you're saying is…it wasn't quite the peaceful getaway I envisioned?"

"Well, the fresh air was fantastic."

"Thank God."

"Oh, but wait, there's more!" Harriet threw her hands up. "Some married guy at the coffee shop decided to flirt with me, and I told him off so loudly the place went silent. I think I gave one woman a full-body shudder."

Charlie hooted. "I'm sorry I missed it." She leaned against the counter, shaking her head. "You know what? I blame Alex."

"What?"

"My idiot brother. This is obviously his fault."

Harriet squinted. "I fail to see the connection."

Charlie gestured vaguely. "If he weren't such a disaster, you wouldn't have needed a de-stressing weekend in the first place. And then you wouldn't have been almost-murdered by an overzealous masseuse."

Harriet considered it. "Fair enough."

"Glad we agree. Now, eat. I promise there's actual food involved. No moss."

Harriet grabbed a spoon and took a bite. "This is why I don't leave home."

Charlie massaged her temples with her fingertips. "You are *impossible.*"

"Hey! I went. I relaxed. I let people touch my body. I did exactly what you told me to do."

"Except it totally backfired." Charlie scooped up a mouthful of noodles. "Ah, the power of cheese and butter. Two of the three best healing powers that exist."

"What's the third?" Harriet asked.

"Alcohol. Naturally."

Charlie retrieved two more bowls from the cabinet and spooned noodles into them.

"Good news is, I wanted to push you out of your comfort zone this weekend, and I think we accomplished that."

Harriet raised an eyebrow, gripping the bowl as though it might float away. "Comfort zone? Let's review, shall we? I'm forty and in the middle of divorcing a man I genuinely thought I'd spend forever with. My kids alternate between treating me like a villain or a personal assistant, thanks to their dad's spectacular disappearing act, and my sister-in-law —who, might I add, is currently the closest thing I have to a friend aside from Greta—is now my housemate. Oh, and my house? A war zone of laundry and broken dreams. So, yeah. I'd say my comfort zone was *obliterated.*" She exhaled sharply and stabbed at her noodles. "But hey, at least there's macaroni."

Charlie stopped eating and stared at Harriet across the table. "You have control issues. And before you try to deny it, let me remind you, you just listed your problems like they were items on a spreadsheet. You probably even have a color-coded system for handling them, don't you?"

Harriet set her fork down. "First of all, it's not color-coded. It's...prioritized. And second, having some structure isn't a bad thing. When everything in your life is falling apart, being able to control even *one* thing can keep you from losing your mind entirely."

"Sure, but what happens when the 'one thing' doesn't cooperate? You can't spreadsheet your way through kids' feelings or a messy divorce. And you can't exactly evict me for being an unpredictable wildcard either."

Harriet frowned. "I wouldn't evict you. You're not..." She paused, her lips twitching with reluctant amusement. "Okay, you're a wildcard. But you're not the *problem.*"

"Exactly," Charlie said, pointing her fork at Harriet. "You can't control me, but somehow, I'm not driving you insane. Maybe it's because deep down, you like having something unpredictable around. Keeps things...interesting."

Harriet laughed softly despite herself. "You're giving yourself a lot of credit there."

"Maybe. But think about it. What's worse? The chaos of life, or holding on so tightly you snap when it doesn't go the way you want?"

Harriet didn't answer right away. Her gaze drifted to the noodles in her bowl. "It's not about snapping. It's about surviving."

Charlie softened, her grin fading. "I get it. But sometimes, surviving looks a lot like letting go."

Harriet's lips curved into a small, rueful smile. "You're annoyingly good at these pep talks, you know."

"It's a gift," Charlie said with a shrug. "Now eat your noodles before they get cold. I'm not dealing with you hangry, on top of everything else."

Harriet said, "I did realize something important during my time away."

Charlie looked instantly buoyed. "Tell me."

"I realized you've been here, what, a month, and I still have no idea what happened with you and Evelyn. You're sleeping in my bedroom and eating the food in my pantry, and I still have no idea why you're here."

"First off, I'm only sleeping in your bedroom because you won't. Second, I'm an open book. All you need to do is ask."

"Okay, then. I am asking."

Charlie scooped up a spoonful of macaroni and shoved it into her mouth, stalling for time. She spoke before fully swallowing, her words muffled but clear enough. "In short, my mother's mortified I'm twenty-seven, living at home, and working retail."

Harriet frowned. "But you love your job."

Charlie swallowed hard and set the spoon down with a clink. "Doesn't matter. I dropped out of college after two years of flailing. That's all Evelyn sees. Not the job I love or that I'm actually good at it and make good money."

"Sometimes it takes a while for people to figure out what they're meant to do." Harriet's words hung in the air. "Sorry. That sounded way less like a fortune cookie in my head."

Charlie snorted. "I'll let it slide this time."

"Do you ever feel like..." Harriet hesitated, her elbows resting on the table. "Like maybe your mom isn't entirely wrong? Maybe—"

Before she could finish, the thunder of footsteps and an unmistakable chorus of "What's that smell?" filled the air.

The kids barreled into the kitchen, noses twitching like bloodhounds on the trail of a feast. Olivia was first, her eyes widening. "Is that mac and cheese? Like, *real* mac and cheese?"

Behind her, Grayson leaned around her shoulder. "Wait, did you actually cook, Aunt Charlie? Or is this one of those 'just add water' situations?"

Charlie raised her spoon like a conductor silencing an orchestra. "Excuse me! I boiled water and cooked pasta and mixed in the cheese and milk and butter. Sure sounds homemade to me."

Olivia's eyes narrowed. "You didn't put weird stuff in it, did you? Like vegetables?"

Harriet sighed, her question slipping into the background as the kitchen filled with chatter and the sounds of bowls clinking against the table. She caught Charlie's eye over the kids' heads, and Charlie gave her a small, knowing smile, as if to say, *We'll come back to that.*

But already Charlie's issues with Evelyn had been pushed back to the recesses of her mind. Now all she could think about was how neither of her children had even said hello.

Heathens, she thought. *I'm raising heathens.*

17

The air in La Jolla carried a late-summer warmth that clung a little too long, like the season didn't know how to bow out gracefully. It was the first week of October, but the coastal breeze did little to cut the lingering heat.

Inside Harriet's house, the atmosphere felt even heavier.

The slightly cooler evenings should have brought some relief, but between her and the kids, the air felt denser than ever. Not even her Saturday mornings out on the court with Liam could brighten her mood. Her weekend away already felt like a distant memory.

Harriet stood in the kitchen, wiping down an already-clean counter to keep her hands busy. Olivia was at the table, hunched over her laptop, her headphones dangling around her neck as if she couldn't decide whether to block out the world or stay tethered to it. Harriet understood the impulse, some days, to want to disappear into something like music and shut out everything else. She would have liked to have done the same thing herself at the moment.

"Did you finish your history project?" Harriet asked, keeping her tone light.

Olivia didn't look up. "I'm working on it."

"That's what you said yesterday."

This time, Olivia sighed audibly. "Why do you care so much? It's my grade."

Harriet paused, the dishrag twisting in her hands. "Because you don't usually let things slide like this, Liv. I'm trying to make sure you're okay."

"I'm fine," Olivia snapped, the words sharp enough to cut.

"No, you're not. You've been moody and snappy for weeks, and I get it—what your dad did—it's a lot. But shutting me out isn't going to make it easier."

Olivia pushed back from the table, the legs of the chair screeching against the tile. "Oh my god. Can you stop? This isn't about Dad."

"Isn't it? Because it sure seems like it. Gray told me you barely talk to him when you're at his place. I wish you'd talk to me instead of sulking around like you're angry at the world."

"You don't understand!" Olivia's voice cracked, her cheeks flushed as tears welled in her eyes. "You don't get what it's like to feel like…like he just doesn't care anymore. And you're here, acting like everything's fine. Like we're supposed to just move on!"

Harriet's heart clenched. "Liv, I'm sorry if that's what it seems like I'm doing. It's not my intention. I'm trying to keep things together—for you and Gray. Because I know how much this hurts. I feel it too."

"No, you don't!" Olivia shouted, tears spilling over now. "You don't know what it's like to have your dad stop showing up! You're not the one sitting here wondering what you did wrong!"

The words struck Harriet like a physical blow.

She took a step forward, her voice softening. "Please listen to me when I say this. You didn't do anything wrong. None of this is your fault. Your father is obviously going through something. And when he comes out the other end of it, I'm sure he'll realize what he's done and course correct."

She could kill Alex for making Olivia doubt herself this way.

Olivia shook her head, backing away. "I don't care. It doesn't fix anything."

"Liv—" Harriet reached out, but her daughter turned and bolted up the stairs, her footsteps echoing through the house before the slam of her bedroom door silenced everything.

Harriet stood in the kitchen, frozen. The house felt impossibly quiet now, the weight of Olivia's words hanging heavy in the air. She wanted to follow, to find the right words to say that would soothe her daughter's pain. Instead, she stayed where she was, her own tears finally spilling over as she whispered to the empty room.

Alex had left over five months ago, and she was only finally crying now.

Her hands gripped the edge of the countertop so tightly her knuckles ached, but it wasn't enough to keep the tears at bay. They came slowly at first, hot and unwelcome, slipping down her cheeks as she let out a shaky breath.

"Finally." Charlie's voice came softly from the doorway, startling Harriet. "I was beginning to think you might be made of stone."

Harriet wiped at her face with the back of her hand, embarrassed to be caught in such a vulnerable moment. "I'm fine," she said reflexively. "It's nothing."

Charlie stepped into the room, shaking her head. "No, you're not. And it's okay." She moved to Harriet's side and rested a hand gently on her shoulder. "You've been holding it in for weeks. Let it out, H. You need to."

Harriet's lips trembled. "I don't have time to fall apart. I have to keep things together for Liv and Gray."

Charlie's grip on her shoulder tightened, grounding her. "You're not falling apart. You're human. It would probably help them to see you cry. It might show them it's okay to feel things."

At that, Harriet broke, a sob escaping her lips as she sank into a chair at the table.

Charlie pulled out the chair next to her and sat down, wordlessly pushing a box of tissues toward her. Harriet took one, pressing it to her face as the tears came in earnest now, years of worry and heartache pouring out in waves.

Charlie stayed quiet for a moment, letting the silence stretch before she spoke. "You're doing the best you can, you know. Even if it doesn't feel like it."

Harriet dabbed at her eyes. "Everything's a mess, Charlie. And I feel like I'm making it worse. Olivia…" She couldn't find the words.

"Olivia's hurting…and you're the closest punching bag."

Harriet cradled her head in her hands. "She thinks I don't understand what she's going through. And Alex…he doesn't even see what he's doing to them."

Charlie rested her elbows on the table, studying Harriet for a moment. "Look, she's fifteen. Her dad just basically said, *'You're not my priority.'* That's a huge wound, and she doesn't know what to do with it. So, she lashes out at you because you're safe."

"Safe," Harriet repeated, her tone flat. "Doesn't feel like it."

"No, but it is. You're the one person she knows won't walk away, even when she's screaming at you."

Harriet exhaled, leaning back in her chair. "So…what? I'm supposed to let her keep screaming?"

"Not exactly. You do what you've been doing this whole time. You keep showing up. You keep listening, even when she says you don't understand. You're her mom, and whether she admits it or not, she needs you. Give her time to figure it out."

For a moment, they sat in silence, the weight of the conversation settling between them.

Finally, Harriet looked up, a faint but determined resolve flickering in her eyes. "I think it's time I have a talk with Alex."

Charlie clapped her hands together. "Oh, *please* let me be in the room when you do."

Truthfully, Harriet had been fine with pretending Alex no longer existed. If it weren't for his sudden change of heart concerning custody of his children, she wouldn't have to think about his stupid new car, or his fresh haircut, or the divorce papers, even. When it came down to it, she'd much rather send him a text or an email, anything other than talk to him face-to-face. But this was the type of conversation that required it. She was doing it for her kids.

She called ahead to his office to make sure he was in. The receptionist assured her he was open for the next two hours. When she knocked on his open office door, he looked bewildered to see her standing there. Did he think she'd stay silent while he treated their kids so badly? His expression wasn't just clueless. It was the kind of stupid that almost dared her to be angrier, and Harriet was more than ready to take the challenge.

She stepped into the office. Alex straightened in his chair, a flicker of confusion crossing his features.

"I wasn't expecting you," he said, his voice a careful mix of surprise and suspicion.

"Really? Well, you should have." She exhaled sharply. "We need to talk."

He leaned back in his chair, his fingers drumming nervously on the armrest. "Talk about what?"

"Don't play dumb," she snapped. "You can't waltz in and out of your kids' lives whenever it suits you. They're not accessories for your Instagram."

Alex opened his mouth, but she held up a hand to stop him. "And don't give me some half-baked excuse about your schedule or your new 'life changes.' I want to know what the hell is going on. You're like a different person...with a ridiculous car."

He blinked. "The car has nothing to do with this," he muttered.

"Of course it doesn't," Harriet said, her tone dripping with sarcasm. "Because when I think of responsible parenting, I always picture a midlife crisis on wheels."

"Do you actually have a concern you'd like to speak about, or did you just come here to insult me?"

At her side, Harriet curled her hand into a fist. "I want to know what's going on with you."

Alex leaned forward and braced his elbows on his desk. "Harriet, I don't owe you an explanation."

Her eyebrows shot up. "Excuse me?"

His expression hardened. "I don't have to explain every decision I make to you."

Harriet felt a flare of heat rise in her chest, equal parts anger and disbelief. "So you can throw our entire custody arrangement into chaos, disrupting your kids' lives, and I'm supposed to shrug and say, 'That's fine, Alex, you don't owe me an explanation?' Is that how this works now?"

"I didn't say it was fine," he countered, his jaw tightening.

"What the hell, Alex? I mean, I don't even recognize you

anymore. You're cheating on your wife and bailing on your kids. What happened to you? You had so much promise—"

"Enough!" His left fist came down on his desk. "I've never been good enough for you. Ever. You know there was no winning with you, right? First, I'm not doing enough for you—not working enough or earning enough. And then, once I was on track, making money and settling in, suddenly I was working too much and not around enough. No matter what I did, there was no way to please you."

Harriet blinked. "That's not fair."

"No, it's not. But it's true—whether you like it or not."

Harriet worked her jaw back and forth. "We're not talking about my perceived faults here, Alex. I'm here to tell you you're messing with the stability I've been working my tail off to build for our children." She swallowed. "How could you possibly think you don't owe me some kind of explanation?"

"What I do or don't do as their father is my business," Alex shot back, his tone sharp now.

No. No, no, no.

"You're wrong. What you do as their father is *their* business, and guess who has to pick up the pieces when you leave them confused and hurt again? Me, Alex. It's always me. So, yeah, I think I deserve to know what the hell is going on."

Alex looked away, his lips pressing into a thin line. Whatever his reason was, he wasn't going to say it. Not to her, and certainly not now.

"This isn't about you," he said after a moment, his tone softening slightly. "I'm trying to do what I think is best for the kids."

She blinked. "In what world is what you're doing best for the kids? Do you even hear yourself? You're not making any sense."

Alex said nothing. He barely even moved.

Harriet turned toward the door, her anger simmering below the surface. "You know what? Fine."

Maybe they were better off with him in their lives less. Maybe this was how things were meant to play out.

As she walked out, she felt her grip on the situation slipping, but one thing was clear. Whatever Alex's reasons were, they were buried under layers of defensiveness and stubborn pride...and she didn't have the time or patience to dig them out. Not anymore.

18

How stupid could she be?

Of course Alex believed he didn't owe her an explanation. He hadn't helped her to understand why he slept with someone else and destroyed their marriage, and he hadn't bothered to explain the flashy car. It was so clear now that Harriet had always had to guess what Alex was feeling. He had never felt the need to tell her himself. And this was no different. It was so thoroughly *Alex*—this new, infuriating version of him. The one who wore arrogance like a new suit and acted like every decision he made was beyond questioning.

Had she known him at all?

How had she not noticed, in the twenty-two years they'd been together, how disappointing he could be? Sure, there had been little moments along the way—how he couldn't seem to remember if their anniversary was April third or fourth, or the way he refused to stand up for her when his mother criticized her time and time again. Then there was the money he assured her he'd bring in but never had, and all the things he'd promised to fix around the house but never did.

Well, there was someone she could pay to do that now. And she would. She didn't need him.

Harriet mulled over this thought during the short drive home from Alex's office—a commute so brief it had been one of the house's main selling points. Now, Alex was living in a rental half the size of their old place, paying fifty percent more than her mortgage. At least the kids had their own bedrooms. Harriet shuddered to think of the complaints if they had to share.

Her own childhood bedroom had shared a thin wall with her parents'. She hadn't known what privacy was until she'd moved out on her own after college. Kids these days…they were so spoiled.

To further prove her point, Harriet opened the front door and walked right into an argument between Olivia and Grayson. Despite not knowing what had prompted it, it didn't take her long to discern it had begun over something stupid. A text, from the sound of it.

Harriet sighed, closing the door behind her with a firm click. "Enough!" she called, her voice sharp.

Both kids froze mid-sentence, turning toward her. Olivia, arms crossed and scowling, stood by the couch with her phone clutched like a lifeline. Grayson sat slumped at the dining table, glaring at his sister as though she had ruined his entire existence.

"Someone want to tell me what's going on?"

"She read my text!" Grayson spat, pointing an accusatory finger at Olivia.

"You left your phone on the table, wide open. It's not my fault you're stupid," Olivia shot back.

"Keep your nose out of my business!"

Olivia snorted. "It was a meme, Grayson. Relax."

Harriet pinched the bridge of her nose and counted to five in her head. "Is this really what you're arguing about?"

Neither responded, but the silence spoke volumes.

Harriet exhaled slowly, feeling the day's exhaustion settle heavily on her shoulders. "Look, I don't care who did what. What I *do* care about is not coming home to yelling. So you have two options: either work this out like civilized human beings, or I confiscate both of your phones for the rest of the night. Your choice."

Olivia opened her mouth to protest, but wisely closed it again. Grayson glowered but said nothing.

Harriet nodded in satisfaction. "Good. Now, go do something worthwhile with your time."

She headed to the kitchen, leaving the kids to stew in their unresolved tension. She couldn't help but think, not for the first time, that parenting was an endless game of managing the ridiculous.

Harriet wiped the last of the counters with mechanical precision, the rhythm of her nightly routine soothing in its familiarity. She placed the sponge neatly in its holder and stood back to survey the kitchen. Everything was in its place, the sink empty, and the faint scent of lemon cleaner in the air.

Turning off the lights, she climbed the stairs, her tired feet creaking against the wood. The house was quiet except for the muffled hum of voices from Olivia's room. Harriet paused, her hand on the banister, straining to catch the words.

"I don't know what to do." Olivia's voice was low and urgent.

"It's okay, Liv," came Charlie's calm response. "Just take it one step at a time. You don't have to figure it all out tonight."

Harriet's stomach twisted.

"Yeah, but what if I mess it up?" Olivia's voice broke slightly.

"You won't," Charlie reassured her. "And even if you do, it's not the end of the world. You're smart, Liv. You'll figure it out. And if you need me, I'm here, okay?"

The knot in Harriet's chest tightened into something sharp. It should be *her* in there, comforting Olivia. But instead, her daughter had turned to her aunt.

Harriet pushed the door open without knocking. Both heads snapped toward her, Olivia's eyes wide with surprise, and Charlie's expression unreadable.

"What's going on?"

"Nothing. We were just talking."

"I could hear you from the hallway. If there's a problem, you know you could have come to me..." She waved a hand toward Charlie, unable to keep the edge out of her voice.

Charlie held up a placating hand. "Liv needed someone to listen."

"I'm here to listen," Harriet snapped, the words sharper than she intended.

Olivia glanced at Charlie and then back at Harriet, her lips pressed into a thin line. "You'd just tell me to stop over-thinking and go to bed."

Harriet's mouth opened, then closed again.

Before she could respond, Charlie stood. "I think it's best if I give you two some space," she said calmly. She walked past Harriet without another word, her footsteps quiet as she disappeared down the hall.

The following silence was heavy, and Harriet suddenly felt the weight of her outburst. Olivia sat on the edge of her bed, arms wrapped around herself, looking younger than she had in years.

"I'm trying to help," Harriet said finally, her voice softer now.

Olivia didn't look at her. "Maybe. But sometimes it feels like you just want me to stop being a problem."

The words stung, and Harriet took a step back as though physically struck. She wanted to argue, to explain, but the exhaustion of the day pressed down on her, and all she could do was say, "You're never a problem, Liv. We don't always see eye to eye, but I love you just the same."

Olivia didn't respond, but she also didn't look away.

Hope buoyed in Harriet's chest as she maintained eye contact with her daughter. Maybe she was going to finally open up about how she was feeling, and Harriet could finally help Olivia begin to heal.

Instead, Olivia said, "Can you close the door on your way out?"

Harriet did as she was told—but she didn't have to like it.

As she made her way to her own room, she passed Charlie in the hallway. She stopped, guilt and frustration swirling together. "Charlie, I'm sorry. I shouldn't have lashed out at you."

Charlie studied Harriet for a moment. "It's okay. I get it. This is hard on everyone."

Harriet nodded, leaning against the doorframe. "It's just... she won't talk to me, but she can talk to you..."

Charlie shrugged. "Sometimes kids need someone to talk to who isn't their parent. Someone they don't think will judge them or try to fix things right away. I'm no better than you. I don't come with all the expectations you do."

Harriet let her words sink in, a lump forming in her throat. "You think I judge her?"

"No," Charlie said gently. "But she might think you do. Or worry you'll try to solve things instead of listening."

Harriet looked down at her hands. "Thank you. For being there for her. And for me."

Charlie gave Harriet a reassuring squeeze on the shoulder. "That's what family's for. Don't beat yourself up too much, okay?"

Harriet managed a small smile. "Easier said than done, but I'll try."

As she turned to head to her room, Harriet felt a flicker of relief amid the lingering frustration. Maybe she didn't have to be the one in control all the time. Maybe it was okay to let go and trust that, even if things weren't perfect, she was still doing her best. And that would have to be enough.

"Hey."

Harriet spun on her heels.

"I think you should come out with me and my friends one night soon. Maybe the next time the kids are with Alex. If Carrie and Laura are going to keep avoiding you like divorce is some disease you can catch through physical contact, we're going to need to get you some new friends."

Harriet opened her mouth, at least ten reasons why she couldn't go at the ready, but Charlie stopped her.

"You know I won't take no for an answer, so I wouldn't even bother."

Harriet's eyes narrowed. "I hate you."

"No." Charlie grinned. "You don't."

19

Harriet had always been bad at saying no. Her entire life was a patchwork quilt of all the moments she should have declined but didn't, stitched together with the thread of her over-accommodating nature.

It was the only explanation for how, ten days after Charlie made the suggestion, she found herself not only allowing Charlie to dress her in a pair of tight, dark jeans and a low-cut black shirt so tight she could barely breathe, but following Charlie out to a shiny silver Mercedes that had pulled up at the curb in front of her house.

Behind the wheel of the Mercedes was a woman with a halo of wild, curly hair, her carefree attitude practically oozing from her posture. In the passenger seat, a bubbly blonde turned to greet them, her black eyeliner as bold as the double gold hoops glinting in her nose.

Once they were settled in the back seat, Charlie made the introductions. Riding shotgun was Jen, and the driver, Sawyer. Harriet smiled faintly, trying to muster enthusiasm. At forty, she felt worlds apart from the trio of twenty-some-things, who exuded an effortless cool she couldn't dream of pulling off.

She tugged at her sleeves, suddenly hyperaware of the cardigan she'd thrown over her outfit, which she feared screamed *mom at PTA meeting.*

Sawyer's grin widened in the rearview mirror. "It's about time we got to meet you!"

"Uh-huh." Harriet's voice was barely audible over the thumping bass rattling the car. She stared out the window as they pulled away.

The car swerved into a lane with too much confidence for Harriet's liking, and she clutched her purse tighter, wishing she'd said no to this whole outing. But how could she? Harriet couldn't bring herself to dampen her sister-in-law's infectious enthusiasm.

Charlie nudged her. "You okay?"

"Yep," Harriet lied, forcing a smile. She could feel Jen watching her from the front seat, probably sizing her up. Did they think she was cool for tagging along, or sad for trying?

Eventually, the Mercedes eased into an unmarked alleyway behind a nondescript taco shop, its sleek body catching the glow of a single streetlamp. Sawyer slipped the keys to the valet with an ease that made Harriet feel like someone's nervous niece tagging along.

Inside, the bar revealed itself like a secret—dim, elegant, with backlit shelves of rare bottles and the low hum of jazz threading through the air. The scent was a heady blend of citrus peel, leather, and something floral Harriet couldn't place. She tried to steady herself, to lean into the ambiance, but felt awkwardly out of sync, like she was crashing a party for people who all knew the password.

Charlie grabbed Harriet's arm, steering her through the crowd. "We need drinks immediately."

The bar was loud, crowded, and suffused with the

kind of energy Harriet hadn't felt in years. Charlie's friends, dressed in short skirts and crop tops, flitted around like brightly colored birds, full of laughter and inside jokes Harriet couldn't begin to follow. At first, she felt out of place, clutching her wineglass like a lifeline and nodding at conversations that moved too quickly for her to join.

Drinks in hand, Charlie waited until the others were involved in their own conversation and turned to Harriet conspiratorially. "I've been meaning to ask, how go the lessons with hot tennis guy?"

Harriet coughed out a laugh. "Good!"

"That's all you're going to give me? You know I looked him up, right? He's *gorgeous.* You definitely need to see if he's interested in a little fun."

"He's twenty-nine."

"More like twenty-*fine!*"

Harriet shook her head, fighting back a smile. "Not going to happen."

"Because you're too shy, or because you don't think he'd be into it? News flash...men dig older women. They know what they like, and they're not afraid to tell you."

"And how would you know this?"

Charlie sipped her drink before responding. "I know things. Many things."

Harriet thought it best not to respond at all, hoping Charlie would lose interest and move on. Or at least be distracted by something shiny and in the opposite direction.

The night went on, and more drinks were consumed, but none of them made Harriet feel any more comfortable. Maybe she should cut her losses and call it a night. But Charlie had a way of making her feel included, even when she didn't want to be.

"Harriet, tell them about the time you were stuck in Italy

for a week," Charlie said, leaning over the table with wide-eyed enthusiasm.

"Oh, it was years ago," Harriet said with a dismissive wave.

"C'mon, you can't just let that story sit there," Charlie teased, and soon Harriet found herself recounting the misadventure—losing her passport, befriending an elderly Italian couple who insisted on feeding her like she was their long-lost granddaughter, and eventually getting home by sheer luck and a last-minute embassy appointment.

The group erupted in laughter at the punchline, and for the first time all evening, Harriet relaxed. The wine helped. So did the realization that maybe she could still charm a room, despite being the oldest.

It was going well—better than she'd expected—until Jen turned to her with wide, expectant eyes.

"Harriet, can I ask you something?"

"Of course," Harriet said, feeling suddenly scrutinized.

"How do you know when it's the right time to settle down? Like, my boyfriend's been hinting at moving in together, but I'm not sure if I'm ready. You've been married forever, right? What do you think?"

Beside her, Charlie groaned loudly.

"Jesus, Jen. What did I say to you earlier? What was literally the *one thing* I told you not to bring up?"

Harriet felt a pang of discomfort. She wasn't sure she was qualified to give love advice these days.

Jen took a sheepish drink and mumbled an apology, which Harriet accepted like the gracious, forgiving person she was.

"Granted, my marriage didn't work out in the end, but I can tell you this: it's different for everyone. I think it's less about timing and more about how you feel with the person. Does he make you happy? Do you feel like you two could grow alongside one another? Are you a better person when you're with him?"

Jen nodded, looking like she was absorbing every word.

The questions kept coming—about careers, mortgages, even skin care routines—and Harriet answered them politely but distantly, feeling her initial warmth toward the group cooling.

It was one thing to have a good time. It was another to be cast as the group's stand-in mom.

When the conversation turned back to someone else's relationship drama, Harriet excused herself, claiming she needed some air. Outside, the night was brisk and clear, the noise of the bar muffled behind the heavy door. Harriet pulled in a deep breath and let it out slowly. She didn't go back inside. Instead, she texted Charlie.

> Harriet: Heading home. Thanks for inviting me out. Have fun.

Then she ordered an Uber and went home alone.

Back at the house, Harriet kicked off her heels, poured herself another glass of wine, and curled up on the couch. Then she went back for some peanut butter.

She thought of Carrie and Laura. Friends her own age who had shared her milestones, her struggles, her jokes about the ridiculousness of parenting and relationships. But recent events had pulled them in different directions.

Harriet still didn't understand what had happened, how they'd dropped her the way they did. The only thing she could think of was that they'd never truly been her friends. Friends don't toss people aside like yesterday's trash.

Feeling a rare burst of bravery, she scrolled through her contacts, and opened an old text chain with Laura and Carrie.

> Harriet: Hey, it's been too long! Want to grab coffee sometime?

She wasn't sure what kind of response she imagined…or if one would come at all. But it felt suddenly important to know whether their distance was intentional or not.

Laura replied almost immediately.

> Laura: Can't do coffee this week, but let's catch up soon.

Carrie simply never responded.

When Harriet put her phone down, she felt worse than before.

Standing on this uncertain ground between her old life and whatever came next, she felt achingly, profoundly alone. She stared at the empty glass in her hand and set it down carefully, as though it might break under the weight of her thoughts. Then she turned off the lights and went to bed, hoping tomorrow would feel less heavy.

20

Harriet's first thought upon waking the next morning was how blissful the silence was.

Next, she thought of her schedule for the day: make breakfast, meal plan, tennis lesson, and groceries. It was easy to forget the events of the previous night and how they made her feel, mostly because she told herself that's exactly what she'd do. She'd already spent too much of her life over-analyzing its daily events and, to be honest, she was a little sick of it. She was a little sick of herself.

Enough was enough. It was time to move on and focus on what truly mattered—like her children.

Harriet knew what she needed to do.

She needed to sign her divorce papers.

She opened the drawer of her nightstand and pulled out the envelope, holding it in her hand, feeling the weight of it. She stared at the papers, her thumb brushing over the edge of the envelope, hoping the answers to her questions might suddenly rise from the surface. How had it come to this? Sure, she'd known it was over as soon as she kicked Alex out, but she'd always thought she would be in control of what came next. She was the one who was cheated on. She was the injured party. She wasn't supposed to be the one to be served divorce papers.

Harriet sighed deeply, the kind of sigh that emptied not just her lungs but something deeper, something she couldn't name. The papers were heavy with memories, promises, and arguments.

Harriet set it down on the bedside table and picked up the pen.

Do it. Rip the bandage off.

Her hand hovered above the pages, but before she could scrawl her name, the sound of shattering glass jolted her. A crash, sharp and sudden, echoed from downstairs, slicing through the quiet like a blade. Harriet froze for a moment. She set the pen down, its tip barely kissing the paper. Throwing on her robe, she tightened the belt as she hurried toward the bedroom door.

Descending the stairs, she found the coolness of the hardwood underfoot and the faint hum of the refrigerator oddly comforting.

In the kitchen, shards of ceramic sparkled across the tiled floor, and the source became immediately clear. Olivia stood frozen with wide eyes, the remnants of a cereal bowl scattered around her feet. Milk pooled in white streaks, trailing toward the corners of the room.

"I'm sorry!" Olivia's voice cracked. Her hands gripped the edge of the counter.

Harriet let her shoulders relax. "It's fine, Liv. Just stay where you are. I'll grab the broom."

As she reached for the closet, Harriet felt an unexpected wave of relief. Relief that the moment had pulled her away from the papers upstairs. Relief that her daughter needed her.

Relief, perhaps, that she still had something grounding her in the mess of it all.

Ceramic shards clinked against the dustpan as Harriet crouched to sweep.

Olivia hovered nearby, shifting her weight anxiously. "I didn't mean to—"

"I know," Harriet interrupted gently, looking up at her daughter. Olivia's hair fell in a curtain around her face, obscuring the furrow of her brow. "It's just a bowl. No big deal."

As the morning rolled forward—eggs sizzling on the stove, the rhythmic thump of tennis shoes as Grayson bolted down the stairs—it was easy to let the crash, the papers, and even the sinking feeling from earlier fade into the background.

But Harriet knew they were still there, waiting. And so was the pen.

The midday sun hung high, casting sharp shadows across the tennis court. Harriet adjusted the brim of her visor and wiped her palms on her skirt as Liam stood at the baseline, effortlessly bouncing a ball on his racket.

"All right, Harriet." Liam's Irish accent wrapped around her. "I'm serving. Let's see if you can return it this time without sending it over the fence, yeah?"

She rolled her eyes. "That was *one* time."

"And yet, it lives on in legend." He grinned, boyish and teasing, his eyes nearly translucent in the sunlight. "I think the squirrels in the park next door still talk about it."

Harriet huffed a laugh despite herself and moved into position, racket at the ready.

They had been at this for weeks now, long enough she knew his habits—the slight lean to his left before a serve, the playful quips designed to throw her off balance. Long enough that she should've been used to the way his presence lit up the court. But she wasn't.

Liam tossed the ball into the air and sent it rocketing toward her, a clean, sharp serve. Harriet darted to meet it, her sneakers squeaking against the court. She managed a solid return, the ball sailing just over the net and landing neatly inside the line.

"Beautiful shot!" Liam jogged forward to keep the rally going. "Where's that been hiding?"

"Maybe I've been going easy on you," she shot back, feeling a flicker of pride.

He laughed as he returned the ball with a controlled forehand. "Ah, so you've been lulling me into a false sense of security. Sneaky. I like it."

Harriet sprinted to meet the ball, managing a decent volley but sending it a bit too high. Liam stepped in, effortlessly smashing it past her. She groaned as it thudded against the court behind her.

"Unlucky," he said, resting his racket against his shoulder as he walked toward her. "But you're getting quicker on your feet. I'll have to up my game soon, or you'll start embarrassing me."

She let out a breathless laugh, brushing a loose strand of hair from her face. "Sure, Liam. I'm *this close* to putting you out of a job."

He leaned slightly closer, enough for her to catch the faint scent of his cologne. "Well, if you do, you'll have to buy me a pint. Fair's fair."

Harriet felt her cheeks warm. She quickly turned away, adjusting the grip on her racket. "Guess you'll have to stick around a bit longer, then. I'm not quite there yet."

Liam chuckled, his voice rich and low. "Don't sell yourself short. You've come a long way."

She busied herself tying her shoelace even though it didn't

really need it. He had no idea how much those words meant. Or how much she looked forward to these lessons, not just for the tennis but for him—the way he joked, the way he saw her, even when she tried to disappear into her own head.

"All right, enough rest." Liam backed up toward the baseline with a playful twirl of his racket. "Let's see if you can handle my second serve. No holding back now."

Harriet smiled faintly, gripping her racket again. "I never do."

The lesson wrapped up with a final rally, Liam slicing a clean backhand that Harriet couldn't quite reach. She laughed as she jogged to retrieve the ball, her muscles humming with exhaustion. "You've got me running marathons out here."

"Good for the heart. And, dare I say, your footwork's looking sharper every week."

Harriet smirked. "Flattery won't get you a tip."

"Who needs a tip when I've already got your sparkling wit to keep me entertained?"

Harriet felt a familiar flush creep up her neck. She wiped her face with her towel and took a sip from her water bottle, using the small ritual to anchor herself. "I'll see you next week?"

Liam nodded, slinging his racket bag over his shoulder. "Same time. And don't forget to stretch tonight. Don't want you hobbling through the grocery store."

"Funny you mention it. Grocery shopping is exactly where I'm headed next."

"Ah, the glamorous life of a tennis star," he quipped, flashing her a quick smile.

Harriet smiled back but didn't linger. "Enjoy the rest of your day."

"You too." He gave a casual wave, his eyes lingering on her a second longer than necessary.

The drive to the grocery store was mercifully short, but as

she pulled into the parking lot, Harriet found herself lingering in the car for a moment. She leaned her head back against the seat, letting the quiet settle around her.

Groceries. Dinner. Kids. A life that didn't pause, not even for a second.

Harriet exhaled and pulled open her car visor to peek at herself in the tiny mirror. Her hairline was damp with sweat and her face red from exertion, but otherwise, she had a glow about her that could only be achieved through exercise—and she felt good about that.

Stepping out of the car, she glanced at the unfamiliar storefront. This wasn't her usual grocery store, just the most convenient, as it was closer to the tennis courts. Next door was a coffee shop she'd never noticed, its windows glowing warmly. She made a mental note to grab something sweet and caffeinated on her way out, a treat for all her hard work.

Inside, the grocery aisles felt like a poorly thought-out maze. The produce section sat smugly where the bakery clearly belonged, and she passed the cereal aisle twice before realizing it had been sneakily labeled "Grains & Breakfast." Her cart rattled in protest as she muttered under her breath, half-shopping, half-orienteering. Yet somehow the chaos was oddly exhilarating, like discovering a secret society where no one knew the rules.

Groceries finally bagged and neatly loaded into her trunk, she locked the car with a satisfied *beep* and turned toward the glowing coffee shop. *Well,* she thought, brushing the dust of disorganization off her soul, *if I survived that, I deserve extra caramel drizzle.*

The moment she stepped inside, the scent of freshly ground coffee hit her like a wave, rich and comforting. She exhaled, letting the familiarity wrap around her. At the counter, she ordered a caramel latte, swiped her card, and moved to the side to wait.

Harriet let her eyes wander, taking in the soft hum of conversation, the low buzz of the espresso machine.

And then she saw them.

Her breath caught, sharp and painful, as her gaze landed on Alex. Her husband. He was there, sitting at a small corner table, laughing softly. Across from him, the woman. *Her.*

The betrayal hit her all over again, a tidal wave crashing down, pulling her under. Her chest tightened as though all the air had been sucked from the room. The sight of them, so casual, so comfortable, burned into her mind.

The woman said something, and then Alex said something, maybe to her or maybe to each other, but Harriet couldn't hear a thing over the sound of her heartbeat in her ears. Alex turned his head slowly, and their eyes met. His smile faltered, disappearing in an instant. He turned suddenly pale and gaunt, like the weight of his choices had finally caught up with him.

The room blurred as tears sprang to Harriet's eyes. She felt the sting of humiliation, the ache of anger, the unbearable weight of heartbreak. She could barely hold herself upright. Her legs wavered, her hand gripping the counter for support as she forced herself to breathe. And then she ran, the late October air hitting her face, her vision swimming with tears. She fumbled for her keys, her hands trembling, her heart pounding so loud it drowned out everything else. Once inside the car, she locked the doors and let the sobs come.

Her hands gripped the steering wheel to anchor her, but nothing could stop the pain that tore through her. It was raw, unrelenting, and all-consuming. She wanted to scream, to rage, to cry until there was nothing left.

Instead, she sat there, gasping for breath, the sound of her ragged sobs filling the car.

21

Harriet could barely breathe.

What a fool she'd been! Not just once, but twice. First, when she'd married Alex, and now.

Of course he was out with *her!* Of course he was moving on! *This* was why he suddenly wanted less time with the kids!

Harriet's thoughts spun out of control as she sat in the car, gripping the steering wheel so tightly her knuckles turned white. The image of Alex smiling—*smiling*—with her, his arm slung carelessly over the back of his chair, felt like a sucker punch to the gut. A cruel, unforgiving slap in the face.

He looked...*happy.* Unburdened and free. Meanwhile, Harriet was crying alone in her car, trying to calm the thudding in her chest.

The weight of the panic—real, raw, and suffocating—settled over her like a blanket of concrete. She hadn't realized how much she'd been holding on, how tightly she'd clenched to the fragile threads of the life she thought she could still control. But now...now it was clear. It was clear how much power Alex still held over her. How much he had the power to shape her emotions and destroy the fragile calm she had painstakingly been trying to build over the last five months.

How is he so damn okay? The thought flared up like fire, stoking the growing rage in her chest. *How is he out there living this fucking charmed life while I'm the one left picking up the pieces?*

She slammed her fist against the steering wheel, the sound of it ringing out in the confines of the car. Her breath came faster, shallow and ragged. *Why wasn't it me? Why wasn't it me who got to be carefree, who got to go out and be happy?*

He didn't *deserve* happiness, not after what he did to her and to his children. She had *fought*. She had *sacrificed*. And what did it get her? A messy separation, a pile of broken promises, and *him*—out there with his new woman, living like nothing had ever happened.

The truth crashed into Harriet, slamming her back into her seat. The pressure in her skull intensified until it felt like the world was closing in. The air was thick and suffocating. She fought to breathe, but her lungs betrayed her.

No, no, no. Not like this. Not now.

Her hands trembled as she reached for the door, but when she tried to open it, her body seized. Her vision flickered again, the edges blurring.

She grabbed the collar of her tennis shirt, tugging at it, desperate for air. Hot tears continued to spill down her cheeks. She was so angry. So furious. But underneath it, the pain still twisted inside her, and it hurt so much, more than anything.

She'd thought she was doing better. Thought she'd been moving forward. But this...this was a reminder that she was still stuck. Still chained to Alex, even in his absence.

Harriet pressed her hand against her chest, trying to push the storm inside her down, but it wouldn't stop. It kept rising, relentless. The panic. The grief. The rage. Everything crashed together, like a storm she couldn't outrun.

Her hands were shaking now, her whole body trembling with the effort to keep herself in the present, to pull herself out of the spiral already beginning to take her under.

He ruined me, she thought. *He ruined everything. And now... now he's free.*

With a sob, Harriet let herself fall forward, resting her forehead against the steering wheel. *How did it come to this?* The question circled, unanswered, as the sound of her own shaky breaths filled the car.

She couldn't be sure how long she sat there, forehead pressed to the steering wheel, her breath ragged and uneven. The car walls pressed in on her, and she knew she couldn't stay.

With a trembling hand, she wiped her face and forced herself to sit up. Her vision blurred with tears, but she managed to start the car, her body moving on autopilot while her mind reeled.

The drive home was a haze. Harriet barely registered the streets or the turns, just the hum of the electric motor and the occasional blare of a horn when her reaction time faltered. By the time she pulled into her driveway, her chest still felt like it was caving in, but she had made a decision.

Inside, Harriet ignored the mess her family had left that morning—the coffee cup on the counter, the open cereal box—and stormed up the stairs. Her footsteps were heavy, each one driven by the anger bubbling beneath her panic. She threw open the bedroom door, her eyes locking on the nightstand like it held the answers to everything.

The divorce papers were still there, exactly where she had shoved them, hoping to avoid the inevitable. Her hands shook as she grabbed them, the paper crackling under her grip. She sat on the edge of the bed, the pen in her hand.

She pressed the tip of the pen to the page. It took more effort than she thought possible, but one by one, she signed her name where it was needed. The letters came out jagged, her hand unsteady, but it was done. Each signature felt like a release, like breaking the chains Alex had wrapped around her without her even realizing.

When the last page was signed, she let out a shaky exhale, staring at the stack in her lap. Her chest still ached, her hands were still trembling, but a flicker of relief cut through the chaos. Without giving herself time to second-guess, she grabbed the papers and rushed back down the stairs.

Outside, the sun was annoyingly bright. Harriet clutched the envelope tightly in her hand as she walked down the driveway toward the mailbox. She didn't make it far before she heard a voice.

"Oh, good. I'm glad I caught you."

Harriet looked up to see Greta standing at the edge of her own driveway with a shovel in one hand. Her eyes flicked to the envelope in Harriet's hand, and her expression immediately shifted to something knowing and mischievous.

"Oh, boy." Greta squinted, shading her eyes. "Looks serious. Is that what I think it is?"

Harriet wasn't in the mood. "I don't know, Greta. What do you think it is?"

Greta leaned on her shovel, giving her a sly smile. "Well, unless you've taken up correspondence with the IRS, I'm guessing those are divorce papers. Am I wrong?"

Harriet blinked. "How could you possibly—"

"Please." Greta waved her hand. "I've been divorced twice. I recognize the look. It's the 'I'm about to mail a chapter of my life to hell' look. Recognized it the moment you stepped outside."

Harriet didn't know whether to laugh or cry, so she did both. A weak chuckle escaped her as she wiped her cheek with the back of her hand. "Yeah, well. That's exactly what it is."

Greta nodded, as though this was perfectly normal. "You know, my second husband actually drove me to the post office when I sent mine off. Claimed he wanted to make sure I didn't change my mind. Can you believe it? The audacity of men."

Harriet sniffed. "Sounds about right."

"Anyway, go on, get that thing in the mailbox before you start overthinking it."

Harriet smiled faintly. "Thanks, Greta."

"Anytime, hon. And if you need a drink later, you know where to find me. Margaritas at seven!"

Harriet shook her head, her lips quirking into a real smile this time. "I'll keep it in mind."

The mailbox wasn't far, and for a brief moment, she hesitated. But then she thought of Alex, sitting there with *her*. The woman he had *betrayed* her for.

She stood by the mailbox, the papers clutched tightly in her hands. Wind bit at her cheeks, but she barely felt it. Her heart pounded, and her thumb brushed over the edge of the envelope. All she had to do was let it go. Just drop it in. But her fingers wouldn't move.

A memory surged to the surface, sharp and unbidden. It was their first year of marriage, and they'd been standing in their cramped kitchen. She had just been offered her first promotion at work, but the stress of the new responsibilities had left her in tears. Alex had cupped her face in his hands, his thumbs brushing away the tears as he looked at her with his steady, confident gaze she used to trust more than anything.

"You're not alone, Harriet," he'd said, his voice low and

sure. "Whatever it is, we'll figure it out. Together. I'm always on your side. Always."

She had believed him then, so completely that the words had become a kind of anchor. Through arguments, sleepless nights, and the ups and downs of life, she'd clung to the promise that he was hers, and she was his.

Now, the memory felt like a cruel joke. The man who had once vowed to stand by her was the same man who had destroyed her.

Her fingers tightened around the envelope as anger burned through her, hot and searing. He hadn't only betrayed her. He had shattered the version of herself who had believed in him.

Tears welled up again, but this time, they weren't just from pain. Alex had already taken so much from her—her trust, her security, her belief in happily-ever-afters. She wasn't going to let him take her future too.

This wasn't for him. This wasn't even about him anymore. This was about her. About finally taking a step toward the person she wanted to be, the person she deserved to be.

With a shaky breath, Harriet pushed the envelope into the slot. The sound of it dropping echoed in her ears. For a moment, the world stood still.

She stood there, staring at the mailbox, and realized she wasn't trembling as much anymore.

It was done.

22

Harriet first met Alex at a mutual friend's party. She was running late, a rare and almost unbearable occurrence. She hadn't been given clear directions and had spent an exasperated ten minutes circling the block before finally finding the right building. By the time she stepped through the front door, her curls were slightly mussed, her cheeks flushed with frustration.

Harriet's brown eyes scanned the room for someone she recognized. When their eyes met, he was struck by how sharp and purposeful her gaze was, and yet there was something unexpectedly vulnerable about her in that moment too.

Alex said he noticed her the moment she stepped into the room, her entrance commanding attention without her even trying, which is funny considering Harriet remembered wanting to leave the moment she joined the party.

She made her way to the drink table, her movements efficient and deliberate. Alex, standing nearby, felt an inexplicable urge to speak to her.

"Long night?" he asked lightly as she poured herself a glass of wine.

Harriet glanced up, startled, then offered a small smile. "The directions weren't exactly…precise."

"Sounds like our host. I'm Alex, by the way."

"Harriet." She set the bottle down. "Nice to meet you, Alex."

Alex tilted his head, a playful grin forming. "So, Harriet, what's the most interesting conversation I can start with you that doesn't involve the weather or the wine selection?"

Harriet paused, feigning deep thought. "How about the one where you tell me what brings a professional conversationalist like yourself to a party full of strangers?"

Alex laughed, leaning in slightly. "Touché. But I'll have you know, I'm only here to meet someone who can keep me on my toes."

"Well, good luck finding her. I'm sure she's around here somewhere." She smiled and began to walk away, but in a show of confidence, Alex reached out and took hold of her arm. Harriet's gaze traveled slowly from his hand on her wrist up to his striking blue eyes.

What followed was an unexpected ease in conversation. They talked about everything and nothing, the initial formality between them dissolving as Alex's humor softened Harriet's guarded demeanor. By the end of the evening, Harriet realized she'd spent more time with Alex than anyone else at the party—a detail that would normally make her self-conscious but instead left her feeling surprisingly content.

Alex drove her home later, kissing her chastely at her door. And when he called her the moment he got home, they talked for three more hours.

Alex had grown up in a home where chaos reigned. His parents' marriage was a volatile mixture of miscommunication and unpredictability. He'd learned to fend for himself, navigating an environment where stability was always out of reach. Meeting Harriet was like stepping into a world he'd only imagined, one where life could be planned, where intentions were clear, and where love didn't have to be a storm.

On their first date, Harriet had chosen the restaurant and picked the wine. "I hope that's okay," she'd said, half-apologetically, though her tone suggested she wasn't accustomed to leaving things to chance.

Alex had laughed. "It's more than okay." And it was. For a man whose childhood had been shaped by unsteady ground, Harriet's approach felt like solid footing.

They slept together that night. Immediately after, Harriet worried Alex would lose interest, but he appeared to be in no rush to leave. In fact, he didn't leave her apartment for the next two days, until Monday morning came around and he had to rush home to change before heading to work. He didn't shower off the smell of her. He wanted to smell like her for another day. For*ever*.

Alex told everyone who would listen how captivated he was by Harriet's decisiveness. He said he'd never met anyone like her before, and he meant it. He told his mother he would marry her one day.

As their relationship progressed, Harriet's meticulousness didn't just charm Alex. It anchored him. She'd send calendar invites for dates, color-code her grocery lists, and had a knack for turning even the most chaotic situations into neatly wrapped solutions. Alex began to rely on her in ways he'd never relied on anyone before. But more than that, he realized her controlling tendencies weren't about dominance. They were about creating a space where life could thrive, a counterbalance to the instability he'd always known.

Harriet, for her part, found Alex's easygoing nature equally refreshing. Where she brought order, he brought a quiet resilience and a surprising adaptability. Together, they formed a partnership that felt almost serendipitous, like the universe had conspired to balance their opposing traits.

"You make me better," Alex admitted one evening as they sat together in her tidy apartment. The light from her carefully curated lamps cast a warm glow over the room, and Alex felt something he rarely had as a child—safe. Seen. "You make me think life doesn't have to be so messy."

Harriet smiled, setting down her mug. "And you make me think it's okay if it is sometimes."

It was the beginning of a love neither of them had anticipated but both instantly recognized as the real thing. Harriet wasn't just someone Alex could love. She was someone who made him believe in a future that was nothing like his past. And Alex's steady adoration allowed Harriet to soften in ways she'd never thought possible. Together, they weren't just a couple—they were a team, each bringing out the best in the other.

Six months after the night they met, Alex proposed. Harriet never worried that it was too soon. By then, she had fallen hard. No one could have convinced her Alex wasn't the one.

They were married on their first anniversary. Harriet wore a simple off-white slip dress with pale gold sandals, and Alex wore the same suit he'd had in his closet for years, even though it was slightly outdated. They said their vows in front of twenty-five of their closest friends and relatives and, two days later, flew to San Francisco for a small honeymoon, where they gorged on fresh seafood and walked the pier with takeout coffees in hand.

From the beginning, Harriet made no secret of her desire to have children. She'd come a long way from pushing her dolls around in a baby carriage, stopping to feed her whenever she cried, but her need to be a mother never faded. She'd been lonely as an only child and couldn't wait to fill her home with little people who called her Mommy.

Alex, however, approached the idea with reluctance. "You

don't understand," he'd said. "I've seen firsthand how poorly things can go when a family isn't built on solid ground."

Harriet frowned. "You don't think we're on solid ground?"

Alex caught himself. "I think kids change everything."

Harriet hadn't pushed the topic. She'd assumed he'd come around in time. She believed their love would eventually change his mind.

Alex focused on establishing himself at work. Harriet deserved the world, and he was determined to give it to her. But the path to becoming the provider he envisioned proved more complicated than he'd hoped. His career so far had been a series of starts and stops. He'd bounced between jobs in his early twenties, dabbling in sales and finance. Nothing had stuck, and while he had the kind of charm that helped him land opportunities, keeping them was another matter. He'd always thought he'd figure it out eventually—until *eventually* arrived in the form of Harriet, and the abstract idea of responsibility became real.

He flipped through job listings, circling a few: Marketing Associate, Operations Coordinator, Customer Account Manager. Each one felt like a step into the unknown. Alex wasn't sure what he was good at—aside from making people laugh at parties and talking his way out of parking tickets. But charm wouldn't pay the bills.

Harriet would come home from work day after day, her blazer slung over one arm and her face flushed, and she would ask about his day.

"I looked at some job listings. Sent out a couple of resumes. I think I might hear back from the place downtown —you know, the one with the ridiculously modern logo?"

Harriet nodded encouragingly. "You'll find something, Alex. I know you will."

Her faith in him was both comforting and crushing. Alex didn't want to just find *something*. He wanted to find the right thing, to prove to Harriet and himself he could be the kind of husband who could carry them through anything.

Two years into their marriage, he secured a new job as an assistant account manager at a small firm. On his first day, he wore a suit and tie Harriet had helped him pick out and arrived twenty minutes early, determined to make a good impression. But by the end of the first week, he was already struggling.

"Just stay organized," Harriet advised when he vented to her about how chaotic his workload felt. "Make a list. Prioritize. You're great with people—that's half the battle."

Alex nodded, but inwardly, he felt like he was drowning. The job demanded a level of attention to detail he wasn't used to, and he found himself making rookie mistakes—forgetting client names, sending emails to the wrong addresses, botching an invoice. His boss, a no-nonsense man named Dennis, pulled him aside more than once to remind him of expectations.

At night, Alex lay awake staring at the ceiling while Harriet slept soundly beside him, the weight of his failures pressing on his chest. He wanted to be like his father in this one way—steady, dependable, the kind of man who worked hard and took care of his family. But instead, he felt like he was floundering, one misstep away from being fired.

One evening, Harriet found him sitting on the couch, his tie loosened and a glass of whiskey in his hand.

"Rough day?" she asked, sitting beside him.

Alex nodded. "I don't know if I'm cut out for this. I feel like...like I'm pretending to be someone I'm not."

Harriet reached for his hand, her grip warm and steady. "You're not pretending, Alex. You're trying. And that's what matters. No one gets it right every time."

Her words were meant to reassure him, but they also reminded him of the gap between them. Despite being an introvert, Harriet was confident, focused, and moving steadily up the ladder in her HR role. Alex, by contrast, felt like he was fumbling in the dark.

But he couldn't let her down. He wouldn't.

He went back to the office, resolving to make it work. He stayed late, asking his boss for advice on how to improve. He wrote everything down, started keeping lists like Harriet had suggested, and forced himself to focus on the details. It wasn't perfect—far from it—but for the first time, Alex felt like he was taking real steps toward becoming the man he wanted to be. Even if those steps were small and uneven, they were moving him forward.

When they found out Harriet was pregnant, nearly five years into their marriage, Alex's reaction was a complex mix of worry and resolve. He was scared—terrified, even. The responsibility, the unknowns, the fear of repeating his parents' mistakes all loomed large in his mind. But he also had faith in Harriet. If anyone could navigate parenthood with grace and competence, it was her.

"You're going to be an amazing mother," he told her one night as they lay in bed, his hand resting lightly on her growing belly. His voice was soft, tinged with both awe and apprehension. "I'm not sure I'll be good at this, but I know you will be."

Harriet placed her hand over his, her fingers warm and steady. "We'll figure it out together."

The babies came—twins, a boy and a girl. And for a while, Alex could convince himself it wasn't so bad, that maybe being a dad was something he could do. He didn't mind changing diapers, and the interrupted sleep wasn't as hard on him as it was on Harriet. He loved his kids.

But then they grew into toddlers who needed more from him. And then they were five and beginning school, begging for his constant attention. And then they turned ten and began asking him all types of questions he didn't have the answers to.

Their sex life suffered. Their once vibrant intimacy, the playful, spontaneous connection they'd shared in the early years of their marriage, became another casualty of parenthood. Nights once filled with laughter, whispered secrets, and stolen moments were now consumed by feedings, laundry, and the unrelenting exhaustion of raising two young children. It wasn't that Alex didn't understand. Harriet was doing everything, balancing her demanding job, managing the twins' routines, and somehow keeping the household running. He admired her for it, but he couldn't help feeling like they were losing something essential.

Harriet missed him in her own way. She missed the way he used to look at her like she was the only person in the room, the way they used to touch without hesitation, the way being together had felt so effortless. She wanted him to reach for her, to close the widening gap between them, but the unspoken barriers felt insurmountable.

Instead, she closed her eyes and let the silence envelop them, wondering how long it would be before they found their way back to each other…or if they ever would.

As the twins grew, the difference between Harriet and Alex's approaches to parenting became clear. Harriet was structured and attentive, always reading the latest parenting books and researching schools, extracurriculars, and developmental milestones. She kept a meticulously updated calendar on the fridge, color-coded with each child's activities, of course. She thrived on planning, ensuring the twins had balanced meals, plenty of outdoor play, and bedtime routines that ran like clockwork.

Alex, on the other hand, became more and more overwhelmed. He lacked Harriet's natural inclination for order, and what had once been a source of admiration now felt like a reminder of his inadequacies. He tried at first, showing up for soccer games, helping with homework, and dutifully following Harriet's carefully laid-out plans, but as the demands of fatherhood grew more complex, he started to falter.

The questions from his children, once simple and endearing, began to feel like tiny arrows pointing out his shortcomings.

"Why don't you ever come to parent-teacher meetings, Dad?" Grayson asked one evening, his voice tinged with hurt.

"Why do you work so much?" Olivia added, her big, curious eyes filled with something Alex couldn't name. It certainly wasn't admiration. He didn't know how to answer them, so he didn't. Instead, he threw himself into his work with a kind of frantic energy, convincing himself he was providing for them. That was enough, wasn't it? A good father worked hard. He set a good example. He made sacrifices.

Harriet noticed the change, of course. She always did. She shouldered more and more of the parenting responsibilities, taking over the roles Alex once attempted to fill. She was patient at first, giving him space to adjust, but her patience wore thin as the years passed.

"Alex, you can't clock out of being a parent," she'd said one evening after he came home late, missing yet another family dinner. Her voice was calm but carried a sharp edge.

"I'm not clocking out." His tone was defensive. "I'm working. For them. For us."

Harriet sighed. "They don't care about the money, Alex. They care about you. They need you."

"What am I supposed to do?" he asked. "I'm not like you. I don't have it all figured out. I don't know how to be...perfect."

"I'm not asking for perfect," she said quietly. "I'm asking for present."

But Alex couldn't even give her that. The more Harriet

stepped in, managing the chaos with her usual efficiency, the more Alex withdrew. He began staying late at the office even when he didn't have to, finding solace in the quiet, structured world of work. Weekends, once reserved for family outings, became filled with catching up on projects.

The twins, then twelve, started to notice their father's absence in ways they hadn't before. Harriet tried to fill the void, but no amount of planning or patience could replace what was missing. Grayson acted out at school, his teacher mentioning "a lack of focus." Olivia grew quieter, her once bright, inquisitive demeanor dimming.

One night, after a particularly chaotic bedtime routine that Harriet managed alone, she sat on the couch, exhausted. Alex came in, his tie loosened, holding his briefcase like a shield.

"You're missing it," she said, her voice heavy with frustration and sadness. "You're missing them."

"I'm doing my best," he replied weakly, but even he didn't believe it anymore.

Harriet didn't respond. She just shook her head and walked upstairs, leaving Alex alone in the silence he had sought but now couldn't bear.

Harriet couldn't be sure how long she stood by the mailbox. By the time she got home, the house smelled like Charlie's takeout leftovers mixed with whatever body spray Grayson had recently discovered. Olivia was holed up in her room with her door closed.

Harriet lingered in the hallway longer than necessary, listening to the faint buzz of music leaking out of her earphones. Her hand hovered over the doorknob, but instead she called, "Liv? Want to watch something tonight? Just us?"

No answer came. Or maybe there was one, muffled beneath the synth-pop beat.

Grayson emerged from his room. "You okay, Mom?" He asked like it was a question he didn't really want answered.

"Fine," Harriet said too quickly. "I was thinking maybe family movie night? Popcorn, candy—the works?"

He shrugged. "Maybe. I've got plans later."

She nodded, forcing herself to act like it was normal, like it didn't sting that the kids had already slotted her into the background noise of their lives.

In the end, she ate the popcorn alone on the couch, Olivia's laughter floating faintly through the walls.

23

Harriet woke on the first Saturday of November feeling nothing at all. Not anger, not sadness, not even relief…just a heavy, numbing void where emotions should be. She stared at the ceiling, the pale morning light seeping through the blinds, and thought of nothing. For a moment, she wasn't sure if she'd actually slept for once, or had simply been lying there, her mind as still and featureless as a blank sheet of paper.

She swung her legs over the side of the bed. The coolness of the wood against her bare feet grounded her, though barely.

Downstairs, the coffee maker sputtered to life, producing a steaming cup of coffee, startling her. She didn't remember turning it on. Carrying the mug to the couch, Harriet sat and stared at the mess strewn across the coffee table. She thought of nothing. She let the numbness settle in.

Eventually, whether it was two hours or two minutes later, she heard footsteps, and Charlie appeared at the bottom of the stairs. She paused, studying Harriet.

True, Harriet looked a mess. Her curls were matted to her

head and there were dark circles under her eyes that hadn't been there a week ago. She was dressed in her rattiest pajamas, the ones with a hole in the bottom seam of her left leg. There was a stain on her right lapel of unknown origin.

Charlie looked at the watch on her left wrist. "It's getting pretty late. Shouldn't you be heading out?"

Harriet blinked. Somewhere in the depths of her mind, there lay the thought that there was something she was supposed to be doing this morning, but it was inaccessible.

She looked at Charlie blankly.

Charlie took a step forward, and then another. "Tennis?"

Harriet said, "Right," but made no effort to move.

She felt Charlie's hand on her shoulder.

"Are you okay?"

Harriet blinked again, and the memory came rushing back. The coffee shop. The muted hum of conversation. The earthy scent of freshly ground beans. And Alex.

The image hit her like a sucker punch to the gut—a cruel, unforgiving slap in the face. Alex, sitting at a corner table, his arm slung carelessly over the back of his chair. His smile. *God,* his smile. Not the guarded, tight-lipped expression she had grown used to, but a real, radiant smile.

It wasn't just the smile that had undone her. It was who he was smiling at.

Harriet couldn't even picture her face now, only the blurry outline of her, sitting across from him, leaning forward like the world revolved around whatever Alex was saying.

"Harriet?" Charlie's voice broke through the fog, her hand still firm on Harriet's shoulder.

She looked up. "I'm fine."

Charlie didn't press further, but Harriet felt eyes on her as she dragged herself upstairs to change. The simple act of pulling on tennis clothes felt monumental, each movement weighed down by the numbness that clung to her like fog. In the mirror, she caught sight of herself. All she could do was laugh.

The drive to the tennis court blurred past. The same roads she'd driven a dozen times felt unfamiliar today, as though she were seeing them for the first time through someone else's eyes. She gripped the wheel tightly.

Harriet sat for a moment after parking, and stared out at the empty court under the bright morning sun. She thought of driving away, of turning the key in the ignition and disappearing somewhere far away. Somewhere quiet. But then Liam's voice carried over the fence, light and carefree as he called out a greeting.

With a deep breath that didn't quite reach her chest, Harriet grabbed her racket from the passenger seat and stepped out of the car. She willed herself to move forward, one shaky step at a time.

She trudged onto the tennis court, her racket feeling heavier than usual in her hand. The sun blazed overhead, warming her through her thin hoodie.

"Let's warm up," Liam called, his voice cheerful as always. His easy grin and relaxed demeanor made him look like someone who never worried about anything. Harriet envied that about him.

Her volleys were sloppy. The ball flew too high, too low, or right into the net. Twice she swung and missed entirely, wincing as the ball bounced against the chain-link fence behind her.

"Don't overthink it," Liam said after her third consecutive miss. He jogged to her side, tossing the ball into the air and catching it again with a quick motion. "You're stiff today. Relax."

"I'm trying." She pushed a strand of hair out of her face for what felt like the hundredth time. It had rained overnight, and the lingering humidity wasn't helping. Her hair stuck to her forehead and neck, curling into unruly spirals she could neither tame nor ignore.

Liam stepped closer. "Here, let me." He reached out, brushing a damp curl away from her eyes with a light, casual touch. His fingers lingered for a fraction too long, and when he pulled back, his eyes were warm, playful.

"You have beautiful eyes."

She blinked at him, blushing. Liam always had that light, flirtatious edge, but today it felt magnified. Like he could sense her unraveling and was trying to reel her back in.

"Thanks," she murmured. But even as she said it, an unbidden thought slipped into her mind. What his skin might feel like beneath her fingers, or the weight of him pressing into her, warm and solid.

The realization hit her like a jolt, and she immediately averted her gaze.

Maybe she had it all wrong from the beginning. Maybe she *was* thirsty.

They finished the lesson with Harriet still fumbling through drills, her embarrassment mounting with every missed shot. Liam remained patient, offering encouragement when she least deserved it, but by the end, she felt more like an idiot than ever.

As soon as the lesson was over, she muttered a quick goodbye and hurried to her car.

The moment she slid into her car, her body sagged, her hands gripping the wheel tightly. She couldn't go home like this. Not with her mind racing and her chest constricting.

Without realizing where she was going, Harriet found herself pulling into a salon parking lot. The sign in the window promised transformation. "Keratin Treatments. Color Specialists. Walk-ins Welcome." Inside, the chemical smell hit her immediately, sharp and sterile.

"What are we doing today?" the stylist asked, her bright smile unnerving.

Harriet strung together a slew of words. It felt reckless, almost absurd, but Harriet didn't back down.

Hours later, she emerged from the salon a different person. Her hair was impossibly straight and sleek, falling in a perfect curtain down her back. The deep black was stark against her skin, a dramatic shift that made her look like a stranger even to herself.

She caught her reflection in the glass door as she walked out. She looked stunning. She looked like someone who could move on.

Harriet sat curled up on the couch, her legs tucked beneath her, staring blankly at the TV. An old movie flickered on the screen, one she'd seen so many times she could recite the lines in her sleep. The dialogue flowed over her like white noise, the characters' movements familiar, predictable, comforting in their sameness.

Behind her, the house buzzed with activity. Olivia, back from Alex's, was in the kitchen, banging cupboard doors open and closed with dramatic flair. Something clattered to the floor, followed by a shriek of frustration.

"Why won't this stupid lid fit?" Olivia's voice carried over the sounds of chaos.

Harriet didn't flinch. A character on the screen was delivering a heartfelt monologue, and her lips moved silently along with the words, the muscle memory automatic.

Upstairs, the dull pounding of bass came from Grayson's bedroom. The sound echoed through the house, heavy and relentless, but Harriet's gaze stayed fixed on the TV.

"Mom!" Olivia's voice was closer now, loud and insistent.

"Did you hear me? The lid won't fit! And there's flour *everywhere*!"

Harriet's head tilted slightly, but her eyes never left the screen. "Use another container," she said, her tone distant and flat.

Olivia stared at the back of her mother's head, hands on her hips, a smear of flour streaked across her cheek. She waited for Harriet to look at her, but Harriet remained still, her focus unyielding. Olivia sighed dramatically before stomping back to the kitchen.

From her spot on the barstool, Charlie observed it all. Olivia muttered something under her breath, slamming a mixing bowl onto the counter. She glanced at Harriet, motionless on the couch, then back at Olivia, who appeared strangely satisfied with her mother's indifference. Charlie leaned forward, resting her elbows on her knees, her coffee mug dangling from one hand. Her gaze lingered on Harriet, taking in the blank expression, the gloss of her dark, straightened hair—that made her look so unlike herself. She looked as though she was sinking into the couch, like she wanted to disappear.

The TV played on, oblivious to the disarray in the house, and Harriet stayed exactly where she was, a statue amid the storm.

Charlie opened her mouth to speak, then thought better of it. She sat back in her chair, her expression unreadable, and watched Harriet the way someone might watch a fragile object teetering on the edge of a shelf, helpless to stop it from falling.

The dialogue from the movie swelled with emotion, but in the living room, the weight of unspoken words filled the air, heavy and unrelenting.

Something had changed.

The doorbell rang, sharp and demanding, followed by two brisk knocks.

Harriet glanced toward the kitchen, hoping someone else might answer, but Charlie and Olivia made no attempt to move. She sighed, pushed herself up from the couch, and padded to the front door.

Evelyn stood on the porch, a polished and uninvited presence. Her perfectly styled hair and tailored coat made her look as though she were on her way to a country club luncheon rather than an impromptu visit to her daughter-in-law's house. Her sharp blue eyes flicked over Harriet's loose sweater, jeans, and socked feet with silent judgment before her face settled into a tight smile.

"Harriet," Evelyn said, her voice honeyed but with the faintest edge of steel. "I was in the neighborhood and thought I'd stop by. Alex mentioned Charlie was staying here, and I simply had to check in."

Harriet stared at her for a beat. Of course Alex had told her. Evelyn's favorite son wouldn't have kept something like this from her.

"Lucky us," Harriet said dryly, stepping aside to let her in.

Evelyn's heels clicked against the hardwood as she swept into the living room. She glanced around the space, her gaze lingering on the folded laundry on the armchair, the slightly crooked throw pillow on the couch, and the stack of unopened mail on the coffee table.

"Well," Evelyn said after a moment. "It's certainly looking...lived in."

Harriet closed the door and leaned against it, crossing her arms. "What can I say? We aim for comfort."

The sounds from the kitchen carried into the room—the clatter of a plate being set down, Olivia's exasperated voice saying, "Aunt Charlie, stop eating the ingredients!"

Evelyn's head turned toward the noise, her expression sharpening like a predator catching the scent of prey. "It's wonderful to see them spending time together, though I must admit, I'm surprised you weren't the one to tell me she was staying here."

Harriet walked back to the couch and sat down, tucking one leg under her. "It must have slipped my mind. Busy and all."

"Busy," Evelyn repeated. She didn't sit, choosing instead to linger in the middle of the room like a queen inspecting her court. "Well, I suppose we all have our own priorities."

Harriet reached for the remote and muted the TV, making no effort to turn it off. "Was there something you needed, Evelyn? Or did you just stop by to remind me I'm a terrible communicator?"

Evelyn ignored the jab, her attention drawn back toward the kitchen. "And Olivia," she said, almost to herself. "She's such a bright girl. I do hope you're encouraging her to apply herself. It's so easy for teenagers to lose focus these days."

"She's doing fine."

"And Grayson? Where is he?"

"Upstairs."

"Is everything all right?" Evelyn said after a moment, her voice softening into a feigned concern that made Harriet's skin prickle. "You're not…overwhelmed, are you?"

Harriet's eyes flicked up to meet Evelyn's. "I'm fine, Evelyn."

There had been a time, long ago, when Harriet would have done anything to please this woman. She would have walked to the ends of the earth and back if asked.

Now, Harriet couldn't wait to get her out of her house.

"I think I'll say hello to Charlie." Evelyn swept into the kitchen.

Harriet leaned back into the couch, waiting for the inevitable clash.

"Oh," Charlie's voice said, flat and completely devoid of enthusiasm. "It's you."

"Hello, Charlotte." Evelyn's tone dripped with forced politeness. "You look...comfortable."

Charlie leaned back against the counter and crossed her arms. "What can I say? I'm thriving."

Harriet smirked to herself and strained to hear better.

"Well," Evelyn continued, undeterred. "It's wonderful to see you spending time with Olivia. Though I do hope you're not letting her pick up any of your bad habits."

"Bad habits?" Charlie repeated, her tone deceptively light. "Like what, Mom? Being honest? Distancing myself from people who criticize me for sport?"

Olivia said, "Solid burn, Aunt Charlie."

Evelyn ignored her granddaughter's jabs and said, "Honestly, Charlotte, could you be any more dramatic?"

Charlie's mouth formed a thin line. "Is there something I can do for you, *Mother*, or can I show you to the door?"

Evelyn turned toward Olivia. "You see the way she talks to me? Would *you* ever speak to your mother that way?"

Olivia, smart girl that she was, only shrugged.

Evelyn held her chin high. "I wanted to make sure you were okay. Is that such a crime?"

Charlie chuckled. "If you think that's what you're doing, then...okay. I'm fine. Now, are we done here?"

Despite her indignation, Evelyn allowed herself to be led back to the front door. She looked back at Harriet, her nose high in the air like she'd smelled something rank, and then she looked to her daughter once again. "Please call your brother. He's really hurting."

Harriet had to physically cover her mouth to stop herself from laughing.

"Sure. Will do," Charlie said. She closed the door behind Evelyn and fell back against it with a *thud*.

Harriet looked at Charlie over her left shoulder. "Yeah, I'm going to need you to tell her she needs to call or text before stopping by from here on out."

Charlie snorted. "Do I look like I can control that woman?"

"Fine, have your brother do it."

Charlie tilted her head slightly as she said, "The golden boy? He'd probably bake her a cake with 'Come over anytime' written on it in frosting before telling her to call first."

Harriet barked out a laugh. "You're right. He'd probably ask for her feedback on the cake afterward too."

Charlie raised her mug in mock salute. "To Mr. Perfect. May he always keep the peace…so we don't have to."

24

The email notification pinged with its usual chipper tone, a sharp contrast to Harriet's mounting irritation. She adjusted her reading glasses and leaned closer to her screen, skimming the subject line of yet another redundant memo from corporate. "Team Synergy and Strategic Realignment"—corporate speak for shifting responsibilities without shifting salaries.

Harriet sighed and rubbed her temples. Her morning coffee had gone cold hours ago, and the lingering odor of someone's microwaved fish lunch in the office break room down the hall wasn't helping her mood. She clicked out of the email and pulled up the document she'd been working on for two hours longer than anticipated, a revised performance improvement plan for an employee who misunderstood the concept of "team effort."

"Harriet…" Her coworker Rebecca's voice chirped from the doorway. "Did you see the update on the travel reimbursement policy? They're cutting allowances again."

"Of course they are," Harriet muttered, biting back a

sharper comment. The company's cost-saving measures had become a running joke, one she was growing tired of.

She added the final paragraph to the document, hit save, and barely had time to stretch before her desk phone rang. The number flashed as familiar—Grayson and Olivia's school. Harriet's stomach dropped.

"This is Harriet," she answered. She tried to sound composed.

"Ms. Young, this is Vice Principal Abernathy. I'm calling regarding Olivia. She and a group of her friends were involved in an incident with another student. It seems they were...unkind, and the situation escalated."

Harriet's heart sank. "What happened exactly?"

"They've been excluding another girl and spreading rumors. Today, it culminated in some particularly hurtful comments during lunch, and the other student became very upset. We'd like to meet with you to discuss how we can address this. Can you come in this afternoon?"

"Of course," she said, masking her irritation. "I'll be there."

Harriet hung up and stared at the phone for a moment before shaking her head. Olivia, her brilliant but sometimes impulsive daughter, had crossed a line this time. That would be a fun conversation.

But first, her unnecessary meeting.

Harriet headed toward Conference Room B, where the bimonthly policy review was already underway. She slid into her seat as her manager, Linda, shot her a pointed glance over the rim of her glasses.

The conversation turned quickly to a policy Harriet had long loathed, the mandatory "workplace efficiency tracker," which essentially turned every task into a quantifiable metric, reducing employees to numbers on a spreadsheet. She'd gritted her teeth for years, but today, fueled by irritation and the perfect amount of not-giving-a-shit, she finally spoke up.

"I'm sorry, but...in my experience, this tracker doesn't improve efficiency. It demoralizes staff and creates a culture of micromanagement. People feel like they're constantly being watched rather than trusted. It's counterproductive."

The room went silent. Linda's eyebrows shot up, and Harriet could feel the eyes of her colleagues darting between them. Even Rebecca caught her eye, her wide eyes urging her to let it go.

But Harriet pressed on. "If we want better results, we need to focus on engagement rather than surveillance. People perform best when they feel valued...not monitored." Seeing the look on Linda's face, she added, "In my humble opinion."

Linda's smile was tight. "That's an interesting perspective, Harriet. Perhaps we can discuss it at another time."

"Or we could discuss it now, while the team is here," Harriet said.

The tension was palpable as Linda moved the meeting along, her clipped tone making it clear Harriet's outburst hadn't gone unnoticed.

As the meeting adjourned, Linda pulled Harriet aside. "We'll need to have a conversation about your approach," Linda said coolly, before walking off.

Harriet didn't regret speaking up. If passive aggression were an Olympic sport, Linda would have a gold medal and her face on a Wheaties box. Even as Harriet returned to her desk, knowing she might have possibly ruined her shot at the corner office down the line and flushed years of brown-nosing down the drain, she felt a flicker of pride. She'd stood her ground.

Still, with Olivia's school visit looming and the weight of her professional risks settling in, the day was shaping up to be one she'd rather forget.

By the time Harriet and Olivia pulled up to the house that evening, Liv hadn't said a word since the meeting with the VP, which suited Harriet fine. She needed the time to think about how she was going to talk to her daughter about her actions without triggering World War III.

Except the closer they got to home, the more Harriet's resolve wavered. She didn't want to get into an argument with her daughter. She didn't want to talk about what had happened at all. Hadn't Olivia already heard what needed to be said at the school? What else was there to discuss?

It was clear that Olivia was acting out, casting her frustration with her father and the divorce outward instead of dealing with it maturely. She was fifteen. She was still learning the definition of emotional maturity. Heck, Harriet was forty, and some days she wasn't sure she'd nailed it down either. If emotional maturity were a class, she'd probably still be asking for extra credit—right after signing up for a remedial course on how not to be an awkward socializer. Maybe they'd offer a discount for bundling the two.

Once inside, Olivia marched straight up to her room. Harriet flopped down onto the couch with a sigh. She spotted movement in the corner. Charlie. Charlie, who never seemed to work, who was always around.

She approached Harriet tentatively. "Everything okay?"

Harriet stared straight ahead at the lifeless television as she said, "Liv got in trouble at school. She and some friends have been bullying some girl."

"Do you want me to talk to her?"

Harriet finally looked at her sister-in-law, who was, naturally, wearing cutoff shorts and an old Coca-Cola shirt she'd sheared off to reveal her flat, twenty-something stomach. "No, I don't."

"Okay. It's just that these things have a way of—"

"Charlie. You're not her parent. I am."

Charlie raised her hands in mock surrender. "Okay, okay. No need to go full momma bear on me." She sank into the armchair across from Harriet, curling her legs beneath her like a contented house cat.

For a moment, neither spoke. Harriet kept her eyes trained on the television, though it wasn't on, while Charlie absently picked at a loose thread on her shorts.

"You know," Charlie said finally, her voice softer now. "I wasn't trying to overstep. I just…remember what it was like being her age. It's not easy."

Harriet turned to look at her, arching an eyebrow. "You mean, what, five years ago?"

"Six, actually," Charlie shot back with a grin. "But seriously, H…kids don't act out for no reason. Maybe she needs something from you that she doesn't know how to ask for."

Harriet rubbed her temples, the exhaustion from the day weighing heavily on her. "Ugh, I know. Believe me, I've been trying. She's angry about the divorce. Angry at her dad for not being around enough. Angry at me for…I don't know, breathing too loud, probably."

Charlie tilted her head, her expression softening. "It's not your fault, you know."

"Thanks, Dr. Phil," Harriet muttered, though her tone lacked venom. She let out a heavy sigh and slumped further into the couch. "Alex is the one who broke this family, but somehow *I'm* the enemy."

Charlie leaned forward. "Maybe that's your in, though. If she's already decided you're the enemy, then you've got nothing to lose by doing something unexpected. Throw her off her game."

"What? Like bake her cookies and tell her I'm proud of her for bullying some poor girl?"

Charlie snorted. "No, obviously not. But maybe try talking

to her like she's your equal. Ask her why she did it, what she's feeling. She might surprise you."

Harriet considered this for a moment, then shook her head. "You make it sound so easy."

"It's not," Charlie admitted, standing and stretching lazily, her cropped shirt riding up even higher. "Lord knows I made things tougher on my mom than they ever needed to be. But nothing worth doing ever is, right? Anyway, I'll be in the kitchen if you want me. Thinking about making popcorn. Or margaritas. Haven't decided yet."

"Maybe both," Harriet muttered as Charlie wandered off, leaving her alone with her thoughts—and the faint, maddening scent of popcorn from the kitchen.

The truth was, Harriet didn't have the energy to fight tonight. Not with Olivia, not with her own swirling guilt, and certainly not with Charlie, who somehow managed to breeze through life as though it were an endless summer vacation. The idea of marching upstairs and confronting Olivia about what had happened at school felt like willingly stepping into a minefield, and Harriet didn't have the stamina to navigate it right now. Every conversation with her daughter lately felt like a battle she wasn't equipped to win.

She closed her eyes and leaned her head back against the cushion, exhaling slowly. *Tomorrow,* she told herself. *I'll deal with it tomorrow.* Maybe with some sleep, she'd be able to find the right words. The ones that wouldn't trigger an explosion. Tonight, though? Tonight, she needed quiet.

From the kitchen, Charlie's voice floated in, cheerful and unbothered. "I decided on margaritas. You want salt or no salt?"

"No margarita," Harriet called back, though the idea was tempting. "Popcorn's fine."

"Boring, but okay!"

The sound of the microwave beeping followed, along with

the hiss of a soda can being opened. Harriet glanced over her shoulder as Charlie reappeared moments later, holding a big bowl of popcorn and a Coke. She flopped down onto the other end of the couch.

"You look like you're about to pass out," Charlie observed, offering the bowl. "Want to talk about it?"

"No, I don't want to talk about anything."

"Fair enough." Charlie leaned back, munching, her eyes fixed on the same blank TV screen as Harriet. "Wanna watch something? I think there's a new true crime doc out."

"Fine, but no murders. I'm not in the mood for that kind of existential dread."

Charlie grinned and grabbed the remote. "Rom-com it is."

Harriet suddenly recalled the feeling of dropping the signed divorce papers into the mailbox. "Fuck rom-coms," she said. "I'm feeling murder-y after all."

25

Harriet should have insisted that Charlie mind her own business. She paused outside Olivia's room, frozen by the sound of their hushed voices. Olivia was talking about the bullying—laughing softly at something Charlie said—and Harriet felt a strange, hollow pang in her chest. Normally, she would have been relieved. Normally, she would have been glad someone else was carrying the weight.

But not tonight. Tonight, she realized she was the one left out. The conversation she should have had, the reassurance she should have given, was happening without her. Parenting a teenage girl was like trying to defuse a bomb she couldn't see, with instructions written in a language she didn't understand. And tonight, she understood that her avoidance had cost her something far more tangible than anxiety: connection.

It stung, sharper than she expected, knowing Olivia had turned to Charlie instead of her. She hadn't just handed off the work of parenting—she'd handed off the chance to matter.

And then there was Gray, who'd been spending less and less time at the house since quitting the soccer team and more time with the girl whose name began with *Mea*. Harriet knew almost nothing beyond that, and it gnawed at her—a mix of worry and helplessness, the kind that made her chest tighten. She wanted to ask, to pry, to fix it, but she didn't even know where to start.

She didn't want to have to think about her kids dating. She didn't want to think about dating at all. Because if she thought about dating, then she'd have to think about sex, and she didn't want to think about how long it had been since she'd had a man's hands on her. Since she'd felt the divine weight of another body on top of hers.

In her bedroom, she closed the door and paused in front of the mirror, studying herself. She was holding up pretty well for her age. There were a few lines across her forehead and the beginning signs of a frown line between her brows, but her crow's feet were minimal, and she didn't appear to be growing jowls. Her jawline was actually still looking quite good. Liv would call it *snatched*—whatever that meant. Harriet only knew it was a good thing.

She'd managed to maintain her slim figure over the years, probably because she was too socially awkward to indulge in post-work cocktails or stuff her face at family gatherings. Instead, she'd spend those events planted in a corner, pretending to be deeply engrossed in her phone or mentally reorganizing her to-do list for the week. By the time she was driving home, her stomach would be staging a full-on protest, growling like it had been personally betrayed. It wasn't intentional. Disassociating was her go-to survival tactic for most public events. Some people mingled. Harriet mentally rearranged her spice cabinet and forgot to eat.

The point was Harriet still looked good. If she wanted to date, she probably could. But the idea gave her chills. That wasn't to say she didn't notice attractive men. She was only human, after all. She'd noticed fathers at school pick up, and her gorgeous, much-too-young-for-her tennis instructor. Liam's Irish accent alone could melt butter, and had, on more than one occasion, left her fumbling her grip on the tennis racket.

Harriet smirked to herself, thinking about their last lesson. He'd told her to "keep her wrist loose" in that lilting brogue of his, and she'd nearly responded with something wildly inappropriate about being flexible. Thankfully, she'd managed to swallow the comment along with her dignity.

Irish, fit, and ridiculously charming…it was unfair. She wasn't sure if he'd been sent to teach her tennis or to test her self-control. Either way, it felt like losing was inevitable.

Harriet let the thought linger longer than she should have. Maybe Liam was exactly what she needed. A no-strings-attached distraction. A fling and nothing more.

Except, there were certainly strings involved. Tennis racket strings. Still, it wasn't like she was planning to marry the guy. If one night with him made things awkward at their next lesson, then she could find someone new to remind her how to perfect her backhand—because, let's face it, it wasn't her backhand she'd been focused on lately.

The more Harriet thought about it, the more perfect for the job he was. He was the kind of man who existed—in her universe—purely for…recreational purposes.

Harriet's cheeks flushed, and she covered her face with her hands, groaning. *Recreational purposes?* Now she really did sound thirsty.

Still, the idea planted itself firmly in her brain. Liam was young enough to keep it casual, old enough to know what he was doing, and charming enough to make her forget Alex and all the baggage that came with him. And that accent…Dear God, the things he could do with words. It was practically criminal.

Stop it, Harriet, she told herself. *The last thing you need is to become some sort of walking midlife cliché, hooking up with the hot tennis instructor.* But even as she scolded herself, a tiny, rebellious part of her thought, *Clichés exist for a reason, don't they?*

It was settled. Harriet had made up her mind. And as she strode purposely across the tennis court that Saturday morning, brushing a strand of her newly black hair away from her face, she felt a rare thrill of anticipation.

The crisp autumn air nipped at her cheeks as she mentally rehearsed her opening lines. She was aiming for something breezy but suggestive, enough to plant a seed in Liam's mind without coming off too forward. Of course, she had little experience in the area of picking up men. It wasn't exactly a skill set she'd cultivated over the years. But from what Charlie had told her during wine-fueled sister-in-law bonding nights, it didn't seem *that* hard.

"Honestly, Harriet," Charlie had slurred once, gesturing wildly with her wineglass. "Men are not complicated. Flash a smile, crack a joke, and for God's sake, lean forward a little. The presence of breasts does half the work for you."

Standing there now, she decided Charlie might have had a point. If leaning forward a little and tossing out a cheeky comment about tennis strings was the ticket to getting Liam's attention, then so be it. Breasts and wit, the ultimate double threat.

The courts were quieter than usual, the weekend chill keeping the casual players at bay. A glance to her left showed she was only one of four people out today—just her, Liam, Diane, a sharp, impassioned woman who'd killed her in a match earlier in the season, and her female instructor. The sky was a patchwork of blue and gray, with the promise of rain in the distance.

Harriet spotted Liam near the far court, bent over a basket of tennis balls. His dark-green hoodie stretched across his broad shoulders, and she allowed herself an unhurried moment to admire him before calling out a "Good morning."

Liam straightened, flashing her one of his devastating smiles. "Morning, Harriet. It's getting pretty cold out. We might need to move indoors soon."

Indoors.

Harriet blushed as she walked toward him. "Indoor tennis could be fun. No wind to blame when my forehand goes haywire."

"You'd never blame the weather. You're far too honest."

Harriet's pulse quickened. "Honest, huh? That's one way to put it."

"And what would you call it?"

She gripped the throat of her racket, feeling bold. "Let's say I try to be...transparent. No use hiding what's on your mind, right?"

Liam's laugh was low and warm. "It's a good philosophy, though I'd say it might land you in trouble now and then."

Harriet smirked. "Trouble's not always a bad thing."

The gentle lift of Liam's brows revealed she'd caught him off guard, and for a moment they stood silently, studying one another.

Eventually, Liam reached for a ball from the basket. "Let's see if you can channel some of that boldness into your swing. Ready?"

"Absolutely." She stepped onto the court, deliberately loosening her shoulders.

For the next few minutes, Harriet hit ball after ball, her focus split between maintaining decent form and gauging Liam's reactions. Each time he stepped closer to adjust her grip or demonstrate a technique, she felt a flicker of electricity. The calm and encouraging way he spoke made her heart race.

As they paused for a water break, Harriet decided to push the envelope a little further. They were now the only pair on the court. "You know, Liam," she said casually, "I was thinking about what you said the other day…about being flexible."

He raised an eyebrow, his expression somewhere between amused and intrigued. "Aye? And what about it?"

She shrugged, taking a deliberately slow sip from her water bottle. "Just that it's good advice. For tennis, of course. And…life." She gave him a pointed look, her lips curling into a playful smile.

Liam's grin widened, and he leaned against the net, crossing his arms. "Is that so? You've been doing some philosophical thinking about our lessons, then?"

"Something like that." She set her bottle down and took a step closer, just enough to test the waters. "Speaking of lessons…maybe we should try a new approach. Mix things up a bit."

His gaze didn't waver. "What do you have in mind?"

Harriet's pulse hammered in her ears, but she didn't falter. "Oh, I don't know. Maybe something a little more…recreational. No racket strings attached."

Liam's lips quirked into a lopsided smile, and he shook his head, chuckling. "You've got a way with words, Harriet. I'll give you that."

She grinned, emboldened by his reaction. "Well, it's good to know I can keep up with your charm."

"And here I thought I was the one teaching you." His tone was teasing, but there was an unmistakable warmth in his eyes.

She was done playing by the rules. She deserved some fun.

Harriet shrugged, the air between them suddenly charged

with possibility. "Maybe it's time we both learned something new."

26

God, how good it felt to be so bad.

Harriet's heart raced as her racket clattered to the court. She looked up at Liam, her breath uneven, her pulse thundering in her ears. The easy smile he usually wore had vanished, replaced by something darker and hungrier.

For a moment, she hesitated, her mind scrambling to remember where she was and who she was supposed to be. But then she noticed the way he was looking at her. Like she was the only thing in the world worth breaking a rule for, and she forgot everything else.

He moved first, a slight step closer that sent her over the edge. Her hand reached for him, and before she could think better of it, his lips were on hers. The kiss was hot, reckless, and brimming with need. Harriet wasn't sure how long it lasted. Seconds? Minutes? Time warped when desire took over.

She pulled away first, her chest heaving and lips tingling. "Tell me you live close by," she said, her voice hoarse, her body betraying her with the way it leaned toward him even now.

Liam smiled, slow and knowing, his hand still resting lightly on her waist.

His two-bedroom apartment was the quintessential bachelor pad, functional but sparsely decorated. The walls were off-white and mostly bare except for a generic framed print of a cityscape and a floating shelf holding a few tennis trophies. The furniture was not new—a black faux-leather couch with a noticeable tear on one arm, and a coffee table that looked like it had seen better days.

A small bookshelf tucked into the far corner held a plant halfway to death and a staggering collection of *Men's Health* and *Sports Illustrated* magazines. A massive flat-screen TV dominated the space, behind which an Irish flag was pinned to the wall. The apartment smelled faintly of laundry detergent and something fried.

The kitchen was small but clean, no dirty dishes in sight and only a single frying pan left on the stovetop. His fridge was adorned with a few grocery store magnets and a lone sticky note with a phone number scribbled on it.

Liam studied her, his eyes hooded and heavy. It may have been a while since anyone had looked at her this way, but Harriet knew what it meant. She knew he wanted her.

He allowed her to move no further than the couch before he pressed his mouth to hers. He tasted like Gatorade, sweet and sugary. There was no hesitation in their movements. Liam's hands slid to her waist, pulling her closer. His breath mingled with hers as his lips moved with a confidence that both startled and thrilled her. The tension in her body dissipated as his hands roamed upward, brushing against her sides, pulling her shirt free from her waistband.

She hadn't realized how much she wanted to feel wanted… until now.

They stumbled into the bedroom, Liam's body pressing into hers with a heat that radiated through her. His lips moved from her mouth to her jaw, then her neck, the slight scrape of his stubble sending shivers down her spine. Harriet's hands found the hem of his shirt and pulled it over his head in one swift motion. His skin was sticky and firm under her touch.

"Are you sure you want to do this?" he murmured, his voice rough but tender.

Harriet's breath caught. She thought of Alex, of her children, of the version of herself she'd been holding onto for so long.

But then Liam's hand cupped her face, and it was just the two of them again. Him, brushing this thumb across her cheek before slipping it between her lips. Her, pressing him against the wall. Him, pushing her onto the bed and kneeling in front of her.

"I'm sure," she whispered.

Their movements became more urgent and desperate as clothes fell to the floor in a tangle. Him, gasping. Her, clawing at his back like the hungry animal she was.

Liam suddenly paused, his breath heavy against her ear. "Wait," he murmured, pulling back slightly. "We should—do you have…"

Harriet blinked up at him, her fingers still gripping his shoulders. She gave a soft smile, her voice steady. "I'm on the pill," she reassured him.

"Okay," he whispered before their lips met again, urgency reigniting between them.

The bed shrank around them, their bodies fitting together with a ferocity that surprised her. Liam's touch was everywhere—her hips, her back, her thighs—as though he couldn't get enough of her.

She let herself go completely, surrendering to the moment and to him. Until...

"Oh...fuck!"

Harriet had no words left. What even were words?

Afterward, they lay side by side, trying to catch their breath.

Liam picked up her left hand, rubbing her fingers absent-mindedly. He pressed down on her ring finger, where her shiny, 1.25 carat diamond used to sit. There was a faint tan line. "You're married?"

She turned to him, blinking. "Separated. Soon-to-be divorced."

"Was it amicable?" He appeared almost ashamed to ask.

"Yes and no," she said. "It's the same old story. Another cheating liar disguised as a good guy."

Liam said, "I'm sorry."

"Have you ever cheated on anyone?"

He shook his head. "No. I don't think I'm capable."

"You're one of the good ones then."

He smirked. "Is that what you would call what we just did? *Good?"*

Harriet exhaled, smiling. "No. What we did was delightful. Sinful. Transformative."

"Transformative, huh?"

"Oh, yes." She murmured gratefully. "In fact, we're going to need to do that again...immediately."

Harriet adjusted her sunglasses, trying to shield herself from the midday sun. Her recent recreational activities had left her hungry and depleted in the best way. The knot in her stomach was a sharp reminder that she hadn't eaten since breakfast.

On impulse, she pulled into the grocery store parking lot, hoping to find something quick to eat.

The warm air inside was a relief as she wandered through the prepared foods section, scanning for a sandwich or salad, something to consume back in the car.

That's when she spotted them. Laura and Carrie.

They were standing near the deli counter, their polished appearances a stark contrast to the functional, hurried shoppers around them. Harriet's stomach tightened. She hadn't seen either of them since Alex moved out, hadn't heard from them since Laura's response to her pathetic text about getting together back in October.

She'd often wondered what she might say to them if they ever crossed paths again. Now, standing just feet away, all the rehearsed lines evaporated from her mind. But instead of retreating, Harriet squared her shoulders and walked straight toward them.

"Harriet?" Laura's voice lifted in surprise, her smile polite but hesitant. Carrie's expression mirrored hers—friendly but guarded.

Harriet folded her arms as she stopped at the edge of the counter. "Imagine my surprise seeing you two here. It's been a while."

Laura shifted uncomfortably, pretending to examine a container of pasta salad. "We've been so busy. Life, you know."

"Sure. Life." Harriet leaned against the counter like she had all the time in the world. It was worth waiting longer for food just to see them squirm. "Busy enough that you couldn't even send a text after Alex and I separated? Busy enough to act like I stopped existing? I'm fascinated. How did you even manage to fit me into your schedule right now? Is this a time-slot snafu?"

Carrie glanced at Laura before speaking, her tone soft and careful. "Harriet, it wasn't personal. We didn't know how to... navigate everything. It was awkward for everyone."

"Awkward for everyone?" Harriet echoed, laughing sharply. "Wow, I'm so sorry my life imploding was inconvenient for you. Must've been awful not knowing what to say. You know, it's wild. I actually didn't know what to say when Alex decided our marriage was a cross-promotion deal he wanted to cancel, but *I* managed. Turns out, showing up is half the battle."

Laura's cheeks flushed. "Be fair, Harriet. We like you both, but...it's not about choosing sides. It's about..." She trailed off, her gaze darting to Carrie for backup.

"Oh, please," Harriet said, rolling her eyes. "It's about convenience. You didn't know how to 'navigate' things because you didn't want to. Because I wasn't useful to you anymore. Let's call it what it is. Alex is shiny and important, and I'm the sad ex-wife who makes everyone uncomfortable at dinner parties. If that's what you think, just own it."

The words hung in the air, sharp and unrelenting. Laura and Carrie exchanged another look, but neither spoke.

"The funny thing is, I used to care what you thought. I spent years molding myself to fit into Alex's world—your world—because I thought that's what mattered. But honestly? I don't need friends who disappear the moment things get hard. And I certainly don't need to spend another second pretending this was ever a real friendship."

Harriet turned and walked away, her strides purposeful, her head high.

She reached her car and sank into the driver's seat, savoring the rare triumph of standing her ground. Full of righteous fury, she was...but still starving.

27

Harriet woke up the next morning still buzzing with the euphoric aftermath of the day before. She could almost taste the sweetness of the decision she'd made, and the clarity that had come with it.

A part of her was alive again, and she couldn't help but smile as she stretched out on the soft sheets. The memory of Liam, his warmth, his touch, and the connection they'd shared felt almost unreal, like something from a dream. She felt lighter and freer, as though she could breathe in a way she hadn't in years.

Then there was the fact that she'd finally—*finally!*—confronted Laura and Carrie!

But as the sun crept through the window, things started to shift. The house was still, but the weight of reality crept in, settling like a cloud over her head. The problem with real life was that it never stayed suspended in those moments of happiness for long.

Harriet stepped out of bed, pulled on a robe, and padded downstairs. The kids were nowhere to be found.

Harriet had known it was only natural for her kids to drift

away from her. But it didn't mean she'd been prepared for how it would feel. Gray, true to his word, was enjoying the freedom that giving up soccer had afforded him. Olivia's mood swings had been harder to track lately, and she was home less and less these days.

When Harriet entered the living room, Charlie was on the couch, her eyes glued to her phone.

"Morning. Have you seen Liv?"

Charlie looked up, blinking like she'd been dragged out of another dimension. "In her room, I think."

Harriet had the sudden urge to unload all her feelings on her sister-in-law. But before she could say anything, Charlie groaned loudly and threw down her phone.

"Evelyn is driving me absolutely crazy."

Harriet took a seat beside Charlie. "I'm here to talk if you want."

Charlie said, "I mean, you know Evelyn. You know how she can be."

"Judgmental."

Charlie nodded.

"Elitist."

"Literally all the time."

"Controlling."

Charlie snorted. "Do you think she has any idea how much she fucked me up?" She took a deep breath, her voice cracking as she spoke again. "Did you know I was an accident? Evelyn and William never really wanted me. Mom was in her forties and had big plans for her career, and I…messed it all up. She was supposed to be a writer. Did you know that? She wanted to go to New York and make something of herself, but then I came along and suddenly all her dreams were ruined. She couldn't do what she wanted…and she reminds me of that every single day."

Harriet was stunned into silence. She had known Evelyn

was difficult, but this? This was a side of Charlie's life she'd never known. How could Alex never have mentioned this?

"Why haven't you told me this before?"

"Because it's mortifying. I'm a grown woman still letting my mother's neuroses affect me."

"I have news for you, Charlie. Our parents' shit always affects us…no matter how old we are."

"Great. Something to look forward to as I age."

Harriet looked pointedly at Charlie. "Deal with it now, and maybe you won't have to at forty."

Charlie's face tightened. "I'll always be a reminder that life didn't turn out the way Evelyn wanted it to." She swallowed hard, tears welling up in her eyes. "She has always adored Alex. Always. He can do no wrong. And I was…There's never been room for me to figure out what *I* want. She's always telling me what to do and criticizing everything about me—my appearance, my weight, the men I date, how I spend my time. I've never been good enough for her. I couldn't take it anymore. That's why I had to leave. That's why I came here."

Harriet was speechless. She had known Charlie had her issues with her mother, but hearing the rawness of it and how deep the pain ran was something entirely different. "Charlie…"

"You don't get what it feels like to never be seen for who you are. To be told you're not good enough and feel like you're always living in someone else's shadow. I've spent my entire life trying to please her, trying to earn her love. And it's never been enough. I'm just…alone."

The tears fell then, silent but powerful, rolling down Charlie's cheeks as she finally let it out.

"You're not alone." Harriet reached out and pulled Charlie into a tight embrace, feeling the tremble of her body as she sobbed. Harriet held her close. She had never seen Charlie this vulnerable before. It was like the dam had finally broken, and everything Charlie had kept inside for years had come pouring out in a rush.

Harriet knew a little something about the feeling.

After a few moments, Charlie sniffled and wiped her eyes.

"Hey." Harriet pulled back slightly. "If you keep crying like this, your crop top's going to need a permanent spot in the laundry. You'll have to start wearing long sleeves to stay dry."

Charlie chuckled through her tears. "Don't you dare. You know my crop top game is strong. It's all about the midriff."

Harriet grinned. "Yeah, I'm sure the midriff is what gets all the attention. But you might want to consider some waterproof mascara next time."

Charlie snorted. "You're ridiculous."

Harriet gave her a gentle smile.

Charlie sat back, staring ahead, lost in thought for a moment. "I've been carrying this weight for so long, you know? And I've let it affect everything. The way I look at people. The way I approach relationships." She met Harriet's eyes. "Maybe even the way I've been trying to help you with Olivia. I don't know."

Even though Harriet was still processing the depth of Charlie's pain, something clicked inside her. Her mind drifted to Alex, and how Charlie had always thought of him as the golden child, the one who could do no wrong in Evelyn's eyes. Alex had always acted so sure of himself, so successful and different from Charlie.

But now, in the wake of Charlie's confession, Harriet felt something shift, like a previously damaged cog in her brain had started working again. Maybe the fractures in Charlie's relationship with her mother weren't so different from the ones Harriet had experienced with Olivia. Maybe the way Evelyn had treated Charlie was a pattern. A pattern that stretched back through generations.

"You know..." Harriet let the connection slowly form in

her mind, "I think I'm starting to understand Alex a little more. I've always been so focused on Liv, on trying to keep our relationship from falling apart…I never really stopped to think about how Alex fits into this. I mean, how much of his life has been shaped by what he's seen and heard and grown up with?"

Charlie raised an eyebrow.

Harriet leaned back, letting the thoughts unravel in her mind. "I think I've always thought of Alex as the one who has everything together. The one who doesn't struggle with things the way I do. But after what you said about your mom and how she's treated you, I wonder if a lot of the pressure she put on you, and all those things she said to you about being a disappointment, maybe she did the same to Alex. Maybe that's why he's so perfect in her eyes. Maybe he *had* to be perfect to get her approval. To feel like he was enough for her."

Charlie worked her jaw back and forth. "I never thought about it that way. Alex has always been the one who had it all figured out. But maybe he *had* to be perfect for her to see him. Maybe he's been fighting for her love just like I have. Maybe he never had a chance to be anything less than flawless."

Harriet had always thought Alex had somehow escaped the chaos of their family dynamics. But now, she wondered if the opposite was true, that Alex had been shaped by his mother's expectations as much as Charlie had…maybe even more.

"I think it's easier to see someone else's pain when you can step back and look at it from the outside."

Charlie nodded slowly. "I guess it's no wonder that either of us turned out the way we did."

Harriet looked at Charlie, wondering if she had ever fully considered the way Evelyn's treatment of her had affected the rest of their family. She had always been quick to judge Alex—especially as of late—but now, the more she thought about it, the more she could see how the same broken patterns had shaped him too.

"Family," Charlie said softly, almost to herself. "It's a mess."

Harriet was suddenly remembering the day Alex had sat her down and told her what he did, how he had betrayed her, and something that was open in her closed up tightly once again. Understanding suddenly dimmed, replaced by something colder. The truth was, *he chose* to hurt her. And in that moment, she wasn't feeling sorry for him anymore.

"And sometimes," Harriet said, "people are just assholes because they want to be." She leaned back, the weight of her thoughts heavy once again.

The empathy she'd been trying to extend to Alex felt foolish now. Understanding familial patterns didn't change the reality of who he was. Some people didn't deserve a second chance.

Charlie sighed deeply. "Evelyn's right about one thing, though. I don't know what the hell I'm doing with my life. I'm twenty-seven. It's not so cute anymore."

"We're all making it up as we go," Harriet said. "I mean, if I had a dollar for every time I've had no idea what I'm doing, I could probably retire in the Bahamas by now."

Charlie let out a small laugh. "Well, in that case, take me with you. I could use a break from all this family drama."

"I'm sure you'd find the best beach clubs," Harriet said. "But I'll take a rain check on the companion. A solo trip might be…less crowded."

Charlie fell silent for a moment, her fingers fidgeting with the hem of her shirt. "I'm serious, though," she said quietly. "I'm just…drifting. I don't even know what I *want* to do anymore. It feels like I'm running out of time, like I'm falling behind everyone else."

"You're not," Harriet said firmly. "You're exactly where you need to be. And trust me, no one's keeping score."

"Except for Evelyn."

"Who we've established is judgmental, elitist, and controlling."

"Your point being?"

Harriet smirked. "It's well past time to stop giving a flying fuck what she thinks."

Charlie raised an invisible glass in salute. "Hear, hear."

28

Harriet felt like a changed woman. Giving in to her desire for Liam, and confronting her so-called friends had torn open something inside of her. She'd finally gotten Grayson to open up about why he'd quit soccer (a girl…it *had* been all about a girl. She should have known!) and had a long-overdue talk with Olivia where she did more listening than talking.

Harriet felt a quiet pride. Bravery didn't always have to be loud. Sometimes, it started at home.

For the next three weeks, Harriet saw Liam as often as she could.

An impulsive spark ignited into a blaze that neither was willing to extinguish. Mornings stretched lazily into afternoons, and evenings often blurred into late nights. Harriet would arrive at Liam's apartment expecting a short visit, only to find herself staying much longer. She lost count of the hours spent tangled in his sheets, the sunlight fading as they learned the ins and outs of each other's bodies.

Liam's easy charm and the intensity of their connection made Harriet feel alive in a way she hadn't felt in years. She'd been with other men before Alex, men who were confident and experienced, who knew what they were doing. But nothing had ever felt like this.

With Liam, it wasn't only about technique or skill. It was the way he looked at her as if she were the only thing that mattered. It was his easy charm and the raw intensity of their connection. It was the way his touch set her nerve endings alight in a way she hadn't known was possible.

She felt the weight of her usual worries lift a little as she basked in the simplicity of desire and the thrill of being desired.

After her time with Liam, Harriet often returned home glowing, her cheeks flushed and eyes bright.

Charlie noticed immediately.

"You've been in a great mood lately," she said one evening as they stood in the kitchen, Harriet pouring herself a glass of wine. "Care to share what's got you grinning like that?"

Harriet paused with her glass poised midair, before deciding there was little point in hiding it. Charlie's perceptive gaze would ferret out the truth eventually.

She lowered her voice. "I've been seeing Liam."

It took Charlie a moment to place the name before her eyebrows shot up. "The tennis instructor?"

"Yeah."

"Seeing as in..."

"Sleeping with," Harriet clarified.

A memory: Harriet straddling Liam at the end of his bed, his hands on her lower back, guiding her forward and backward. Her breasts crushed against his chest, her hands landing in his hair.

A blush rose to her cheeks.

Charlie's lips curved into a wide smile. "Good for you! About time you had some good ol' fashioned fun. Honestly, it's been years since I've seen you this light."

Harriet felt a mixture of relief and delight at Charlie's approval. "It's…easy with him. No expectations, no pressure. Just…"

"Fun?" Charlie supplied.

"Exactly."

"Hot?"

"*So* hot."

Charlie lifted her own glass in a toast. "Here's to Liam, then. May he continue to keep you…*smiling*."

Harriet grinned. "Is that what they're calling it these days?" She clinked her glass against Charlie's, silently toasting to more than Liam. She was toasting to herself, to this unexpected chapter of happiness, and to the woman she was rediscovering within. To the parts of her, long dormant, that were now awake.

Charlie emptied her glass and set it down with a flourish. "Now tell me. How big?"

Olivia appeared seemingly out of thin air. "How big is what?" She tugged open the refrigerator door and pulled out a La Croix and then looked at her aunt expectantly.

"How big was the water bill." Harriet turned to Charlie. "I told you, you can't keep taking such long showers."

Olivia's eyes glazed over. She sipped her drink, her eyes on her mother, then said, "Can I have twenty bucks to go to the movies this weekend?"

Harriet's eyes widened. "That's what it costs to go to the theater these days?"

"Pretty much," Charlie said.

Olivia held out her hand. "So?"

"Who all's going?"

Her daughter pouted. "Why do you always ask me that? Why can't you trust me?"

Harriet shook her head, smiling. "I look forward to the day

you have your own kids and finally understand that I'm not trying to be nosy. I'm just trying to know you."

Charlie's chin dropped to her chest.

Olivia said, "Okay…"

Harriet exhaled softly and then went to fetch her purse. She slid a crisp twenty into her daughter's hand. "And…I do trust you, Liv."

Olivia took another pull from the can and then set it down on the counter. She looked at her mother for a moment, her lips pressed together in thought. Then, without a word, she stepped forward and wrapped her arms around Harriet in a quick, tight hug.

Harriet's eyebrows shot up in surprise, but she returned the hug, her hands running up and down Olivia's back.

When Olivia pulled away, she studied her mother's face curiously. "You look…different,." Her eyes flicked over Harriet's features like she was trying to solve a puzzle.

A smirk tugged at the corners of Charlie's lips. "Kids notice everything."

Olivia's gaze bounced between them. "Wait, what am I missing?"

Harriet shook her head. "You're not missing anything." She looked to Charlie for backup.

Charlie leaned in conspiratorially toward Olivia. "She's just feeling good from all the exercise she's been getting lately."

The look of boredom returned to her daughter's face. She reached for her soda can again. "Well, you look…happy."

Charlie coughed out a laugh.

Harriet shot her a sideways glance but couldn't fight the grin creeping across her face. She absolutely intended to *exercise* as often as she could.

Sunday afternoons remained a sacred refuge for Harriet. The ritual of meal planning and prep offered a soothing sense of control, a quiet anchor to her week. On Sundays, she could forget about looming deadlines and the weight of unfinished projects...and maybe even the chaos of her own thoughts. She could simply *be*.

She had her favorite playlist humming softly in the background, her neatly organized recipe cards spread across the counter, and a detailed grocery list already checked off and filed away. In spite of her new extracurricular activities and the soon-to-be-ending drama of her marriage, Harriet's routine was her anchor in an unpredictable world.

Today was no different. She was slicing strawberries for the week's breakfasts when her phone buzzed on the counter. The interruption was unwelcome, a tiny ripple in her carefully curated afternoon.

Alex.

The name lit up the screen, accompanied by the kind of hesitation only a history like theirs could bring. Her instinct was to ignore it—after what she'd seen that day in the coffee shop—but she wiped her hands on a dish towel and picked up.

"Hi." His voice was steady but edged with something she couldn't quite place. "I was hoping you had a minute to talk about Christmas."

That's right. Christmas was only a few weeks away. Between cleaning up after Charlie and all those hours "perfecting her form" with Liam, she'd let time get away from her.

"What about it?"

"The kids want us to spend it together. As a family."

She blinked, caught off guard. "They told you that?"

"They did."

Interesting. Not a peep to her about their sudden enthusiasm for a temporary family reunion special.

She said, "Alex..."

"I know it's a lot to ask. I'm not trying to make this about us or dredge up old stuff. It would obviously mean a lot to them."

Harriet arched a brow. "Well, I'm glad to hear you listen when they talk. I'll try not to be too shocked if I witness it with my own eyes."

She was greeted with silence from the other end of the line.

Harriet's grip tightened on the phone. The thought of Christmas—of Alex in the house, the weight of their shared history hanging over everything—made her itchy. But then she thought of Liv and Gray, their faces lighting up at the idea of a family Christmas.

"I'll think about it," she said after a moment.

"Thanks, Harriet. Really." There was a pause, and then he added, "I'll let you go. Just…let me know what you decide."

"I will." Then, before she could stop herself, she added, "And Alex, so we're clear, don't even think about bringing your mistress. This isn't a holiday rom-com."

She ended the call before he could respond.

29

Christmas morning snuck up faster than a kid on a sugar high, leaving Harriet with little time to think about the gift wrap…let alone the family dynamics. The air in Harriet's living room was thick with the kind of silence that made her skin feel too tight. The tree sparkled, and opened presents littered the room, but everyone was shifting uncomfortably in their seats.

Charlie sat on the couch, her usual warmth muted today, her Vans hoodie no doubt hiding a crop top underneath. Her arms were crossed as she glanced between Harriet and Alex like she was watching a tennis match.

Grayson and Olivia sat at opposite ends of the room in an attempt to avoid even the hint of family closeness, despite this gathering having been their idea. Grayson's eyes were glued to the television, where *A Christmas Story* played, while Olivia was, predictably, on her phone. Whoever it was she was frantically texting with had her smiling in a way that made Harriet's stomach churn. Alex was by the window, his eyes trained on the view as if he could somehow wish the tension away.

And then there was Greta.

Despite her stubborn streak and habit of cutting through the crap with a knife-sharp wit, Harriet couldn't stand the idea of her being alone on Christmas, so she'd extended her an invite to join them.

Greta looked around the room, eyes darting from person to person, her lips quirked up in a knowing way. She cleared her throat dramatically. "Well, isn't this cozy?" she said. "I don't know about you all, but if I didn't know any better, I'd think we were at a wake, not a Christmas celebration."

Charlie choked on her coffee. The kids froze, their heads snapping toward the source of the disruption. Alex stiffened, his jaw tightening, but Greta didn't give him the satisfaction of reacting.

"Honestly," Greta continued, "if you're going to make it this awkward, at least put on a movie we haven't already seen a thousand times."

Harriet glanced at Alex, whose face was carefully neutral, but she could see the edge in his eyes. She was the one who should be looking like that! She was the one who'd been wronged! She was the one who wanted to crawl into a hole and die on the rare occasion that their paths crossed!

"Greta," Charlie said with a half-laugh. "Maybe we should just enjoy the holiday and not focus on the, um, *subtle* atmosphere."

Greta gave her a look that said she wasn't fooled. "Subtle? Honey, this is like a Christmas miracle…if you count the miracle of everyone here somehow managing not to strangle each other with their own scarves."

Alex held back a snort as Grayson and Olivia continued watching the movie.

"How about some drinks?" Charlie said finally, rising to her feet. "There are no rules about when it's appropriate to start drinking at Christmas."

Greta watched her move. "Well, *someone's* trying to make

themselves useful." She leaned back, her arms folded as she studied the room once more. "Make mine nice and strong."

As the hours wore on and the wineglasses emptied, the tension in the room started to loosen. The awkward silences were filled with the occasional awkward chuckle, and the conversation, while still carefully sidestepped, appeared to flow a little more easily.

The first glass of Chardonnay helped. The second helped even more, and by the time the third arrived, Harriet found herself leaning into the familiarity of the room. Charlie was telling one of her outrageous stories about a family trip while Grayson pretended not to roll his eyes. Alex had finally relaxed a little, his shoulders easing as he reached for his own glass.

For a few minutes, at least, the weight of the past year lifted. But then the conversation turned, as it inevitably did when Alex's name was mentioned, this time in the context of some "new friends" he'd made after the separation.

Something shifted in Harriet's gut, a cold reminder that some things were never quite behind you. It was subtle at first. A word here, a laugh there, all centered around Alex's adventures post-separation. The wine wasn't helping this time. No amount of Chardonnay could soften the sting.

Harriet's mind flickered back to a conversation with her mother when she was younger. The day her mother had confided in her, eyes wide with bitterness, about how her father's infidelity had torn apart not only their marriage but the very foundation of trust they'd spent years building.

"You never forget that feeling," her mother had said, her voice raw with pain. "Once someone shows you they can betray you, there's no going back."

The memory gnawed at Harriet's insides as she looked across the room at Alex, laughing a little too freely. She hated how the mere thought of Alex with someone else still made her stomach churn. Time had yet to heal this particular wound.

Charlie stood suddenly, looking like she'd had enough of the merry, boozy charade. She moved toward Alex, her face unreadable, a certain kind of determination in her step.

Harriet's breath hitched as Charlie approached her brother, and then, with a quiet but firm tone, began to speak. The words were low, meant only for his ears.

Alex shifted on his feet, his expression unreadable, but Harriet could see the slight tightening of his jaw, the subtle sign that he wasn't entirely immune to the weight of his sister's words.

"Charlie," he said finally, the words a warning. "It's not the time."

Charlie didn't back down. "No. It's exactly the right time."

Harriet stilled. "What's going on?"

"It's nothing," Alex said at the exact moment Charlie said, "Alex wants to talk to you."

Harriet glanced at the kids, who had long ago moved from watching Christmas movies to fighting over some new video game, and back at Alex.

Charlie continued, her voice low. "You owe Harriet the truth, Alex. A real explanation. Not an excuse…not this half-hearted guilt you've been carrying around."

Harriet could feel the heat rise in her chest as she watched them. This wasn't about *them* anymore. It was about something far deeper, something she'd buried under layers of patience and politeness. She could see Charlie's point, but it only made her angrier. How was it that everyone else knew what Alex owed her, but he couldn't bring himself to face it?

Since the day she charged into his office, she'd struggled to let it go, telling herself it didn't matter. Alex was going to do what he wanted, and she had little control over it.

Now, she might finally get some answers.

Harriet's fingers tightened around the edge of her glass as she stared at Alex.

He looked down at his hands. "I don't even know where I'd start."

Charlie shook her head slowly. He was twelve years older than her, but was, in many ways, so much less mature. "Your words don't have to be perfect. You just have to tell her."

Alex stood, and Harriet followed him. Alone in the den, Alex sat, clenching and unclenching his fists. Harriet waited for him to start talking.

30

Harriet pushed away the unsettling thought that one of the other four people in the house might be listening outside the door and settled her gaze on Alex. "Well?" she said, her tone giving away her impatience. It was so quiet they could have heard a pin drop.

Alex didn't look at her. His hands twisted together in his lap, knuckles white, his body coiled as if bracing for an impact.

Harriet's fingers toyed with the stem of her wineglass, her skin hot with the deceptive courage of enough alcohol. It gave her a veneer of control, but she still felt as though she were balanced on the edge of a fraying rope.

Her body would make one hell of a *splat* when it hit the ground far below.

"Tell me. Whatever it is."

Alex drew a shaky breath and finally lifted his eyes to hers. They were filled with a storm she hadn't seen in years. "I didn't know how else to let you go," he said so quietly that Harriet could barely hear him.

Harriet blinked, uncomprehending. "Let me go?"

His Adam's apple bobbed as he swallowed. "There was no affair, Harriet. I didn't cheat on you."

The words landed in the space between them like a bomb.

Harriet's mouth fell open. "What—" Her voice was barely a whisper now, her grip tightening on the glass until she worried it might shatter. She dropped her head back and stared up at the ceiling, blinking before saying, "What in the actual fuck!"

Alex flinched, probably because Harriet almost never swore. Eventually, he said, "I'm going to need you to use your words right now so I know whether I should brace for impact or start running."

"Don't do that. Don't try to be cute. Not right now."

Alex exhaled sharply, scrubbing a hand over his face. "I know. I…I don't know how else to do this."

She let out a humorless laugh. "Try starting with the truth, Alex."

Silence stretched between them, heavy and suffocating.

Alex leaned forward and ran his hands through his hair. "I made it up. All of it. I thought…I thought if you believed I'd done something unforgivable, it would be easier for you to walk away. That you'd hate me enough to leave without looking back."

She tried to process what he was saying, but her pulse thudded in her ears, loud and unrelenting. "You let me believe…" Her voice cracked.

She stood abruptly, needing the physical distance, needing to breathe.

Alex stood too, his hands outstretched as though he could somehow pull her back from the edge of her disbelief. "I thought I was doing the right thing. We were falling apart, Harriet, and I didn't know how to fix it. We were so unhappy, and I thought—"

"You thought *lying* to me was the answer?" she snapped.

"I thought it would be better than dragging this out and hurting each other over and over again," Alex said, his voice breaking now. "I thought you'd be free to move on."

Harriet paced the small room. Her thoughts raced, colliding with one another, leaving her dizzy and unmoored. "All this time," she said, her voice trembling. "You let me hate you for something you didn't even do. Do you have any idea what this has done to me?"

"I know." His voice was heavy with regret.

She stopped pacing and faced him again. Her eyes were blazing now, a mix of anger and pain she couldn't contain. "You broke us, Alex."

"That's not true," he said, his voice raw. "We were already broken."

PART TWO
ALEX

31

There was a story about Alex's marriage that he had once told anyone who asked, and it went a little something like this: His childhood was marked by loneliness.

An only child until the age of twelve, he spent far too much time alone, earning praise for his independence. But Alex didn't want to be self-sufficient. He wanted to feel loved by his parents.

Things changed when Charlie was born, twelve years his junior, but not in the way he had hoped. His mother, once vibrant and ambitious in her burgeoning career as an author, became a shadow of her former self. Struggling to balance her children and an absent husband, she was forced to abandon her writing. She withdrew into a quiet, numbing routine.

Alex had no choice but to step in as a caretaker for his little sister. He raised her as best he could, and Charlie became the bright spot in his life. The one good thing he dared to hold on to. Charlie was the only person he'd been capable of loving, and the only one capable of loving him in return.

And then, after college, he met Harriet. Finally, here was someone who could love him the way he needed to be loved, who could be present, caring, and giving.

That first night, he worked up the courage to introduce himself. The banter that followed had been equal parts thrilling and humbling. Harriet went beyond sparring. She swept in for the intellectual checkmate before Alex even knew the game had started. He spent the night trying to keep up as she dismantled every topic he brought to the table with a mix of intellect and wit, leaving him equal parts impressed and intrigued.

By the end of the night, his ego was bruised, but his interest was piqued.

She's the kind of woman you marry, he'd thought. Turned out, he wasn't wrong.

From the beginning, Alex told everyone who would listen how captivated he was by Harriet's decisiveness. She knew what she wanted, whether it was a glass of Malbec or a debate partner, and she didn't waste time pretending otherwise. He'd never met anyone like her.

Within a month of dating, Alex had told his mother he would marry her someday. Evelyn's response was exactly as Alex had expected, which was to say she said nothing much at all.

Harriet liked to joke that she had all the romance of a well-formatted spreadsheet, and at times, Alex would agree. But she made life better—and not in the sweeping, movie-montage kind of way. She made life better by scheduling things and knowing where everyone's keys were, and never running out of peanut butter—their favorite.

Her meticulousness didn't just charm Alex. It grounded him.

He quickly found himself relying on Harriet's systems and

structure. She wasn't controlling. She was creating spaces where life could thrive, where the chaos and unrealistic expectations he'd grown up with could finally settle. For Alex, who'd spent most of his childhood navigating the unpredictability of his parents' lives, Harriet's steadiness was nothing short of a revelation. She made *him* better.

He didn't just love her. She made him believe in a future nothing like his past. Harriet was the kind of person who didn't just keep things running smoothly. She made them worth running at all. So when they found out she was pregnant with twins, he was able to put aside his fear of parenting, of repeating the same mistakes his own parents had made, knowing he was embarking on this journey with her.

He was lost…but *she* would know exactly what to do.

There was nothing they couldn't do as a team. He'd told himself that for years, and it had always felt true.

But now, standing at the edge of a family Christmas that felt more like a minefield than a celebration, Alex couldn't shake the question that had been gnawing at him for months.

Where had it all gone wrong?

Harriet stood frozen, her expression one of dazed confusion. For a moment, Alex thought she hadn't heard him, but then he saw it—the slow widening of her eyes, her lips parting slightly as though the air had been knocked out of her. She blinked, and her hand came up to her chest, her fingers brushing the delicate chain of her necklace. He noticed she wasn't wearing her rings.

"You pretended to have an affair…" She trailed off, her voice failing her. She took a step back. Her gaze darted to the floor, then back to him, searching his face. "What am I meant to do with something like this, Alex?"

Alex's shoulders curled forward instinctively, bracing for impact.

Harriet's face was set in the careful, neutral expression she wore when she didn't trust herself to speak freely. Alex had to look away for fear the shame might cause him to combust on the spot.

"This is why...Charlie shouldn't have said anything. I should never have told you."

It took her a moment to gather her thoughts. "So...what? You were going to let me go on believing you cheated on me? Why? So I could be the villain? The one who decided to end our marriage?"

Alex shook his head. "No. *I'm* the villain in this story."

He had thought he would feel better once he told her the truth, that the guilt he'd been living with all this time would suddenly vanish. Or, at the least, diminish. But he felt no different than he had before. He felt worse. He had gone and hurt Harriet once again, something he swore to himself he'd never do.

Harriet studied him for a long moment. He grew quickly uncomfortable under her gaze. Being back in the house with her and the kids, sharing a room with her, had been tougher than he'd imagined it would be.

"What?" he asked finally, unable to bear the silence.

She glanced down at her hands, fingers running over the faint indentation where her wedding band used to be. "Are you going to tell me why you did it, or am I supposed to guess? Because if I have to guess, we could be here a while, and feelings could get hurt...more than they already have."

From the other room came a loud crash, followed by Greta's muffled apologies. Harriet didn't flinch. She kept her eyes on Alex.

"Just tell me why you did it," she said, her voice quieter now.

"I thought it would be easier this way."

"Easier for who?" Harriet shot back.

"I don't know," he admitted, his voice barely audible.

But he did know. It had been easier for him.

His lie wasn't the only betrayal. It was everything leading up to it.

The cracks had started forming long before he pretended to cheat.

32

A memory: The clatter of keys had echoed through the small house. Alex, freshly eight years old, had sat cross-legged on the kitchen floor, a mismatched pair of socks on his feet and an open jar of peanut butter in front of him. A butter knife rested nearby, smeared with the remnants of his last attempt to make a sandwich.

The pantry was half-empty as usual. His dad promised to pick up dinner on his way home from work, but Alex hadn't known when that would be. His dad's promises often came with vague timeframes—"after the meeting," "once I finish this project"—and those timeframes had a way of stretching well past dinner. His mom was home, but she might as well not have been. She'd been in her study with the door half-open, fingers flying across her typewriter keys. She muttered to herself occasionally, her words punctuated by the ding of the typewriter's carriage return.

"Mom?" Alex called, loud enough to be heard but not so loud as to disturb her rhythm.

"I'm on a roll, Alex," she said without looking up. "What do you need?"

"Nothing," Alex lied. He knew better than to ask again. Instead, he climbed onto the counter to grab the loaf of bread. It was slightly stale, but he didn't care. He spread a thick layer of peanut butter on a slice, folded it in half, and ate it over the sink, watching crumbs fall into the basin.

Once, he'd tried making dinner for himself. He'd boiled pasta, just like he'd seen his mother do hundreds of times, and added a jar of sauce he'd found in the back of the pantry. He'd burned his hand on the pot, and when he showed it to his mom, she'd smiled.

"You're so independent," she'd said. "I don't know what I'd do without you."

Then she closed her office door.

After cleaning up his mess, Alex wandered into the living room. A stack of early copies of his mom's debut book sat on the coffee table, waiting to be signed. He picked one up and flipped through the pages, the words blurring together nonsensically. People were already talking about it. One of his teachers had mentioned it to a colleague, and one of their neighbors told him she was going to be famous. He wanted to be happy for her, but her writing was just another thing that kept her from noticing him.

He picked up the TV remote and turned it on, keeping the volume low. His favorite show was starting, but he found it hard to concentrate with the sound of the typewriter.

Hours later, when the typing finally stopped, he perked up, hoping his mom might come into the living room to sit with him. But the door to her office stayed closed.

That night, he brushed his teeth and gotten ready for bed by himself, like most nights. He pulled the covers up to his chin and stared at the glow-in-the-dark stars stuck to his ceiling. They reminded him of the ones in the planetarium his dad had promised to take him to, though the trip never happened.

In the silence of his room, Alex whispered the same promise he made to himself every night: *Tomorrow, I'll do better. Tomorrow, she'll notice.*

Alex had been eleven when he found out his mother was pregnant. His parents hadn't told him. He'd figured it out on his own after hearing his mother vomiting for days. She'd stopped eating and had grown thin, except for the slowly protruding roundness of her belly. Though his parents tried to hide it, they'd argued about the pregnancy relentlessly, hushed exchanges he could hear through the walls. Evelyn was forty. She hadn't planned on having more children. They were already struggling with the one they had.

It was during one of the faint conversations Alex wasn't supposed to hear that he first heard the word abortion. He didn't know what it meant, only that it made his mother growl in rage. His father's voice was a low and steady current, insistent but not quite angry.

"Evelyn, we're barely holding it together now. This isn't the time for another baby."

"And whose fault is that?" Evelyn snapped back. "You think I wanted this? You think I planned this?"

"You don't have to go through with it," his father said quietly. There was the scrape of a chair, then the sound of his mother pacing. "It's not too late."

Evelyn let out a sharp, bitter laugh. "Not too late for what? To carve up my body and live with it for the rest of my life? To spend the next twenty years hating myself? That's not an option, no matter how much you think it is."

Her words cut through the silence like a knife, leaving Alex frozen in place. He didn't understand everything, but he knew enough. His mother was angry, and his father desperate, and none of it felt like something a family was supposed to talk about.

Evelyn's first novel, *Firelight in Winter,* had been her breakout success, landing her a coveted spot in the literary world. Starting over with another child felt like a cruel joke.

She didn't know if she held the capacity to love it, but the thought of getting rid of it made her feel hollow inside.

Her husband didn't understand. To him, the baby was a problem to solve, a burden to shed before it could weigh them down. But to Evelyn, it wasn't so simple. The baby was already there, growing inside her, altering the very fabric of her existence. Giving it up felt like severing a piece of herself.

But as she sat in the dim light of her dining room, she couldn't help but wonder if her writing—the thing that had always defined her—would have to be the sacrifice.

Eventually, Alex had thought of becoming an older brother as a blessing. He would have someone else to play with, someone else to love. Someone else who could love him in return. And from the moment Charlotte came into the world, Alex was enamored. Everything the baby did was bewildering and incredible to his twelve-year-old self. He couldn't believe how small her tiny toes were, how impossibly soft her skin and hair.

As she grew older, Alex took care of her more and more. He helped her learn to use the toilet, learn her letters, and how best to speak to their parents so as not to anger them. Charlie was his best friend.

By then, Evelyn, once vibrant and ambitious in her burgeoning career, became a shadow of her former self. Struggling to balance two children and an absent husband, she abandoned her writing and withdrew into a quiet, numbing routine. Her mood was a storm cloud that hovered over the house, darkening everything in its path. She yelled at Alex for leaving his shoes by the door, scolded him for watching TV too long, and complained about the mess in his room even when it wasn't messy.

"You think I have time to clean up after you? You're old enough to do it yourself, Alex."

Alex nodded, swallowing the lump in his throat. It wasn't only her words but the way she said them, the edge in her voice making him feel like he was the reason she was unhappy.

But it wasn't only Alex who bore the brunt of her frustration. She was equally frustrated by her daughter as well.

"For God's sake, Charlie, don't slurp your cereal," she barked, her voice cutting through the quiet of the kitchen.

Charlie froze, her spoon suspended midair. She kept her eyes on the bowl. Evelyn looked tired, her face pale and her eyes ringed with shadows. Charlie didn't argue. She never did. She just finished her cereal in silence and slipped out the back door with her brother before her mother could find something else to criticize.

As Alex and Charlie grew, their age difference became a struggle. Charlie loved her big brother and wanted to follow him everywhere, but Alex no longer wanted to be a substitute parent. He constantly pushed Charlie away, too old now to have her following him around like a shadow.

It was different at school. Alex had always been good at blending in. He kept his head down in class, aced his tests, and stayed out of trouble. But when Susie Meyer smiled at him from across the chemistry lab in the tenth grade, something shifted.

She was untouchable, effortlessly confident, always surrounded by a group of laughing friends. Yet, for some reason, she kept looking his way.

"You're really good at this," she said one afternoon, peering over his shoulder. "I'd probably fail without you."

Alex felt his cheeks heat. "It's just practice," he muttered, barely able to meet her gaze.

But Susie didn't move away. She stayed, asked him questions, and laughed at his awkward jokes. By the end of the semester, they became partners not just in chemistry but in walking to class, eating lunch, and lingering outside after school.

For the first time, Alex felt seen.

She invited him to her house to study, introduced him to her parents, and even held his hand during a movie night. He started to believe that maybe he wasn't as invisible as he thought.

Then came the winter formal.

"You're going with me, right?" Susie asked one day, her voice casual, like it was the most natural thing in the world.

Alex's heart thudded in his chest. He nodded quickly, his mouth too dry to speak.

That night, after leaving his house—there was no one at the foot of the stairs asking for photographs, or even anyone to see him in his suit—he stood on Susie's front steps, his palms sweating as he clutched a corsage he'd spent an hour picking out. Susie was stunning in a silver dress.

For most of the evening, Alex was on cloud nine. They danced, laughed, and shared whispered jokes. But as the night wore on, Susie began drifting toward her friends. By the time the slow songs started, Alex found himself standing alone near the punch table, clutching two plastic cups.

Eventually, one of Susie's friends, a tall guy from the football team whose name Alex couldn't remember, told him Susie was leaving with him.

Alex's stomach dropped. He scanned the room, but Susie was nowhere to be found. His chest tightened as he realized she hadn't even said goodbye. He left the dance early, walking home in the cold without his jacket.

For weeks after, Susie barely spoke to him. When she did, it was all excuses—"I've been busy," or "You're so serious, Alex. Can't we just have fun?"

By the time she officially ended things, she was already dating someone else. Alex assured himself it didn't matter. That there would be other girls. But deep down, it confirmed what he feared most, that no matter how hard he tried, no matter how much he gave, he would never be enough to keep someone's love.

Alex decided, then and there, it was safer to keep people at arm's length. If he never let anyone in, they couldn't leave him.

College wasn't much different from high school, except Alex had to drive a beat-up old Honda Civic clear across town to attend his much bigger classes. The anonymity of the campus suited him fine. No one paid much attention to the quiet guy sitting near the back, scribbling notes, and raising his hand only when he was sure of the answer.

He declared a major in business because it was practical and because his dad nodded approvingly when Alex mentioned it at dinner one night during his freshman year.

"Good choice. You'll never be out of work with a business degree."

That was enough for Alex. He didn't know what he wanted, but he knew what he didn't: his dad's disappointment.

Still, Alex struggled to find direction. He spent hours in the campus library, poring over textbooks, but it all felt hollow. The concepts had been clear, the numbers adding up, but nothing sparked any real interest.

He tried joining a few clubs, one for aspiring entrepreneurs and another for marketing students, but he always felt like an outsider, unable to match the energy or enthusiasm of the other members.

Money was tight, and so Alex picked up a part-time job at a local diner to help cover his gas and books. His parents were paying his tuition, so he wouldn't dare ask for anything more.

By the time graduation rolled around, Alex had a respectable GPA and a degree in hand, but no real idea of what to do with either. He spent the next few months floundering, sending out resumes to every company he could think of and being rejected more often than not.

The jobs he had landed interviews for felt uninspiring—entry-level positions in offices that smelled like stale coffee and glared with fluorescent lights. But he reminded himself that the goal wasn't passion or fulfillment. It was to make money, to prove he was capable.

To prove to his parents that he could be someone worth loving.

33

The memory came rushing back. Alex had leaned against the kitchen counter and stared at the two mugs of coffee Harriet had prepared.

She always made his first, letting it brew for exactly four minutes before adding a splash of milk, the way he liked. He found it endearing and slightly amusing that she turned even coffee-making into a precise art. It was one of those small gestures that quietly spoke volumes about how she cared. Only six months into their marriage, and already he couldn't imagine life without her.

Harriet had breezed into the room, her phone tucked between her ear and shoulder as she jotted something onto the calendar pinned to the fridge. Alex was in awe, marveling at how she could carry on a conversation about a work deadline while simultaneously reorganizing their grocery list. Her hair was pulled into a loose bun, and she wore one of his oversized hoodies, sleeves rolled up to her elbows. To Alex, she looked like home.

Hanging up, Harriet glanced over at him. "You've got that

look again," she said, reaching for her mug. "What are you thinking about?"

"How amazing you are," Alex said. It wasn't the first time he said it, but the sincerity never waned.

Harriet rolled her eyes, though her cheeks flushed pink. "Flattery will get you everywhere," she said, taking a sip of her coffee. "But if you're buttering me up to avoid cleaning the bathroom this weekend, think again."

Alex laughed, a genuine, warm sound that filled the small kitchen. "No ulterior motives. Just…thanks. For everything you do."

She leaned against the counter beside him, her expression softening. "You know I'm not keeping score, right? We're a team."

A team. The words landed in Alex's chest with more weight than Harriet probably realized.

He hadn't always felt part of a team. Before her, his life had been a series of fragmented efforts, his parents leaving him feeling like he was always scrambling to fill the gaps. With Harriet, it was different. She hadn't just patched the holes. She'd built something sturdy enough for both of them to lean on.

"I know," he said quietly, meeting her gaze. "It's…new for me. In a good way."

Harriet reached over, her fingers brushing his. "You're doing great, you know. This whole marriage thing? We've got it down."

"Yeah, except for the part where I nearly burned the pancakes this morning."

"You were multitasking," she said, smirking. "Who irons a shirt while making breakfast, anyway?"

"Someone who's married to the world's most organized human and doesn't want to disappoint her."

Harriet laughed, a sound that always made Alex's heart feel

lighter. "Disappoint me? Alex, I married you fully aware of your…creative approach to time management. But you've improved. Honestly, I think we're rubbing off on each other."

"You're saying I'm making you less organized?"

"No, I'm saying you're making me more fun."

Later that evening, Harriet sat cross-legged on the couch, her laptop balanced on her knees, while Alex sorted through a box of old photos they'd brought back from his parents' house. He pulled out a picture of himself as a kid, standing awkwardly in a too-big suit at some long-forgotten event.

"Look at this," he said, holding it up.

Harriet glanced over and snorted. "Adorable. You look like a miniature accountant."

"That's…not far off. I think I was pretending to be one, actually. My dad always said I was the serious one."

Harriet tilted her head, studying him. "Maybe that's why we work," she mused. "You've got the serious streak, and I've got the spreadsheets. Perfect match."

Alex laughed, but her words stayed with him long after they'd gone to bed. Lying beside her in the dark, listening to her even breaths, he felt something settle within him. Harriet didn't just fit into his life. She made it make sense.

And as he drifted to sleep, he found himself thinking, not for the first time, that she wasn't only his partner. She was his home.

And then the kids came.

Olivia came out first, screaming and furious. Grayson followed two minutes later, quieter but no less determined. Harriet, exhausted and drenched in sweat, looked at Alex with a weary, triumphant smile, and he thought, *We made a family.*

But the truth was that Alex wasn't ready. He'd grown up fending for himself in a house where the only thing predictable was the silence. Parents who were there but not present, praise handed out sparingly, love measured in accomplishments. When people told him later how "resilient" he'd been, it had sounded like a compliment. But to Alex, it was a reminder that no one had noticed how scared and small he felt.

Becoming a father terrified him. He didn't know how to be something he'd never really had.

For a while, Harriet made it look easy. She knew exactly what the kids needed—what *Alex* needed, too. She juggled the chaos with the efficiency of a general. Alex told himself he was lucky to have her, but slowly, not all at once, his gratitude morphed into something else.

By the time the twins were toddlers, his resentment had multiplied. Alex threw himself into work, telling himself he was providing for his family, but really, he had been hiding. Hiding from the noise, the mess, and the relentless demands of fatherhood. He was hiding from the way his wife had begun to look at him—like, maybe, she hadn't made the right choice in choosing him after all.

Harriet took notice, of course. She always noticed.

"Alex, you can't clock out of being a parent," she said one evening after he came home late, missing yet another family dinner. Her voice was calm but carried a sharp edge.

"I'm not clocking out. I'm working. For them. For us."

Harriet sighed. "They don't care about the money, Alex. They care about you. They need you."

"What am I supposed to do?" he asked. "I'm not like you. I don't have it all figured out. I don't know how to be...perfect."

"I'm not asking for perfect," she said quietly. "I'm asking for present."

Alex only stared at her.

"Do you even want to be here?"

The question hung in the air between them. Alex didn't answer. Once the kids grew out of diaper changes, midnight feedings, and *Goodnight Moon*, he didn't know what he was supposed to do. The twins only wanted Mom. They wanted her to make their sandwiches for school, and Grayson wanted her to find his favorite red shirt—it was always in the laundry.

By the time Liv and Gray started school, Alex had perfected the art of avoidance. He stayed late at the office, buried himself in projects, and distanced himself from Harriet in ways so subtle they hadn't felt like cruelty until they'd piled up into something unrecognizable. It hadn't been any one thing. It was the little moments—when he bristled at Harriet's reminders about the kids' parent-teacher conferences, or when he snapped at her for forgetting to pick up his dry cleaning. It was the way he flinched when she tried to comfort him after a bad day at work, ashamed that she'd seen him fail. It was the simmering anger he held onto until it boiled over, leaving him shouting about something small and insignificant while Harriet stood there, stunned.

At eight, Gray stopped wanting to play baseball—the only sport Alex was ever interested in—and began playing soccer.

Alex didn't know how to be the dad who came to his kids' games right from the office, cheering them on from the sidelines. He didn't know he was supposed to offer to take them out for ice cream after a particularly good game.

He hadn't been so naïve as to believe that mothers had it any easier, but they had something that Alex hadn't—a community. He didn't have male friends he could talk to about what to do when your daughter started talking about boys, or when it was time to tell your son he needed to start applying deodorant. His friends and colleagues were good for only two things: watching sports and drinking while watching sports.

The bad moments piled up, weighing more and more heavily on Alex's shoulders.

There was the night Harriet had spent the evening wrangling the twins through homework and baths while juggling a work deadline on her laptop. By the time Alex walked in, the house smelled of garlic and melted cheese, but the tension in the air was thick enough to cut.

"You're late," Harriet said, not looking up from the kitchen counter where she was assembling dinner. Her voice was flat, tired.

"I had a meeting run over." Alex shrugged off his coat and hung it over a chair.

"Of course you did."

Alex stiffened. "What's that supposed to mean?"

"It means you always have a meeting," she snapped, slamming the oven door shut. "Or a deadline. Or some excuse to be anywhere but here."

"Here we go," he said, his voice sharp. "I work late because someone has to pay for all this." He gestured vaguely around the kitchen, as though the house itself had been a burden she'd forced upon him. As though she didn't contribute to their finances in any real way.

Harriet turned to face him, arms crossed. "Don't you dare act like this is just about money. You don't even try anymore, Alex. You come home late, you barely talk to me or the kids, and when you do, it's like you're a million miles away."

"I'm trying!" he snapped, his voice rising. "Do you think this is easy for me? Balancing everything?"

"You're not balancing anything. You're avoiding it. Avoiding us."

The words hit him like a punch to the gut, not because they weren't true, but because they were.

And yet, instead of admitting it, he lashed out.

"Maybe if you didn't micromanage every second of everyone's lives, I wouldn't feel like I'm suffocating in my own house," he said, the words venomous and ugly.

Harriet's face froze. "Suffocating?" she repeated, her voice barely above a whisper.

Alex wanted to take it back, but the damage was done. "I didn't mean—"

"You know, you used to like me the way I am." Her voice broke ever so slightly, as she struggled to keep her composure. "You *chose* me because I am the way I am. You had an idea of the kind of life you wanted, and you could have that with me." She pressed her lips together, her gaze falling to the floor. "You wanted this, Alex. So don't you even dare try to tell me it's not what you expected. I have always been the same person. *You* are the one who changed."

The look in her eyes—guilt mixed with hurt—was unbearable.

To Alex, nothing had truly ever felt the same after that. He would never be able to go back, only stare longingly into the rearview mirror.

34

Now, Harriet looked as though she might be sick.

"I thought if you believed I cheated, it would be easier for you to leave." Alex's stomach churned like he'd swallowed glass. He couldn't meet Harriet's eyes, the weight of his guilt pressing him into the chair like it might crush him entirely. He closed his eyes, thinking, searching for some way to undo the damage.

Harriet stared at him, stunned. "You thought *lying* to me was the solution?"

"You don't get it," he said, so softly he could barely hear it himself. "I could feel myself turning into my parents. I was distant and angry, and making everything else a priority except you and the kids. I didn't want to hurt you guys anymore. I didn't want to screw them up the way my parents screwed me up."

Harriet's nostrils flared. "Because what you did was so much better."

"I didn't know how to stop it, Harriet!" Alex's desperation was clear. "I didn't know how to fix myself! I still don't! And I couldn't stand the thought of you watching me fail again and again."

For a long moment, Harriet said nothing. From the other room came the sound of the twins laughing, oblivious to the tension between their parents.

Alex stared at the closed door separating them.

"You should have told me," she said eventually. "You should have let me in."

Tears welled in Alex's eyes. "I didn't think I deserved to."

A memory: Alex adjusted the Bluetooth in his ear, laptop bag digging into his shoulder as Harriet's voice cut through the house: "Alex! We need to leave now if we're going to make it before the crowds!"

The twins were already at the door, buzzing with excitement for the zoo. Harriet stood at the bottom of the stairs, arms crossed. "You promised them this," she said. "You can't keep doing this. They're your kids."

He muttered something about responsibility, about his father never taking a day off.

Harriet's reply lodged like a knife: "Then why does it feel like you're never here?"

Later, in the silent office, Alex stared at the blinking cursor, then at the framed photo of the four of them in Vegas. Harriet was laughing, the twins beaming. He was there too—phone in hand, smile stiff, already half gone.

His father's mantra rang in his ears: *The job comes first. Everything else is a luxury.*

The slammed doors, the missed birthdays, the ache of always coming second—he'd lived it all, and now he was passing it on. He had become the man he swore he'd never be.

Shoving his chair back, Alex grabbed his bag and stepped

into the hot afternoon sun. For a moment he let the warmth sink in, then pulled out his phone. His fingers hovered over Harriet's name. He didn't know what he'd say, only that he couldn't keep doing this.

He pressed "Call" and held his breath, hoping it wasn't too late.

But it was.

After that, Alex had tried to be a better father. He tried to be the one to drive them to school when it fit his schedule, to remember that just because they appeared old enough to do everything on their own didn't mean they had to. He'd tried to suggest ways the three of them could bond after dinner, like by playing board games. He sat cross-legged on the floor as Grayson and Olivia, both twelve and each wearing expressions of muted skepticism, sat across from him.

"All right," Alex said, holding up a die like a trophy. "The rules are simple. Roll the dice, move your piece, and—"

"We know how to play, Dad," Grayson interrupted, leaning back against the couch. His voice was flat.

Alex's grin faltered.

"Right. Of course." Alex rubbed the back of his neck. "Who wants to go first?"

Olivia glanced at her brother, then back at Alex. "Can't we play something else? Or watch a movie?"

"But this is fun," Alex said, his enthusiasm forced. He gestured at the colorful board. "Family bonding, you know?"

Grayson shrugged. "I guess."

The kids exchanged a look that Alex didn't quite catch. He cleared his throat and rolled the die himself, making a show of moving his piece across the board. "See? Easy! Now you try."

Olivia picked up the die. The sound of it clattering on the table filled the awkward silence.

Harriet had invited Charlie for dinner, probably as a

buffer between them. She watched from the kitchen doorway, arms crossed over her chest.

She stepped into the room as Olivia took her turn. "How's it going in here?" She asked, her voice light but her eyes sharp.

"Great!" Alex flashed her a strained smile.

Grayson and Olivia said nothing, their focus already drifting toward their phones sitting on the edge of the table.

Charlie raised an eyebrow. "Looks like it." She crossed the room and sat down on the armrest of the couch. "Hey, kids, why don't you grab a snack or something? I need to talk to your dad for a minute."

The twins didn't need convincing. They were up and out of the room before Alex could protest. And Harriet? Charlie had no idea where she'd gone off to.

Alex sighed and leaned back against the coffee table, avoiding Charlie's gaze.

"You're really trying, huh?" Charlie said, her tone laced with gentle sarcasm.

"What's that supposed to mean?" Alex shot back, though his voice lacked any real heat.

Charlie slid down to sit next to him. "It means I can see you're making an effort. But it's like you're…I don't know. Holding back."

Alex stared at the board game in front of him, tapping his fingers against his knee. "I'm not holding back. I'm just…not good at this stuff. Harriet's better at it."

Charlie frowned. "That's a cop-out, Alex, and you know it."

"I'm trying."

"Yes, I see that."

Alex worked his jaw back and forth. "What do you want from me, Charlie? I've got Harriet in one corner telling me I need to be more present and then, when I am, you're telling me it looks forced."

Charlie tilted her head, studying him. "Listen. I know

Mom and Dad fucked you up. They fucked me up, too. But at some point, we have to grow up and stop blaming them for our problems. And I know you don't want to repeat their mistakes."

"If you say so."

Charlie frowned. "Come on. Don't be like that."

Long after Charlie had gone home that night, after Harriet and the kids were asleep, Alex allowed himself to think about his sister's words. He hated that she was right.

He should have told her this was how he was. That he kept his distance when things got messy because he had a bad habit of making them worse. It wasn't like the kids were ignored. They had Harriet, and she was a wonderful mother. She had her own way of doing things—often, the better way, in fact. Alex should have told Charlie this...and then he should have told her to come back and give him parenting advice when she had her own children.

But then he'd remembered she had had to survive a childhood with the same set of parents, and maybe he ought to give her a break.

It occurred to him then that maybe all these issues with being a father wouldn't have been so bad if not for the fact that he started feeling like he was holding back in his marriage as well.

Every time Harriet came home with a new promotion or a salary increase—or, he may as well be honest, she simply came home in a great mood after having had a good day—he'd felt a little tingle deep in the pit of his stomach that could only be one thing.

He'd been jealous! Jealous that she was doing well in her career while he was stagnant. Jealous that her colleagues recognized her as someone they wanted to keep around. And he'd certainly been jealous she had found a career that made her happy and satisfied.

Alex had never felt any of this before, and instead of being happy for his wife, her success only tore open the tiny hole Alex deemed to have been poked long ago in their marriage.

It was a hole he, despite his best intentions, had not intended on stretching to the brink.

Besides, Harriet liked being the breadwinner. She never explicitly said it, but Alex could tell from the way she pulled out her credit card at the store, and the way she reached into her wallet any time the kids asked for money. She paid the mortgage and set the bills to autopay from the account she had before they were married. She did all the grocery shopping and Christmas shopping and registered the kids for summer camp.

She was too nice to ever admit to anyone outside of the two of them that she made almost double what Alex brought home, but Alex had known how it made her feel. So long as she brought in more money, she was able to justify being the one in control.

She had loved the house as much as he had, and she had been the one to send him the listing for the electric SUV they'd ended up buying, even though she told everyone it had been his idea.

And for someone who claimed not to like any kind of attention on her, she sure had liked to shop at all the pricey stores she'd once teased Laura and Carrie for spending all their time in. Harriet could claim to be awkward and shy all she wanted, but only she saw herself that way.

Harriet was wonderful in so many ways, and yet she failed to see just how broken Alex was. How he clung to her from that first night, knowing she was a promise of everything he hadn't had as a child. She was peace and calm and organized chaos, and she loved him. But she didn't see him. She couldn't have.

She didn't see how it pained him to make so much less

money than she did, and she hadn't been able to tell that he hated his job. She failed to see how lost he felt—in life, in his marriage. He let her tell her story about the shiny new car because it made him look like he had more of a say in their marriage. Look, he bought us this fancy car. Look, he wanted the house too. Look, he thought that summer camp was a great experience for the kids.

And then he concocted the scheme to pretend he had an affair, all so that he could get out of his marriage and maybe, finally, be able to breathe again.

35

A memory: five years earlier. The house had been quiet, save for the faint hum of the dishwasher in the kitchen. Alex had spent the morning cleaning the kitchen while Harriet tackled the laundry upstairs. They barely exchanged words, their movements around the house choreographed like strangers sharing a space rather than a life.

Harriet was folding a stack of freshly dried towels at the kitchen table, her motions brisk and methodical. Alex sat on the edge of the couch, his elbows on his knees, staring blankly at the coffee table. A half-finished mug of coffee sat nearby, forgotten.

Harriet's voice broke the stillness, sharp and edged with frustration. "Hello?" Her tone was controlled, but barely. "I'm trying to talk to you, and you're sitting there like…" She gestured vaguely, the words escaping her. "Like you're somewhere else."

He looked up, his gaze heavy and reluctant. "I'm listening."

"No, you're not."

Alex sighed and leaned back against the couch, his head tilting toward the ceiling. "What do you want me to say, Harriet?"

"I want you to say something real," she said, her voice rising slightly. "I want you to tell me what's going on in your head instead of shutting me out."

The accusation stung more than it should have, though it wasn't new. "I'm not shutting you out," he said. But even as the words left his mouth, he doubted them.

Wasn't that exactly what he'd been doing?

"Yes, you are." Harriet stepped closer, her eyes searching his face for something resembling vulnerability. "You've been doing it for months. Maybe longer."

Alex's jaw tightened. "I'm doing the best I can."

"Are you?" The weight of Harriet's words hung between them. "Because it feels like you've already given up. Like you've decided this is how it's going to be. You in your corner and me in mine."

He opened his mouth to respond, but nothing had come. What could he say? That she was right? That he had started to believe there was no fixing this? No fixing *him*?

The silence stretched. Alex felt Harriet's disappointment deepening.

"See? This is exactly what I mean. You don't even fight anymore. You don't try. You just…withdraw."

This was something he'd heard before.

Alex rubbed his temples, his frustration bubbling below the surface. "Just tell me what you want me to do," he said, his voice tinged with defeat. "Because clearly whatever I'm doing isn't enough. It's never enough."

A flicker of sadness broke through her anger. "I need you to *try*. To meet me halfway."

"I don't know if I can," he admitted, the words barely audible. "I feel like no matter what I do, it's wrong. I'm tired of failing you, Harriet. Failing the kids. Failing myself."

She hesitated.

Alex felt her eyes on him. He'd known, perhaps for the first time, that she was finally seeing the depth of his self-doubt, the cracks in the armor he'd so carefully constructed.

"I don't know what to say." Her voice was barely above a whisper.

His nod had been a small, resigned motion. "Me neither."

The room fell silent again, the air thick with unspoken words. Harriet turned and walked toward the kitchen, leaving Alex alone on the couch. He stared at the coffee table, the sunlight now fading into dusk, and felt the weight of inevitability settle over him.

For the first time, he allowed himself to think the thought he'd been avoiding.

Maybe there wasn't a way back. Maybe this was how it ended—not with a bang, but with a quiet unraveling.

The apartment was quiet except for the scrape of Grayson's fork. Olivia had already shut herself in her room, music thudding faintly through the walls.

"Is it okay if Meagan comes over?" Grayson mumbled.

Alex blinked. *Meagan?*

His son's cheeks flushed, and Alex's stomach sank. Harriet probably already knew all about her—who she was, what she liked—while he sat here clueless, a stranger at his own table.

"Does your mom know?" he asked.

"Does that matter?"

The words cut deep. Alex tried to ask if Gray felt like he could talk to him, but his son only looked confused. The truth threatened to choke him: *Because I don't know you. Because I'm failing you, just like my dad failed me.*

The thought spiraled, gathering momentum. He wasn't only awkward. He was a failure. He didn't know his children's friends, their schedules, or their favorite shows. He didn't know how Olivia liked her coffee or whether Grayson preferred Coke or Pepsi.

Harriet probably knew all of it. She probably knew Meagan's birthday and what kind of flowers she liked and whether she and Grayson had kissed yet.

He snapped, too loud: "It matters to me! I don't know what you need, how to reach you anymore—and it's killing me, Gray. It's killing me because I love you, and I don't know how to show it."

"Dad," Grayson said quietly, his voice unsteady. "We don't hate you."

The words hit Alex like a punch to the gut. He wanted to believe them, but the doubt was too deeply rooted. He shook his head, a bitter laugh escaping. "You don't have to say that."

"I'm not just saying it." Grayson's chair scraped the floor as he stood. "I mean, yeah, you mess up sometimes. But it's not like Mom's perfect either. We get it, Dad. We do."

The words landed like a blow—merciful and undeserved. Alex stared at his son, his chest aching with a mixture of shame and love so intense it nearly overwhelmed him. He only managed: "I want what's best for you."

It was in that moment he knew what he had to do.

Now, Alex could barely lift his eyes to meet Harriet's.

The signed papers had arrived weeks ago and he'd quickly dropped them into his desk drawer. He didn't want to be constantly reminded of what he'd done.

"I don't get it," Harriet said. "I know things weren't perfect, but I never expected them to be. I never put that kind of pressure on anything, let alone a marriage! You should have been an adult and talked to me. Instead, you decided for both of us. You decided…" She swallowed and set her wineglass down with a shaky hand.

"I decided to cheat on you."

36

For months, Alex had wrestled with the same thoughts, the same accusations echoing endlessly in his mind. *You're a failure. You're ruining them. They deserve better than this.* True. His children's faces—their laughter, their tears, their questions he couldn't always answer—flashed before his eyes. And Harriet…He loved her, this much he knew, but love wasn't always enough.

It all led to one decision. He would be the bad guy. He would make it easy for her to leave, to hate him, to move on without looking back.

He didn't wait long. Once he made up his mind, there was no going back.

He sat Harriet down at the kitchen table, the weight of what he was about to do having already settled heavily between them. She looked tired, her curls loosely tied back, a faint crease between her brows.

"What's up?"

Alex swallowed, his throat dry. "We need to talk."

Her smile faded, replaced by concern. "Okay."

"I've been..." The words stuck to his tongue. He forced them out anyway, each one like a shard of glass slicing through him. "I've been seeing someone else." The words were like ash in his mouth, delivered in a voice so hollow and detached he almost didn't recognize it as his own.

Harriet blinked, her expression frozen in place. Had she heard him correctly?

When she finally spoke, her voice trembled. "What?"

"I never meant for it to happen." He avoided her gaze, staring instead at the table between them. "But it did."

The blood drained from Harriet's face. "How long?" she whispered.

Alex hesitated, the air around them thick with tension. "A while," he said finally.

Best to make her think it wasn't a mistake. Best to make her hate him.

Her lips parted slightly as though to speak, but no words came. When she found her voice again, it cracked. "Who is she?"

He froze. He hadn't thought this far ahead, hadn't prepared for the specifics. Desperately, he grasped for a name —any name. "Rebecca."

The moment the name left his lips, Harriet's face twisted into something raw and unrecognizable. She'd met Rebecca and had shared drinks with her after an office party.

The betrayal cut deeper now, the wound jagged and bleeding.

The silence between them was deafening. Harriet sat motionless, her breath coming in shallow, uneven gasps. Then the tears began, spilling silently down her cheeks. She didn't try to hide them, didn't bother to wipe them away. Her eyes locked on Alex's, and what he saw there would haunt him forever.

"Why?" she finally choked out.

She would never forgive him.

Their marriage was over, just like he knew it would be.

Harriet would ask him to leave. It had been a matter of time.

Alex opened his mouth, but no words came. What could he even say? That it wasn't true? That he made it all up to give her an easy way out? No, this was the point of no return.

"I'm sorry," was all he managed.

The minutes dragged on, each second more agonizing than the last.

When Harriet had finally moved, it wasn't to leave the table but to push herself to her feet, her hands trembling. The breaking of plates had come later, after dinner.

"Is this what you wanted?" she demanded, her voice rising, sharp with anger and pain. Another plate hit the floor, splintering into jagged shards. "To destroy everything? To humiliate me? To rip apart our family?"

Alex didn't answer. He couldn't.

He stood there, frozen, as she hurled another plate, her sobs now uncontrollable. Each shattered plate echoed in his chest, but he made no move to stop her. He didn't deserve to.

When she finally stopped, her chest heaving, the kitchen was a battlefield of broken ceramic. Harriet stood amid the wreckage, her hands gripping the edge of the counter for support.

Her voice, raw and hoarse, had broken the silence. "Get out."

Alex hesitated.

"Get out!" she screamed, her voice cracking, her pain so palpable it left him breathless.

He nodded numbly and turned to leave, the sound of her sobs following him as he walked out the door. The weight of what he'd done, of the lie he'd told, settled over him like a suffocating shroud. He'd done what he had thought was right. He was the villain of their story. And now, he would have to live with the aftermath.

He found himself behind the wheel, driving without direction. It wasn't until he pulled into a familiar parking lot that it dawned on him where he'd been heading…and who he was going to see.

Inside the boutique, he wandered awkwardly among the racks until Charlie spotted him. Her gaze lingered long enough to suggest she understood his presence there wasn't a good sign.

Without hesitation, she grabbed his arm and led him out of the store. Once outside, her expression shifted, concern flashing across her face like a storm cloud.

Alex told his sister what he'd done. She had stared at him for so long, he was certain she hadn't heard a word, until finally, she stepped back, propping herself up against the wall.

"Alex, what the hell are you talking about?"

"It was the only way," he told her. He needed Harriet to leave him. To hate him. It was the only way she would move on.

Charlie stared at him. "Are you insane?"

"We're better off this way. I—" He'd broken off, swallowing hard. "I'm… I can't do it anymore."

Charlie's voice was firm. "Alex, you can't lie to her like that. Do you have any idea what this will do to her?"

"She'll be happier eventually. She will. It was the right thing to do."

Charlie shook her head. "No. It's not. It's cowardly, Alex. And it's cruel. Harriet loves you, for God's sake."

He didn't respond. He couldn't. Because deep down, he didn't believe her.

"It's done," he said.

Charlie's voice softened, but the edge of frustration remained. "She deserves the truth. Even if it hurts."

Alex looked down at the floor. "I can't tell her, Charlie. It's better this way."

"For who? You? Because it sure as hell won't be better for her when she finds out you lied. And she will find out."

He flinched at her words. "She won't," he said finally, his voice quieter now, almost pleading. "Not if you don't tell her."

Charlie narrowed her eyes. "You want me to lie for you?"

"It's not lying. It's just…not saying anything."

"I don't agree with this," she said after a long pause.

"Thank you," he murmured, though the relief that had washed over him had felt hollow.

"I'll keep your secret, Alex. But only because I don't want to make things worse for Harriet. Not because I think you're right."

He nodded, unable to look at her. He knew she didn't understand. No one would. But that was fine. This wasn't about him. It was about protecting the people he loved—even if it meant destroying himself in the process.

Now, Alex lifted his gaze from his lap and looked squarely at Harriet. "We weren't happy, Harriet."

Her voice was sharp and unwavering. "Don't put words in my mouth."

The couch let out a groan as Alex shifted uncomfortably. "We were falling apart, and you know it. I saw the writing on the wall, and I wasn't willing to go through all of that."

"So you lied to me. You made me believe you were a cheater." She drew in a shaky breath. "Knowing exactly what my mother went through and how it would destroy me."

"I didn't want to drag it out. I thought…I thought it would be easier if—"

"Easier?" Harriet brushed a tear from her cheek with a fierce swipe. "Well, congratulations, Alex. This ending hurts so much less than if you'd just been honest."

And then, to Alex's surprise, she was laughing. It wasn't a laugh of amusement but something raw and bitter, like the sound was clawing its way out of her throat against her will.

She paced a few steps away, her hands on her hips, shaking her head as the laughter gave way to a sharp exhale.

"What's funny?" Alex asked cautiously.

She turned to face him, her expression somewhere between incredulity and pain. "You," she said. "You and your genius plan to spare me the pain. I mean, who thinks like that? Who decides lying and pretending to be a cheater makes breaking up a marriage somehow easier?"

"I thought…"

Harriet waved him off. "Don't try to explain it again. Please. You've said enough." She let out another mirthless chuckle, shaking her head. "God, I've spent months blaming myself. Thinking I wasn't enough. Wondering what I could've done differently. And the whole time, it was you playing some warped hero in your own head."

Alex's face twisted with guilt. "I never wanted you to feel like that. I didn't know how else to—"

"*Stop.* You didn't care how I felt. You cared about what was easiest for you. You literally just said so."

Alex's gaze dropped to the floor.

"And to think, I actually turned to your sister for support. Do you know how many times I cried on her shoulder, how many times she told me I was strong enough to get through it?"

At the mention of his sister, Alex's head snapped up. "Charlie was just trying to help."

Harriet froze, her breath catching. “What?”

Alex realized his mistake too late. “I didn’t mean—”

“No, say it,” she said, her voice low and deadly.

Alex looked like he wanted to sink into the floor. “She... she knew,” he admitted reluctantly. “I told her what I’d done.”

PART THREE
HARRIET

37

No. *No, no, no.* Harriet had to have heard him wrong.

She stared at Alex, her expression shifting from disbelief to anger. "She *knew*? Your sister knew... and she didn't say anything?"

"She didn't agree with it," Alex said quickly. "She told me it was wrong and—"

"And what?" Harriet snapped. "She sat here, under my roof, and watched me unravel! She let me think I'd been betrayed!"

"She begged me to tell you the truth."

Harriet let out a short, bitter laugh. "Do you have any idea what it's like to find out that the people you trusted most—my *family,* for God's sake—were lying to me the entire time?"

"Harriet, I made the decision. This isn't on her."

"No." Harriet shook her head. "You don't get to decide that. You don't get to tell me who's responsible for breaking my trust." She took a step back, her voice quieter but no less sharp. "I can't even look at you right now."

"Harriet, please," Alex began, but she cut him off with a raised hand.

Without another word, she turned on her heel and pulled open the door. "Charlie!"

Charlie appeared, her face pale and unsure. "What's going on?"

"Get in here." Harriet's tone left no room for argument. She turned sharply, the sound of Charlie's hesitant steps following close behind.

Harriet slammed the door behind her. Alex flinched on the couch, his gaze darting between the two women.

"All this time..." Harriet's voice was a mix of disbelief and fury. She gestured wildly at Alex. "Why would you let me think all this time..."

Charlie's words faltered before they even formed. She looked at her brother and then down at the carpeted floor. Finally, she said, "It wasn't my place to say anything."

"Not your place?" Harriet laughed sharply. "I welcomed you into my home when you had nowhere to go! I've defended you when no one else would, and this is how you repay me? By keeping something like this from me?"

"I didn't want to get in the middle. You were already so hurt."

"You didn't think I deserved the truth?" Harriet's hands balled into fists. "Do you even understand what you've done?"

Charlie's eyes glistened. "I...I'm sorry."

"Sorry? That's it? That's all you have to say?" Her anger burned hotter. "Maybe Evelyn was right about you." The words tumbled out before she could stop them. "You *are* floundering, and you're too old not to know what you're doing. Can't please anyone, can you?"

Charlie's face crumpled, the mention of her mother's criticisms hitting hard. "That's not fair."

"Fair?" Harriet barked a laugh. "You and Alex...You're two sides of the same coin. Liars and cowards."

The weight of Harriet's words hung heavy in the air. She

didn't wait for a response, just turned abruptly and stormed out, leaving Charlie and Alex in stunned silence.

The sound of laughter and clinking glasses drifted from the living room as Harriet joined the others. Grayson and Olivia had finally managed to pull themselves away from the television and were seated at the table with Greta, who sipped on a glass of sherry.

Harriet plastered on a smile, though her hands trembled as she poured herself a drink.

Charlie stepped out of the den and let out a shaky breath. "Maybe I should go," she said quietly. "I think I've outstayed my welcome."

Harriet worked her jaw back and forth. "Oh, you most definitely have."

Alex looked at his sister, guilt etched across his face. "You can stay with me."

Harriet snorted and then tipped her head back and emptied half her wine in one gulp. "I hope the two of you are very happy together." She turned to Greta and her kids and lifted her glass in salute. "Merry *fucking* Christmas!"

Greta barked out a laugh. "Well," she said with a mischievous grin, "if this isn't the most dramatic Christmas I've ever seen, I'll eat my hat."

For someone so perceptive, Greta took an awfully long time to pick up on Harriet's cues that it was time for her to leave. Even after Alex and Charlie slunk out with their proverbial tails between their legs, it took Greta nearly thirty minutes to finally excuse herself.

"Harriet," she chirped. She looked over her shoulder to make sure the kids weren't within earshot. "A pleasure, as always. Glad to see you've stayed strong and not let that man crawl back into your bed."

Harriet resisted the urge to groan, her mood shifting as a sudden realization hit her. She didn't need patience or platitudes—she needed a distraction. She needed sex. Quick, rough, and dirty. And she knew exactly where to get it.

The problem was she couldn't leave the kids. Not on Christmas.

The evening trudged on as Christmas nights with teenagers often do—halfhearted attempts at tidying up, a *Friends* rerun they barely watched together, and scattered conversation as she, Grayson, and Olivia wandered between their phones and their bedrooms. By the time they'd retreated upstairs, murmuring good nights, the house was finally still.

Harriet stood in the kitchen, nursing the last sip of her wine, staring blankly at the quiet mess in the living room. Wrapping paper still littered the floor, the tree lights blinking lazily in the dark. It had been an exhausting and eye-opening day...and Harriet needed to forget about it as soon as possible.

She reached for her phone and tapped out a message.

Harriet: Come over. I'll make it worth your while.

She hit send before she could second-guess herself, the buzz of adrenaline cutting through the sluggish weight of her earlier mood. She didn't have to wait long for a response.

Liam: Be there in 20.

Harriet: Don't ring the bell.

When Liam arrived, well after eleven, looking impossibly tan for the time of year, Harriet ushered him inside with barely a word, pulling him into her bedroom with a hunger that permitted no discussion. On the television across from the bed, a Christmas movie played for cover. Harriet glanced briefly at the scene—Jude Law slipping on a pair of glasses in Kate Winslet's English cottage—before pressing her mouth to Liam's. He tasted of bourbon and cinnamon, and Harriet wanted to devour him.

Then his mouth was on her neck, and her hands were in his hair. Him, pressing her into her mattress. Him, peeling off her underwear with his teeth. Him, diving between her legs as she grabbed fistfuls of bedsheets. He was everywhere—on and in and over and under—and she was hissing his name between clenched teeth. It was exactly what she needed—raw, heated, and utterly consuming.

They lay tangled in the aftermath, chests heaving with each heavy breath. Outside, the sudden growl of a muscle car stirred her, and Harriet pulled away, the practical side of her brain reasserting itself. She dug around in the near dark for her robe, which she threw around herself.

"You should go before the kids hear you," she whispered. "You can sneak out the way you came in."

Liam's easy smile faded. He sat up slowly, pulling on his shirt. Harriet admired the taut muscles in his back.

When he turned to face her, his jaw was tight. "Harriet, I like you. A lot." His tone made her pause. "But this…" He gestured between them. "It's starting to feel like I'm only here for convenience. Like I'm some kind of distraction for you."

Her stomach tightened, guilt cutting through the post-coital calm. She opened her mouth to protest, but he was right. A distraction is exactly what he was to her.

"I'm not saying I don't enjoy being with you, but…I'm not the kind of guy who does this sort of thing. I don't do casual. I want more than this, and if you're not ready for something real, that's okay. Just…call me when you are." He touched her chin so lightly she almost thought she imagined it. Then he pressed a chaste kiss on her lips.

He finished dressing and then paused in the bedroom doorway long enough to give her a small, sad smile. "Merry Christmas, Harriet."

Harriet granted herself five minutes to feel sorry for herself before getting into the shower to wash the day from her skin, and then she went to bed because there was nothing else left to do.

38

Harriet's first thought upon waking well after ten the next morning was how much she loved the silence. No snoring, no blaring alarm, no children bickering over the last bowl of overpriced, over-sugary cereal.

Since she had far too much to drink the day before in an attempt to forget everything that had happened, it took her about five minutes too long to realize there was something wrong with the silence.

Swinging her legs out of bed, she shoved her feet into the slippers—a rare gift from Grayson, the right shoe said "Mama" and the left "Bear." As she shuffled to the top of the stairs, the eerie quiet settled around her. No kids. No sounds of the TV blasting bad reality TV or the unmistakable noise of Olivia's TikTok on full volume. Nothing.

She glanced across the empty living room, her heart beginning to thud unevenly. "Olivia? Grayson?" she called out, her voice catching slightly.

No answer.

A heavy weight settled in Harriet's stomach as she made her way to Grayson's door. She knocked once, then opened it to find him sprawled out on his bed, headphones in, a controller in hand. The faint sounds of explosions and shouting voices from his game filtered through.

He tugged one bud out of his ear.

"Why is it so quiet? Where's Liv?"

"Dunno," Grayson muttered, his eyes glued to the screen.

Harriet stared at him for a second, debating whether to confiscate the controller and force him to engage. She decided against it...for now.

Instead, she headed to Olivia's room. When she knocked and got no response, she pushed the door open. The bed was perfectly made, the way Olivia always left it, but something about the untouched pillow and the absence of the usual mess of clothes on the floor made Harriet's pulse quicken.

"Olivia?" she called out again, louder this time, hoping for an answer that didn't come.

Harriet's skin prickled. She pivoted and marched back to Grayson's room, throwing the door open without knocking. "Gray, *where* is your sister?"

He glanced up. "I said I don't know!"

"Try again. And this time, say it like you mean it. Is there something you're not telling me?"

Grayson sighed dramatically. "Mom, seriously, I have no idea."

"Grayson," she said, her voice sharpening. "This isn't the time to test me. Her bed wasn't slept in last night. If you know anything about where she might be, you need to tell me now."

He squirmed, avoiding her gaze. "I mean, she...she might be with someone."

A pang of dread hit her so hard she stumbled back against the wall. "What do you mean, 'someone?'"

"A guy."

For a moment, Harriet couldn't speak. Her daughter had a boyfriend? Since when? How had she missed this? She took pride in being a reasonably attentive parent. Maybe not helicopter-level attentive, but still.

"Grayson," she said, regaining her composure. "Do you know his name?"

Grayson hesitated. "Tyler. I…I made her give me his address a while back. Just in case, you know? She said he's older, and I didn't trust him."

Harriet blinked, momentarily floored. "You did what?"

"I told her if she was going to see some older guy, I needed to know where he lived. I didn't tell you because she swore me to secrecy, and I didn't want her to stop talking to me."

Harriet stared at her son, a mixture of anger, pride, and sheer panic swirling inside her. She reached out and pulled him into a quick, fierce hug. "You're a good brother," she said. "But I'm going to need you to give me that address right now."

He nodded, retrieving his phone and scrolling through it before handing it to her. Harriet took a screenshot and texted the image to herself.

As she turned to leave the room, she pulled out her phone and texted Alex the address.

Harriet: Meet me here ASAP. Liv needs us.

Harriet steeled herself with a deep breath. She had no idea what she was about to walk into, but one thing was certain. She was going to find her daughter, and if this Tyler kid thought he was getting away with anything, he was about to meet the full force of Harriet's maternal wrath. She wasn't above dramatic threats, bad cop impressions, or confiscating every gaming console in a five-mile radius if it came to that.

God help him if he had a cat she could threaten to adopt.

Alex was kind enough not to comment on the state of Harriet's hair or what she had chosen to wear. After the words "He's older, and I didn't trust him" came out of Gray's mouth, Harriet had gone into autopilot—text Alex, get dressed, find keys, get into car, drive. It was a miracle she'd remembered to change into real shoes from her slippers.

Alex slammed the door of his precious sports car as Harriet approached him from across the street. Together, they looked up at the small two-story house in front of them. The front yard was overgrown with weeds, the paint and stucco chipped in numerous places, and in the driveway sat a muscle car that could only be described as a mother's worst nightmare.

A memory of this car tugged at her from the recesses of her mind, but she couldn't place it.

"I'm going to need you to go do the talking," Alex said.

Harriet looked at Alex. He did, in fact, look like he might be looking to throw a few punches should the need arise.

She pushed past him and walked up the front steps to ring the bell. Finding it broken, she balled her hand into a fist and pounded on the door as loudly as she could. Immediately, a dog started barking.

After what felt like three minutes, the door opened to reveal a tall, lanky guy who looked like he'd been interrupted in the middle of a nap…or worse. His hair was a tangled mess, and his T-shirt bore the faded logo of a metal band Harriet didn't recognize.

He blinked at her, confused, before leaning against the doorframe with an air of disinterest. "Yeah?" He held the dog back with a hand at his side.

Harriet took a second to size him up. He couldn't have been older than twenty—not quite the ancient predator she'd been bracing for, but still plenty unsettling.

Her maternal instincts and years of dealing with teenagers

kicked in. "Tyler? We're here for Olivia," she said, keeping her tone firm but polite. "Is she inside?"

The guy frowned, his gaze darting to Alex, who was standing with his arms crossed like an enforcer in a crime movie. "Who's asking?"

"Her parents," Harriet said, plastering on a smile she knew didn't reach her eyes.

He straightened up. "There's no Olivia here."

Alex took a step forward. "Let's try this again. Either you invite us inside and we have a calm, reasonable conversation, or I call the police and let them ask you where my underage daughter is. Your choice."

Tyler hesitated, glancing back into the house. Harriet caught the movement and leaned forward. "If you're thinking about slamming this door in my face, I'd reconsider. I'm a mother on a mission, and nothing terrifies grown men more."

"All right, all right," Tyler muttered, stepping aside to let them in.

The interior of the house was somehow worse than the outside. The furniture was mismatched, the smell of stale pizza lingered in the air, and the coffee table was covered in empty cans and cigarette butts. Harriet didn't want to touch anything for fear of contracting something.

She turned back to Tyler, who was hovering near the door. "Where is she?"

Tyler shrugged.

Alex stepped forward, his imposing frame filling the small space. "See, you've already let us in, *bro*. You wouldn't do that if she weren't here. Unless you really are that stupid," he said. "So I'll make this easy for you. You tell us where she is, and we leave. Or you keep playing dumb, and we make this a lot harder for you."

Tyler raised his hands in mock surrender. "Fine! She's

upstairs. But she came here on her own, okay? Nobody forced her."

A sharp ache bloomed in Harriet's chest. She shot Alex a look that said *Brace yourself, hero* before lunging for the stairs, her voice ringing out sharply as she called Olivia's name.

The filthy, uneven steps groaned under her weight as she took them two at a time, the musty air thickening with each step. By the time she reached the top, Olivia's head was poking out from the doorway of one of the rooms. Her hair was a wild mess, and she was wearing nothing but an oversized long-sleeved shirt and skimpy underwear.

Harriet's brain short-circuited, a thousand thoughts colliding in a pile-up of motherly panic. But one thought broke through loud and clear, practically screaming, *For the love of God, where are your pants?*

"Get dressed. Right now. We're leaving." Harriet's eyes flicked over her daughter, scanning for signs of distress or injury, but it didn't stop the knot of anger tightening in her chest.

Olivia hesitated, considering an argument, but Harriet's expression brooked no debate. The silent command in her mother's eyes was more than enough.

Olivia disappeared back into the room without a word, leaving Harriet standing in the hallway, trembling with the effort it took to hold herself together.

Her heart was still pounding when she felt Alex's presence behind her.

"She okay?"

Harriet nodded, though the knot in her chest tightened further. "She will be."

Neither spoke as Olivia emerged a minute later, now dressed in leggings and an oversized hoodie. She avoided their eyes, her face flushed with embarrassment.

Harriet opened her mouth to speak, but no words came.

Instead, she placed a hand on Olivia's shoulder and guided her toward the stairs.

The descent felt heavier than the climb. When they reached the front door, Harriet turned to find Alex lingering in the doorway, his jaw tight. His eyes swept over the house one last time, cataloging every crack, every shadow, every filthy inch, like he could burn the whole place into memory by glaring at it. She knew that look. It was his way of holding back the explosion, of gripping onto what little control they had left with white-knuckled determination.

He settled his gaze on Tyler. His voice was low and sharp as a blade. "You stay away from my daughter."

Outside, the fresh air hit Harriet like a slap, the chaos of the last twenty-four hours threatening to overwhelm her. Olivia slid into the back seat of the car without a word, and Harriet stood frozen on the sidewalk, staring into the middle distance.

Alex's voice broke through the haze. "You okay?"

She turned to him, her expression unreadable. "No. But I'm dealing with it."

His brow furrowed, but he didn't press her. Instead, his hand brushed hers for the briefest of moments. It wasn't much, but it was enough to remind Harriet of the weight of his recent confession.

The memory resurfaced, sharp and raw, and for a fleeting second, she thought she might shatter.

Instead, she squared her shoulders. "Thank you for coming," she said, her voice steady.

"Where else would I be?" Alex looked as though saying it pained him.

AthomewithCharlieAttheofficeOutpretendingtocheatagainAnywherebuthere.

She stared at him for a moment before finally looking

away, down at her feet. It was a cruel twist of fate that she even had to see him again so soon after his confession.

"Well. Bye."

"Wait—" He looked at her, a thin line forming between his brows. "Shouldn't we…you know…talk to her? Together?"

Harriet snorted. "So now you want to be a parent?"

Alex swallowed. "Okay. I deserved that."

"I think you've made it quite clear that your role as a parent is, well…less involved than mine."

He reached for her hand. "I'm trying, Harriet. Our daughter needed us, and I came."

Harriet exhaled, the fight draining out of her. She was too tired for this—too tired for the same old argument, the same old hurt.

She rubbed her temples. "Fine. Meet us at the house."

As she slid into the driver's seat and started the engine, she glanced at Olivia. Her daughter's arms were crossed, her gaze fixed out the window.

Harriet's chest ached with the realization of how much she didn't know—not just about Olivia, but about Alex and Charlie, about everything she thought had been solid in her life. She allowed herself one small, bitter smile. It looked as though the universe was determined to keep her on her toes.

She looked past Olivia and out the window, where Alex stood motionless beside his car. She said to Olivia, "I want you to tell me what you think you were doing, and you better not even think of lying to me."

Olivia shrank further into her seat. "I didn't mean to spend the night. We fell asleep."

Harriet released a deep breath. Oh, how she wanted to strangle and hug her daughter in equal measure. *Stop growing,* she thought to herself.

She put the car in drive and pulled away from the curb.

39

Harriet pulled into the garage with a weary sigh, the kind that came from a day far too long and a patience stretched far too thin. If she'd ever been happier to be home, she couldn't remember when.

Olivia sat slumped in her seat, eyes half-closed and face pale with exhaustion. The whole night had taken its toll, leaving them both looking as bad as they felt.

Harriet glanced in the rearview mirror. Dark circles. Messy hair. A smudge of something—probably mascara—beneath one eye. Great.

A second later, Greta materialized behind the car, her sweater pulled so tight around her shoulders she looked like she was bracing for a winter storm, despite it being sixty-five degrees. Her sharp eyes scanned them like a mom at parent-teacher night, concern etched into every wrinkle on her brow.

"You found her! What happened? Is she okay?"

Harriet blinked, momentarily thrown, before remembering her frantic doorbell-ringing spree that morning. She'd stopped by Greta's place, half-hysterical, asking if she'd seen Olivia. Of course, Greta was here now.

Harriet felt a pang of guilt. If there was one person she shouldn't be neglecting in her train wreck of a social life, it was Greta. The woman was the real deal—reliable, selfless, and entirely unbothered by Harriet's chaos. Unlike the *friends* Harriet had been wasting her time with, Greta didn't come with drama or hidden agendas. Just casseroles, unsolicited advice, and the occasional judgmental stare.

"She's okay, Greta. Thanks. Just...a little misunderstanding."

Greta didn't look convinced. "You both look like you crawled through a dumpster." She reached out instinctively, like she might check Olivia's forehead for fever, but stopped herself.

A pair of headlights swept across the driveway, followed by the sound of a car pulling up to the curb. Harriet didn't have to turn around to know who it was.

Greta's mouth opened slightly, her eyes flicking between him and Harriet. "Huh. Didn't see that coming."

Harriet didn't have the energy to explain. There would be plenty of time for that later, seeing as Greta would come knocking, looking for answers. Instead, she took Olivia's hand and headed toward the door. Behind her, Greta greeted Alex warmly.

"I'm surprised to see your face around here so soon after last night."

Harriet heard only, "Greta, listen..." before she was through the door with Olivia.

Harriet led Olivia to the couch, where she sat with her arms crossed and sank back against the cushions, her jaw tight and expression defiant.

Alex shut the door behind him, his movements stiff, controlled, like he was holding something back. He glanced at Harriet, but she didn't return the look. Her focus was on Olivia, the weight of exhaustion settling deep into her bones.

Harriet chose her words carefully. "Liv...what were you thinking?"

Olivia rolled her eyes. "Oh my god, Mom. Can we not—"

"We *have* to. You disappeared. You didn't answer your phone. Do you have any idea what that was like for me?"

"I was *fine*—"

"You were at Tyler's," Alex snapped. "An older boy's house. *Overnight.*"

Olivia turned to him then, her eyes burning with something between anger and betrayal. "Oh, so now you care?"

Alex flinched, but his jaw tightened. "I've always cared."

Olivia let out a bitter laugh. "Bullshit."

Harriet pinched the bridge of her nose. "Olivia..."

"No! He doesn't get to waltz in here and suddenly pretend to be *Dad of the Year.*" Olivia shot up from the couch, her voice rising. "Where was this energy before, huh? When I needed you? When you missed our birthday, or my school play, or—god, I don't know—every major event in my entire life?"

Alex opened his mouth, but Olivia wasn't done.

"You don't get to act like some concerned father now just because it's convenient. You barely *know* me, Dad. You don't get to *judge* me."

Alex swallowed hard. For a second, he looked like a man who'd lost the battle before he even stepped onto the field. But then he straightened. "You're right. I haven't been here like I should have been."

Olivia scoffed, turning away.

"But it doesn't mean I'm just going to stand by and let this happen," he said. "Tyler is too old for you, Olivia. This isn't a *relationship.* It's dangerous."

Olivia turned back, eyes flashing. "You don't know *anything* about him."

"I know enough. Enough to know he's a grown man with no business being with a fifteen-year-old girl."

Harriet's stomach twisted. She knew Olivia was furious, hurting, and feeling betrayed. But Alex wasn't wrong. She had to step in before it escalated further.

"Olivia," Harriet said, her voice quieter, but firm. "I get that you're angry. But your dad is right. Tyler *isn't* okay. You sneaking around and lying isn't okay."

Olivia's eyes welled up, but she blinked fast, swallowing it down. "I love him."

Harriet pinched her eyes shut, her heart aching for her daughter, but she kept her voice steady. "Oh, sweetie. You just *think* you do."

Olivia shook her head, jaw clenched, fists tight. "You can't control me."

"You're right. I can't. But I can protect you. And that's exactly what I'm doing."

Harriet took a slow, deep breath and kneeled slightly to meet Olivia's stormy gaze. Her heart twisted at the raw anger and hurt etched into her daughter's face.

"Olivia," she began carefully. "Why him?"

Olivia's face hardened defensively, her lips pressing into a thin line. "Because he listens to me," she said finally, her voice quivering with emotion. "He...he actually hears me. Not like you two. You're always too busy fighting or worrying about rules. Tyler...he gets it. He gets me."

Harriet exchanged a pained glance with Alex, who remained rooted in place, his jaw tight. She forced herself to stay calm, even as the words cut her deeply. "Help me understand, Liv. What does he get that we don't?"

Olivia hesitated. "He knows what it's like. His parents are divorced too. He knows how hard it is being stuck in the middle while everyone's angry or sad or pretending it's fine. He doesn't treat me like I'm a kid who doesn't get it."

Harriet felt like she'd been punched in the chest. When she

looked up at Alex, the anger in his eyes was replaced with something far heavier. Something like guilt.

"Liv," Harriet said gently. "I'm sorry we made you feel that way. I'm sorry if it feels like we aren't listening or that we don't care about what you are going through. But Tyler…he's not the answer. No matter how much it feels like he is right now."

Olivia sank into the couch with a sharp exhale. The defiance on her face melted into something smaller and sadder. "I don't expect you to get it," she mumbled.

Harriet sat beside her, keeping a cautious distance. "We don't have to get everything to care about you, Liv. You're our daughter. We want you safe."

Olivia's lip quivered, but she forced herself to look up at her parents. "Then why couldn't you guys stay together? What happened between you two?"

The room went still. Harriet looked at Alex, her heart hammering. She didn't want to do this, didn't want to unpack years of complicated, painful truths in this fragile moment.

But Alex spoke first, his voice low but steady. "It was my fault."

Harriet's head whipped toward him, surprise flashing across her face, but Alex kept his gaze locked on Olivia.

"If you want to be mad at someone, be mad at me," he said. "I made mistakes. I messed things up in ways I can't take back. And your mom…she did the right thing by telling me to leave."

Olivia blinked. "What did you do?"

Alex shook his head, his voice heavy. "What matters is that your mom deserved better, and I couldn't be what she needed. That's on me."

Gratitude and sorrow washed over Harriet. She wanted to say something, to ease the weight of Alex's words, but this wasn't the moment to untangle it all.

Olivia stared at him for a long moment, her anger visibly softening. "I don't hate you," she said quietly.

Alex's lips twitched into a sad smile. "You have every right to."

Olivia shook her head, her voice breaking. "I just...don't understand why everything has to fall apart."

"Sometimes people aren't meant to be together forever." Harriet reached over and placed a hand on Olivia's knee. "I think Dad and I were meant to be together to bring you and your brother into the world, and raise you to be thoughtful, smart, caring individuals. Now that we've done that, our time together has come to an end."

"But no matter what, Liv, we're always here for you," Alex added. "Both of us."

Olivia's face crumpled, and before Harriet could say anything more, she leaned into her mother, her arms wrapping tightly around her. Harriet held her close, stroking her hair as Olivia finally let the tears fall.

Alex stood nearby, his own eyes shining with unshed tears. "We love you, Liv."

A heavy silence settled between them. Olivia's chest rose and fell, her face crumbling for half a second more before she pulled away from Harriet and brought herself to standing.

"Can I go to my room?"

"Of course."

Olivia walked past them and up the stairs.

Harriet finally let out a breath, rubbing her temples.

Alex sank onto the couch, elbows on his knees, staring at the floor. "Well," he muttered. "That went great."

Harriet shot him a look but didn't have the energy to argue.

"We need to keep her away from him," he said.

"I know."

"And she needs to be punished for sneaking out."

"I know."

"And I'm so sorry. For what I did to you."

Harriet blinked, momentarily thrown. "What?"

Alex looked up at her then, and something in his expression—something raw, unguarded—made her stomach twist. "For all of it," he said. "For leaving you to do this alone. For making you feel like I didn't care. For every time you needed me and I wasn't there."

Harriet's throat was tight. She hadn't expected this. Not now. Not ever, really.

Alex exhaled, running a hand over his face. "I knew I was failing you. Failing *them*. And I convinced myself that the only way to fix it was to distance myself. Because that's what I do. But the longer I stayed away, the harder it got to come back. And then time just...kept passing." He shook his head. "I don't know how to make it right."

Harriet crossed her arms, staring at him, feeling something she couldn't quite name—anger, exhaustion, maybe even something close to relief.

"I'm not sure you can," she said finally.

Alex nodded. "But I want to try."

Harriet studied him for a moment, trying to decide whether she believed him. If it even mattered. "You don't get points for saying the right things, Alex. It's what you *do* that matters."

"I know."

She let out a slow breath. "Then prove it."

They stood in silence, the weight of everything stretching between them. Upstairs, a door creaked—a reminder that the kids were still there, that this wasn't just about them.

Harriet finally turned away, rubbing her tired eyes. "You should go."

Alex's eyes cast around the room as though he were taking it in for the last time. "Yeah."

He didn't move right away, though, and neither did she. Because despite everything, despite the years and the hurt, this felt like something. A shift.

When Harriet opened the door to let Alex out, Greta was standing there, poised to ring the bell. She stepped aside to let Alex pass her, her eyes on his back as he walked to his car. Then, without missing a beat, she turned to Harriet.

"Harriet, love. Can I give you some advice?"

"Do I have a choice?"

Greta grinned. "You can pretend you do."

Harriet expected Greta to walk in and make herself comfortable on the couch or at the kitchen table. Instead, she merely stood just inside the door.

"I know you never really knew my late husband, John," Greta said. "He was too sick by the time you moved into the neighborhood. But Alex reminds me a lot of him." She folded her arms, her expression shifting into something softer, more reflective. "John was a tough nut to crack. He had trouble with PTSD from his time overseas and never truly got any kind of help for it. He never outright said it, but I *knew* he felt like he was failing his family. And no matter how hard I tried to prove to him that wasn't the case, it was like he was incapable of hearing me."

Harriet stood still, rooted to the floor beneath her.

Greta swallowed hard, her gaze distant as a complex emotion flickered across her face. "He was a confused and deeply unhappy man, but I loved him in spite of it." A pause and then a slow inhale. "I only wish I'd loved him enough to make him get the help he needed."

Harriet's throat tightened. "Greta..."

The older woman waved a hand dismissively, batting away her own grief. "The point is, men like Alex and John...they carry their failures like boulders on their backs. No one else sees the weight, but *they* feel it with every step." She looked at

Harriet again, her eyes steady. "What is it you need from Alex?"

Harriet shook her head lightly. "I don't know."

Greta hummed knowingly. "But I think you do." She didn't break eye contact, holding Harriet in place with that sharp, perceptive stare. "Think."

Harriet met her gaze, determined not to look away. If Greta wanted to play mind games, fine. She'd play. She'd—

But then it hit her, like a truth that had been waiting for her to say it out loud.

"I need him to be a proper parent."

Greta's lips curled into a small, satisfied smile. The kind only winners wear. "See. I *knew* you knew."

Harriet exhaled through her nose. "Now I have to figure out how to make a grown man act like he is, in fact, a grown man."

Greta smirked. "You've handled a teenage girl. How much harder can it be?"

Harriet snorted. "One of them thinks they know everything and refuses to listen to reason. The other one is my daughter."

Greta let out a laugh. "You're screwed."

Harriet sighed. "Yeah. Tell me something I *don't* know."

40

SEVEN WEEKS LATER...

Harriet sank deeper into the couch, her legs curled up beneath her, a spoonful of peanut butter hovering below her chin. She was wearing an oversized T-shirt—one of Alex's old ones, soft from years of washing, its sleeves practically swallowing her arms. The neckline slipped off one shoulder as she absentmindedly scooped another spoonful from the jar, a habit that used to make Alex wrinkle his nose in mock disgust. Her gaze stayed locked on the TV, where the Australian Open final replay was playing.

She licked the peanut butter off her spoon as the final moments unfolded. A crisp ace down the T. A fist pump. A forehand winner Zverev barely moved for. And then, on match point, a clean backhand down the line that left Zverev frozen in place. Game, set, match.

Sinner let out a small yell, a rare show of emotion, and the crowd roared.

Harriet exhaled, scraping the bottom of the peanut butter jar with her spoon. She wasn't sure what she'd expected from this morning—from this match, from this particular Sunday—but the feeling settling over her now was an odd one.

Something final, like the click of a puzzle piece sliding into place.

She stretched as she got up from the couch, the T-shirt swaying around her like a sleep-deprived ghost. The peanut butter jar sat abandoned on the coffee table, an empty monument to her questionable life choices. She padded into the kitchen, shivering as her bare feet hit the cold tile. Toast. Yes. Safe. Responsible. Grown-up.

She grabbed the bread and shoved two slices into the toaster, staring at it like she could speed up the process with sheer willpower. While she waited, her eyes flicked to the whiteboard on the fridge—last week's to-do list, which was now this week's problem. *Dentist appointment*. Ugh. She squinted at the time. Tuesday, 2:00 p.m., right smack in the middle of the day. She should have scheduled something first thing in the morning. Would she be numb and drooling through dinner? Something soft then. Soup? Mashed potatoes? Just straight-up regret?

Then there was the recall. *Check with Alex re: electric car issue*. Right. The Drive Motor Battery Pack Control Module. Harriet had no idea what it was, but it sounded expensive, like something that would either (a) explode or (b) cause her car to roll gently to its death in the middle of an intersection.

The toaster popped, startling Harriet like she'd been caught committing a crime. She grabbed the toast, balancing it on a plate, but before she could slather on her beloved salted butter, she suddenly remembered she hadn't yet done her meal planning for the week. She grabbed her notebook, flipped to a fresh page, and began brainstorming.

- *Monday: Something healthy to make up for the peanut*

butter binge. A salad? No, who was she kidding? Maybe a frittata.

- *Tuesday: Soft food.*
- *Wednesday: Stir fry. Must use up sad, neglected broccoli.*
- *Thursday:????? (To be decided by Future Harriet, who hopefully had her life more together.)*
- *Friday: Takeout. Because some things in life should be predictable.*

Her plate of toast sat untouched on the counter, growing colder by the second, much like her will to be productive. She flipped to another page and scribbled her weekly reminders. Dentist—ugh. Car recall—would they have a loaner for her? Groceries. Reach out to Charlie? This one she was still debating, even though she sensed she owed her an apology. Apologize to Liam, now that she'd established she wasn't ready for a relationship. With him or anyone.

Harriet exhaled dramatically, glancing around the kitchen like a woman on the verge of a breakdown. Somehow her high from watching tennis had already faded, her brain always finding a way to turn the day into a bureaucratic nightmare.

She looked down at her toast. Cold and hard. Harriet shrugged and brewed herself a strong cup of coffee instead.

Alex's sports car pulled up out front of the house long before there was a knock at the door. She hadn't seen him in weeks, not since the incident with Olivia the day after Christmas. He looked taller. Brighter somehow.

She opened the door, and there he was, an envelope in his hand and something steadier in his eyes than she'd seen in a long time.

"Hey."

"Hey," she echoed. She stepped aside. "Come in."

He made himself comfortable, settling into the couch. He looked at it mutely for a moment, and she wondered if he was finally going to say something about it.

She'd picked it out after she'd kicked him out all those months ago. It was electric blue and velvet, the opposite of what had been in its place, the boring beige couch he'd taken with him to his new place. He brushed his hand absently over the fabric and glanced up at her.

"Are the kids home?"

Harriet motioned toward the stairs. "They're upstairs. Do you want me to get them?"

"No. Not yet." He slowly extended his arm, holding out the manila envelope for her. He gripped it a little tighter before offering it to her. "Here. I'm sorry it took me so long."

Harriet opened the envelope and removed a slim stack of papers.

Petition for Dissolution of Marriage

She met Alex's eyes. "I've already signed these."

Alex exhaled through his nose. "Not exactly. They're… revised."

Harriet arched a brow. "Revised how?"

"Everything's the same as before…except for the custody section."

Harriet felt the beginnings of an anxiety attack creeping in. Her hands shook, making it harder to read. The words swam in and out of focus.

The Petitioner, Alexander Young, and the Respondent, Harriet Langley Young, respectfully agree to share joint physical and legal custody of the minor children. Both parents shall have equal physical and legal custody of the children, with shared decision-making authority regarding the children's health, education, and welfare.

Major decisions concerning the children shall be made jointly, ensuring both parents have an equal voice in matters affecting their well-being. The children shall reside with each parent on an alternating weekly basis. Both parents shall share responsibility for making major decisions regarding the children's upbringing.

Both parents acknowledge that this shared custody agreement is in the best interests of the children, ensuring they maintain strong and meaningful relationships with both parents.

Harriet hadn't realized she was crying until her tears hit the paper. She blinked, trying to catch her breath and steady the overwhelming swirl of emotions—relief, sadness, and something dangerously close to hope.

Alex cleared his throat. "Split custody. Officially." His voice was even, but there was something else there. Something careful.

He leaned forward, forearms resting on his knees, and Harriet felt herself mirroring him before she could stop herself. "And I need to apologize." His fingers laced together as he exhaled. "Serving you with divorce papers out of the blue…it was cold. I'm sorry."

Harriet let out a shaky breath, glancing down at the papers again, then back at him. His face was open, unguarded in a way that made her chest ache.

"I've been going to therapy," he added, like it was something he needed to get out before he lost the nerve. "I know it doesn't fix everything, but…I'm trying. I want to be better. For the kids. For me." A pause, then softer, "For you too. If it's not too late to matter."

This gave her pause. Not because she was surprised—okay, maybe a little—but because it was the first time he'd communicated this plainly. No defensiveness, no expectation of praise, just…a fact.

Harriet studied him for a long moment, weighing his

words, the way he sat still under her gaze instead of rushing to justify himself. Finally, she wiped at her cheek, gave a watery half-smile, and said, "Well, miracles do happen."

Alex huffed a quiet laugh. "I had a feeling you wouldn't make this easy."

Harriet sniffed, dabbing at her eyes before shooting him a smirk. "Oh, did you think personal growth was gonna buy you an easy time? Adorable."

She looked down at the papers once more and brushed an errant tear from her cheek. Then, without a word, she picked up a pen from the counter and signed. When she slid them back to him, Alex didn't hesitate either. He signed his name, then exhaled like he'd been holding his breath for years.

Harriet had always imagined endings would feel more dramatic. Explosive, maybe. Like a car crash you saw coming but couldn't stop. But she felt...quiet. Settled. The house was peaceful in a way it rarely was—just the hum of the dishwasher, the distant sound of Olivia playing music in her room, the steady rise and fall of Alex's breathing at the other end of the couch.

A month ago, she would've braced for a fight. Six months ago, she would've paced the room, overthinking every possible outcome. But today, she simply got up, poured two cups of coffee, and set one in Alex's waiting hands.

Wrapping her own around the other, she took a slow sip. Then, finally, she said, "I get it now."

Alex looked at her over the rim of his mug. "Get what?"

"Why you did it." There was no confusion as to what she was speaking of. "You were right to end things. Not to drag it out."

Alex stared into his coffee like it might give him the right words. "I thought I was doing you a favor," he admitted. "I thought if I made myself the villain, it'd be easier for you to move on." He shook his head, letting out a quiet laugh. "Turns out, I'm an idiot."

Harriet hummed, tilting her head. "Well. That was never really in question."

He chuckled.

A beat of silence passed before she spoke again. "So... would you like to stay? Hang out for a bit?"

His head snapped up, hope flickering across his face. "Yeah, of course. I mean—"

But she was already walking away, disappearing upstairs. A moment later, the kids came barreling down the stairs, filling the space with their usual energy, and Alex's attention shifted.

In her room, Harriet took the time to change slowly, enjoying the muted sounds of the kids and Alex downstairs.

For the first time in a long time, she wasn't bracing for something to go wrong. Instead, she let herself enjoy the moment—the easy rhythm of their voices, the simple fact Alex was here, present, doing what he should have done long ago. Getting help. It had taken time, and more heartache than she cared to dwell on, but he was finally stepping up. Not just showing up, but truly being there for their kids. And that meant something. She was actually excited to see the father he could become, the one she'd always known was in there somewhere.

With a small smile, she tightened her ponytail and headed downstairs. She retrieved her racket from the front hall closet and headed to the kitchen in search of her water bottle.

Alex froze when he saw her, his mouth forming the shape of an O.

She smirked, catching the way he started to say something —probably some smart-ass remark—but stopped himself.

Instead, he nodded. "Charlie told me you were playing again," he said. "Good for you."

"What can I say? Turns out whacking things at high speed is great for my mental health." She picked up her keys and added, "And don't think I didn't catch that almost-comment. Personal growth looks good on you."

Alex huffed a quiet laugh. "Have a good time, Harriet."

She smiled, real and easy in a way that felt almost foreign. "I will."

She stepped outside, racket in hand. The coastal air carried the familiar mix of salt and blooming bougainvillea, the sound of waves faint against the cliffs not far below. This was La Jolla—steady, resilient, always waiting—and it felt like the right place to begin again.

Harriet had thought her new life had begun the moment she and Alex had separated. But now, with each step forward, she recognized the truth.

Her new life was only just beginning.

A LOOK AT

CHARLIE IN PROGESS
(LOST AND FOUND BOOK 2)

Some women find themselves...Charlie crashes into herself—morning sickness and all.

Charlie Young has always been someone else's something—Alex's younger sister, her parents' afterthought, the fun distraction in a man's life but never the main event. Now she's hoarding a major secret: she's pregnant. By accident. With a man who made her feel safe—until he politely made it clear that fatherhood wasn't in his plans.

Back in her childhood home, wedged between a disapproving mother, an absent father, and the constant reminder that her brother is the family favorite, Charlie has two options: keep pretending she's fine, or have a full-blown identity crisis at the dinner table. (Honestly, it could go either way.)

Between secretly throwing up at work, questioning whether she even wants to be a mom, and finally realizing she's really good at her job, Charlie starts to wonder: has she been waiting for permission to take her own life seriously?

With biting humor and raw honesty, CHARLIE IN PROGRESS *is a deep dive into family dysfunction, self-discovery, and what happens when you finally stop playing the supporting role in your own damn life. Perfect for fans of* All Adults Here *and* Fleabag, *this is a story about growing up late, letting go of expectations, and finally stepping into the spotlight of your own life.*

AVAILABLE APRIL 2026

ACKNOWLEDGMENTS

Thank you to my writing group: Katie, Darci, Lauren, and Ciaran.

Thank you, always, Jordan Hansen.

Thank you, Love N. Books Press.

And thank you to my two Dominics, the loves of my life.

Rachel Celeste (also writing as Rachel Del Grosso) was born in Ontario, Canada. She began writing at a very young age, but has since learned to write in complete sentences. She writes the stories women need when they're in the middle of becoming someone new.. Rachel lives in Las Vegas with her husband and son. Harriet In Waiting is her fourth novel.

Find her on Instagram *@rachelceleste* and sign up for her newsletter at *rachelceleste.substack.com* or www.racheldelgrosso.com.

www.ingramcontent.com/pod-product-compliance
Lightning Source LLC
LaVergne TN
LVHW100516110826
845146LV00002B/666

* 9 7 9 8 8 9 5 6 7 6 8 9 9 *